THE O'MALLEY SAGA

Book One:
The Blood Oath

THE
O'MALLEY SAGA

Book One:
The Blood Oath

•

TOM AUSTIN

WESTERN
AUSTIN
c. 1

AVALON BOOKS
THOMAS BOUREGY AND COMPANY, INC.
401 LAFAYETTE STREET
NEW YORK, NEW YORK 10003

© Copyright 1996 by Tom Austin
Library of Congress Catalog Card Number: 96-96757
ISBN 0-8034-9175-1

PRINTED IN THE UNITED STATES OF AMERICA
ON ACID-FREE PAPER
BY HADDON CRAFTSMEN, SCRANTON, PENNSYLVANIA

This writing is dedicated to Louie, Kathy, Beau, and Angelique L'Amour

Acknowledgments

The author would like to recognize the following people who gave invaluable assistance in this endeavor: Dr. Robert McPherson, Professor of History, who jump started me a long time ago; Kristin Lindstrom, without whose considerable skills I would still be withering on the vine; John Ramsey Miller, who logged many electronic hours encouraging and entertaining; and Merry Austin-Adams, personal editor, who always believed in her big brother.

The Beginning

I seen the smoke from the ridge top where I was huntin' a squirrel for supper. The war was near four years old, and we hadn't been touched much by it in our little valley. Most of the menfolk were gone, including my three brothers and Pa, but we hadn't seen no fightin' close to home.

I knew as soon as I saw the smoke that it come from our place. Fear jumped up in my throat, and I took off down the trail like I had a fire under my feet. Ma was at the house, and she was alone.

Branches whipped my face as I raced through the woods, but I paid 'em no mind. My Sharps rifle was slowin' me down, but I didn't dare drop it. I might have need of it when I got to the clearing. It seemed to take forever, that run down the hillside, and when I finally run clear of the trees I could see our cabin was on fire, as was the little barn. I run past the old blue sow that was layin' with her feet in the air, deader than a sack of meal. My eyes were startin' to blur and my breath was comin' in ragged gasps. I turned the corner of the burnin' house and stopped in my tracks. Neighbor O'Donnel was standin' by the clothesline with his boy what had been wounded at Shiloh. They was standin' over Ma, and she was dead.

I'd never heard tell of an O'Malley man cryin', but I reckon I did. Right there in front of Neighbor O'Donnel and his boy I did a sight of cryin'. I knelt down next to Ma, touched her still warm face, and thought of all the pleasures she'd done without livin' with Pa on his hillside farm and raisin' us boys. The tears came hard and fast, and though I was ashamed, I couldn't stop 'em.

I bawled a long time 'til O'Donnel's boy cleared his throat and said real quiet: "I got one of 'em, Matthew. He's layin' over yonder, and I don't think he's plumb dead."

I looked up at him and then looked to where he was pointin'.

1

A man lay in a crumpled heap near the rail fence that marked the boundary between our two farms.

"You go see to him, Matt," O'Donnel said to me. "I'll get my woman to come over and lay out your Ma proper."

I stood up and stepped back. O'Donnel knew what needed doin', and I surely didn't. I'd been to buryin's before, but I had no idea what come before the buryin'. I nodded my head and walked down to where the man lay. I rolled him over and jumped back 'cause his eyes were open. I stepped back up to him and heard his breath whistle through his teeth. It had a kind of windy rattle to it so I reckoned he was lung shot and not long for this world. I mightily hoped that he'd go straight to hell when he died.

"How old are ye, boy?" His voice surprised me and I jumped again.

"Fifteen," I managed to stutter.

"When I was fifteen I was walkin' behind a lop-eared mule in Tennessee, and fishin' in the creek." He turned his head with a grimace as he looked at me. "How come you ain't in the fight?"

"My three brothers and my Pa done left, but I had to stay and take care of my Ma and the farm. You killed my Ma," I managed to say without my voice crackin'.

"I'm sorry, boy, but it weren't me. I was part of the raiders, but I ain't never killed a woman, ever." The man was rocked by a fit of bloody coughing and he was visibly weaker when he'd finished.

"Who killed my Ma?" I asked him. All of a sudden the identity of the man who'd pulled the trigger had become mighty important to me.

"I reckon it was Falcon Beck," the man said without hesitation. "He's the one that claims leadership in our gang, and holds the claim by killin' anybody who takes exception."

"He's mine," I said in a hushed tone. The words hadn't seemed to be mine, but they'd come from me.

"Don't you even think on it, boy. Falcon Beck is poison mean, and he's leadin' a band of the worst kind of outlaws." The man stopped talkin' a minute and took a deep moist breath. "I don't know how I ever fell in with such company, but I did and this here's the end of it. They ain't fightin' for neither the blue nor the gray. Beck's gang is just runnin' around the country usin' the war as an excuse to rob and kill." The man took another deep breath. "You stay shut of him, boy. He'll eat you up quicker than a toad gets a fly."

"I'm takin' a blood oath right here and now, mister," I said. I took out my belt knife and slashed myself deep and wide across my right forearm. "I'm takin' a blood oath that I'm gonna kill Falcon Beck, or die tryin'. He's got to pay." The blood dripped from my arm onto the man's already bloody coat. He didn't hear me. He wasn't ever gonna hear anything in this world again.

We had us a buryin'. It was a rough row, but I held together 'til I was alone. Neighbor O'Donnel built a hand-shaved red oak box that he spent considerable time on; and Mrs. O'Donnel gave Ma her own silk party dress since all our stuff'd been burnt up, and she fixed her hair real purty. I dug the grave myself, and put it right under the big oak near the corral. Ma'd always set store by that tree and it seemed fittin' that I put her there. I dug it deep and the sides were smooth as was the bottom.

Folks come from up and down the valley for the buryin'. I heard a lot of 'em say how natural Ma looked before we shut the box. She didn't look natural to me. She looked dead and nothing was gonna change that. The words was spoke and I dropped the first dirt on her. It near killed me. Then I looked at the livid cut on my arm and felt the fire shoot through my guts.

I thanked everybody as they fixed to leave, and a few of the ladies left off clothes, food, and other truck they figured I'd need. I particular thanked the O'Donnels and reckoned them for the best neighbors a body could ask for. Everybody took out 'cept the Parson. He was a God-fearin' man, but given to preachin' hellfire and damnation, which I had a hard time with. He walked over to me and laid a hand on my shoulder.

"I hear you took a blood oath of vengeance, Matthew." One thing about him he didn't beat around the bush none.

"Yep," was all I said. The slash on my arm was readily apparent and anybody that knew the O'Malleys or even the Irish clans for that matter, knew what that cut meant.

"I know your blood runs hot, son, but a blood feud's not the way to remember your Ma. I know she wouldn't want you doin' what you've bound yourself to do. Remember that the Lord said that vengeance was his."

"Not in this case, Parson," I said quiet. "We O'Malleys have always taken care of our own. I'll let the Lord take care of the other folks."

"It'll sour you, boy. Hate does that, and it does it fast."

"Then I reckon I'm gonna sour," I said. My jaws were startin' to get tight and he could see it.

"God love ya, son. You're gonna need it." The preacher turned on his heel and, without a look back, walked over to his single-hitched buggy. I turned and looked at the raw earthen hump under the big oak, then I looked down at my arm. The wound was still raw and had barely started to heal, but it was nothin' to the way my heart felt.

I planned on huntin and killin' me a man named Falcon Beck, and I didn't even know what he looked like.

Chapter One

I was in trouble. The man standing on my hand was big and he looked mean.

"Mister, that's my watch you're standing on." My voice kind of squeaked as I said it, and that made me mad.

"I'd say that watch belongs to whoever picks it up, sonny."

If I agreed with him, he'd sure take Pa's watch, and then probably rob and beat me anyway. It was near the only thing I'd brought with me from home. Pa'd given it to me when he left, and I didn't want to lose it. I was in trouble, and when I looked around I could see that there was no one in the eating house that was going to help me. Kansas, after the Civil War, was a hard country, and a man was expected to take care of his own trouble. There sure wasn't going to be help comin' from the law. The only law that counted was the gun a man carried, and I'd left mine on the mule tied out front. I kept callin' myself a man as if I had to be reminded that I was sixteen and tryin' hard to fill a man's boots. I'd been doin' a man's work for quite a spell.

"You hear me, boy? I said that watch belonged to whoever picked it up."

"Okay, mister, get off my hand."

He stepped back, and I fetched it to him. Pa always told us boys that there was a time for jawin' and a time for fightin', and there was no sense in discussion if the man was intent on gettin' whipped. I reckoned this big, mean looking feller was pure intent on getting whipped, only I wasn't sure I was the man to do the whippin'. I hit him hard, and he was fair surprised. I'd been splittin' fence rails, cuttin' wood, haulin' hay, and workin' hard since I was knee-high to a short duck. I wasn't as big as he was, but I wasn't the littlest fella in the place either. I hit him flush on the jaw, and it sat him on his butt. Then I picked up Pa's watch and put it in my pocket. As the big man slowly got to his feet he reached for his belt and pulled out a knife that would have passed for a short sword.

"I'm goin' to open you up, boy. Nobody's ever hit me and lived to brag on it."

I didn't have a knife, and both my old Sharps rifle and Pa's horse pistol were out on the mule. I started backin' away from him a step at a time, watching the knife in his hand. I backed until I was up against the wall. He made a big grin, then lunged at me. I jumped off to one side and he missed, but it was close. He near cut my shirt off me.

"That's enough." The voice was quiet, but had a quality that carried all through the room. The man with the knife turned toward the voice.

"This is no affair of yours, O'Malley."

"I'm 'fraid it is. That's my brother, and us O'Malleys always take up for each other. It's bred to us."

The big man was surely between a rock and a solid spot, because Owen O'Malley was holding a .36 Navy pointed roughly at his belly. The man might not know it, but back home in Pennsylvania the O'Malley boys were known to hit what they was aimin' at. There was four of us all told. Dan was the oldest, then come Mike two years after Dan, then after Mike come Owen with two years between 'em, and then I come along four years later. All us boys had been raised up to shoot straight—Pa was right particular about us wastin' good powder and ball.

The big man was starting to sweat; then he sheathed his knife and moved toward the door. I let out a breath that I'd been holdin' for a spell.

"This ain't over, O'Malley," he said over his shoulder as he slammed out the front door.

"Thanks, Owen. You saved my bacon."

He turned to look at me, and I could see anger on him.

"You best carry a gun all the time and not be scared to use it. You made Beck look bad, knockin' him down that way, and he means to kill you for it."

"I'm glad to see you too, Owen."

"I'm sorry, Matt, but you just made a killin' enemy of one of the worst men in the territory."

"He didn't give me a choice, Owen." I thought back on what my brother had said to the big man, and I reckoned sure I'd heard him call the man Beck.

'Fore I could ask, Owen spoke again. "Let's get out of here before he comes back with some of his men."

Folks had gone back to eating since there hadn't been a killin', and we walked out the door with Owen going out gun foremost. We stopped by my mule.

"What are you doin' in this part of the country, and where's Pa?" Owen asked.

"I don't know where Pa is. He never come back. Fact is, I ain't heard from anybody but you, and that was over a year ago. Far as I know Pa nor the other boys don't even know that Ma was killed. Me and Neighbor O'Donnel been workin' the farm, with me doin' most of the work. Last winter I told myself that when the grass showed green on Ma's grave I was comin out to find you. Come spring I took out. I went to the town where you sent the letter from, and folks there said you were headed for Kansas." My tone was bitter. Owen looked up at me.

"I'm sorry, Matt. None of us have had an easy time of it. What happened to the farm?"

"I rented it to O'Donnel. I needed the money, and he needed the ground for two of his boys that come home."

"Two of his boys?"

"The other three won't be comin' home. Two died for the Union, and the other died for the Confederacy."

I looked away from Owen. The O'Donnels had been our closest neighbors all our lives, and we'd grown up with the boys bein' our best friends.

"A lot of men died," Owen said quiet. He'd know. He'd joined the Grand Army of the Republic early and stayed 'til the last dance was called. He'd ended up a captain in the cavalry.

"What happened with Pa, Matt? He promised he wouldn't go to the war."

"He tried to stay home, Owen, but we heard rumors that Danny'd been wounded, captured, and sent to Andersonville, and that Mike had been killed at Shiloh. Pa was pacing the floor every day and could talk nothing but what was happenin' with the fight. One day he comes in, hands me his watch, and says, 'Matt, you work the place. I'm going to find the boys.' He patted Ma on the shoulder and told her he'd be back directly, then he climbed up on the bay mare and took out south. He stopped down the lane a ways and yelled back that I was to give him a while after the war ended, then I was to come out and fetch all the brothers back

to the farm. "Go find the boys and bring them home, Matthew,"
he said to me.

"Well I waited 'til the grass was showin' green, and when he
didn't come home I threw a leg over the buckskin mule and took
out for the last place I knew you'd been. I stopped here to eat
and get directions, and after I'd finished my meal, and fetched a
gold piece out of my pocket to pay, I hooked the watch chain
with my finger and dropped the watch on the floor. I guess you
saw the rest."

I glanced at Owen, him lookin' off toward the west. His square
jaw still jutted out, and his green eyes had that misty look, only
they were a mite hard now. I had no idea where my other two
brothers were, but I'd made good on a third of my promise to
Pa. I'd found Owen, or rather he'd found me, and I was downright grateful that his timing had been so good.

The other boys had been gone near as long as Owen and nary
a word from them. I'd not heard officially from the government
either, the way some folks had when their kin was killed. We'd
heard the rumor on Mike from a man who said he knew him and
seen him go down at Shiloh. I held to a slim hope that they'd
made it through the war. It was a mighty slim hope. A lot of men
had died. They lay in unmarked graves, their names unknown.

"It's a hard land you've come to, Matthew. You'll find few
friends in this country. I've made enemies here, lad. The Jayhawkers are hunting me and the men I ride with."

I looked in his face and saw trouble lines around his eyes.

"Why they hunting you, Owen? You crosswise of the law?"

"The men I'm with are fine men. Some of them rode with me
during the war, and some of them rode for the other side. The
boys that rode for the Gray lost, but that doesn't make them bad
people. Only in this part of the country it does." Owen stopped
for a minute and looked down the dusty street. "The Jayhawkers
started out fighting the pro-slavery Missourians before the war,
and now they're trying to keep the war going with men who
fought for the losing side. I fought for the Union, but the day the
war ended we became one nation, one people again. We met five
Rebs that were riding the same way we were, north and east. We
joined up together, shared food, shared water, shared joy that the
war was over and we were going home."

Owen took a deep breath and turned back toward me. "I listened to three of the five men talk about their homes in Kansas
and how they missed them and their people during the war. We

had a brush with the Cheyenne, and one of the Kansas boys saved my life. He was still wearing his gray coat, and me my blue. He saved me and risked his life in the savin'. When we got to Kansas, and near their home places, we kept hearing rumors how the Jayhawkers had confiscated the land of people who fought for the South. When we got to the first homestead of one of our Kansas boys, we found out the rumors were true. It was the same for the other two. They had the misfortune to own good land and come home to find Jayhawkers perched on their ground. Homes that they'd worked hard to build, and thought of through the long years of the war, were being lived in by people that had no title to them.'' Owen rubbed his day's worth of dark beard then looked at me.

''We started doing some checking and found that several of the places confiscated had been taken by men who had ridden with Quantrill and his irregulars. They weren't really Jayhawkers. They were thieves and killers, but had taken the name to give them popular support.'' Owen's hand went down unconsciously to the gun in his belt, and his voice was full of emotion. ''People didn't know, or didn't care. All they knew for sure was the boys riding with us had worn gray, and that made them wrong. It worked into a fight, and us that are fighting are considered outside the law. They're hunting us, and there's times when we're hard pressed. There's been some killin'.''

I looked hard at Owen. I'd never heard tell of an O'Malley that was an outlaw, except for Grace O'Malley in Ireland about 1550 or so. She'd been a pirate, or so Pa had told us.

Owen turned. ''We got to leave, Matt. Practically every hand is against us. We come to town for supplies, but if we stay too long they'll build a force against us and trouble will be on us. My friends are down the street. I saw that buckskin mule tied here at the rail, recognized the scar on his flank, and thought it was Pa. I was some surprised to see you fightin' with the likes of what you'd tangled with.'' Owen stopped for a minute, and his gaze landed on the white scar on my arm. He looked into my face questioningly.

''I took a blood oath to kill the man what killed Ma, Owen. His name is Falcon Beck.'' Owen's eyes widened and a low whistle came from him.

''Well, boy, you taken on a mouthful, I'll give you that. You just met him. He was the big man you knocked on his butt.'' Owen rubbed his whiskered cheek and looked down the street.

"I probably should have killed him while I had the chance. Beck is the leader of the so-called Jayhawkers."

"I'm glad you didn't, Owen. That's for me to do. I took the oath."

"I hope you're up to it, Matt. Falcon Beck is poison mean. Folks say that he's killed over twenty men, and some of them were in standup fights." Owen looked to my mule and then back at me. "I hate to have you come with us, but after the trouble you've had, we've little choice."

"Where we goin'?" I asked as I untied my mule. "I'd like to stick around and find Beck."

"You forget about Falcon Beck for the time bein'. You keep passin' the word around that you're huntin' him, and you're gonna find him before you're ready. We're heading for the breaks of the Arkansas River. It's rough country, and pretty much unpopulated," he said as we walked down the street. We stepped around a corner and came up to eight hard-faced men looking close about them.

"Who's the kid, O'Malley?" one of them asked.

"He's my youngest brother, fresh down from Pennsylvania."

"He's riding a mule, Owen," another man said.

The tone of his voice made my hackles come up. I'd just near had my guts spilled on the ground and been turned into an instant outlaw, and my O'Malley pride was strong on me. I had my Sharps in my hand, and it just naturally seemed to be pointing at the man's brass belt buckle.

"Mister, I may just have come down from the farm, and I might be riding the mule that used to pull our plow, but I been over the hill and through the meadow. The farm is miles behind me, and I know how to shoot this here rifle, so I'd suggest you don't make no more comments about my mule." I didn't raise my voice. I didn't figure I needed to. The Sharps was talkin' for me.

Owen had a big grin on his face, but I was dead serious. My O'Malley pride was on me, and I was tired of being treated like a kid.

"You better pull back there, Major. I think the boy is serious, and he's like the rest of the clan. He just plain don't miss what he shoots at. There was a time or two back home when he even outshot me."

The man called Major broke into a big smile that was like the sun after a thunderstorm. "Don't be so sudden, son. I meant nothing by it. I seen the time when I'd given the shirt off my back for a chance to straddle a mule. I only commented on the mule 'cause we have to ride fast, and mules aren't fast movin' critters.''

"Matthew O'Malley, this here's Bob Daly, lately Major Daly of the Confederate Army. He passes for the leader of this bunch of misfits,'' Owen said to me.

Well, leave it to me to do some damn fool thing like brace the leader of the men I was going to ride with.

"I'm sorry, Major Daly. I'm a might touchy since the trouble I had with Falcon Beck.'' I saw curiosity flash across his face, and he turned to Owen.

"I'll tell you about it on the road, Major. We best get movin','' Owen said to him.

The Major turned back to me. "I accept your apology, but a friendly word from a man who has seen the backside of the world. You pull a gun down on a man, and you best be ready to kill him 'cause somewhere, sometime, someone is going to try you just to see if you got any sand in your craw.''

He turned to the other men. "Let's move out.'' They reined their horses around almost as one man and trotted down the road. I felt the fool and took a position at the back, being in no mood for questions or conversation. I could hear Owen and the Major talking at the front, but couldn't make out what they were sayin'.

We rode most of the day until the brush got thick and the country was broken by sand hills and plum thickets. I'd never seen such country, and I figured if anybody chased after us, as rough as it was, they really wanted us. We got to an island in the river about an hour before nightfall, and it was plain to see that these men had ridden together for a spell. Each man seemed to have a self-appointed job that went with fixin' the meal or setting up camp. I stirred around and gathered up some driftwood, trying to make myself useful. Major Daly did the cooking and explained to me when I dropped an armload of wood close up to the fire, "We used to share the cooking, but I decided to take the job over after tasting what everyone else in this pack made. None of the rest of them can fix anything worth eatin'.''

That brought a chorus of hoots from the other men, but no one argued either. It was a friendly, pleasant time that made me glad to be there; we all forked down the jackrabbit stew that the Major had thrown together. He did a fair job of it, and there was enough left over for breakfast.

After we ate, things broke up as men started hunting their blankets. They'd introduced themselves around while we were eatin', so I had a name stuck to each man. The two across the fire were Nat Leavy and Joe Turner. They were two of the Kansas boys trying to get their farms back. On the far side of the island, stretching out their beds, were brothers, about a year apart in age. Their names were Earl and David Chapman. They'd ridden with the Major for three years during the war and simply had nothing better to do than follow him. Owen had told me they had no family left in Tennessee, and were completely loyal to the Major. They figured on working on his farm with him if he got it back. Two of the men that interested me most were a man named Kiowa, and Chunk Colbert.

Kiowa was a full-blood Kiowa Indian who had operated as a scout for Owen's cavalry unit for most of two years. He rarely spoke, but I noticed that he took in everything around him. I'd seen Indians before, but they'd been what folks called tame Indians. It was plain to see that Kiowa was no tame Indian. He was dressed most like everyone else, but there was a look to his eyes.

The guy that called himself Chunk Colbert had attached himself to this group by his own invitation. Owen said that he'd been a loner since he'd joined. He had spoken of the war, but had declared no allegiance nor mentioned any particular engagements that he'd participated in. Just as I looked at him, he stood up, moved toward the back of the clearing, and started acting mighty curious. No one else paid any attention to him, but I was fascinated. Most everybody who lugged a short gun carried it in his belt, in a pocket, or in a holster on his saddle. If they carried a belt holster, it was usually army issue with a flap over it to protect the gun. Colbert had taken an army holster and made it over so it hooked to his belt on the right side. He'd also cut off the flap and cut the leather down so the hammer of his Rootes Colt wouldn't be hampered. He was standing there with his feet spread wide, shucking the Rootes out of the holster so fast it was a blur. He saw me watching and waved me over.

"I guess Owen told you that we've had some gun trouble with folks hereabouts?"

I nodded my head.

"Well, I got a brother down in Texas, and he showed me how to set this up. Seems he's got the same kind of problems with the carpetbaggers down there that we got with the Jayhawkers up here. Anyhow, he's faster at peelin' it out of the holster than I am, but I'm a lot faster now than when I started.''

His hand streaked down again to the holster and pistol, and I was fair impressed at how the gun seemed to jump into his hand and come level on target. He'd made his point with me.

I wandered over to my blankets and crawled in. I lay there lookin' up at a night sky nearly covered with stars. Sleep was slow in comin'. The trouble with Falcon Beck came back to me, and I could feel the tension in my gut. The way things were goin' I'd best learn Colbert's secret to getting a gun in my hand, or leave the country. Maybe I could talk Owen into leaving. I had me a blood oath to fill, but from what everybody'd told me I might not be up to it right now. I wouldn't have admitted it out loud, but I wasn't sure I was ready to do what needed to be done. Falcon Beck would still be around when I'd learned a few things more, and I was in a fair sweat to find out what had happened to my other brothers, not to mention Pa. I didn't like to think I was runnin', but maybe if we left the country, Beck would forget that I'd knocked him on his tail. On the other hand, thinking back to the look of hate on his face when we parted company, maybe Falcon Beck would never forget me. No matter what.

Chapter Two

They came on us just as day was breaking. There was a yell, then a rush of horses. A single shot sounded and then a volley. I rolled out of my blanket and grabbed my Sharps. Shots sounded around me, and I was knocked down by a horse. I rolled over and looked up into the face of Falcon Beck. He was pulling back on his reins trying to steady his horse, and his rifle was pointed at my chest. I rolled just as he fired, and the bullet blew dirt into my face. I triggered a shot, mostly by instinct, and he dropped from his horse. I knew I'd missed, but it'd been close. I jumped to my feet and picked up Pa's horse pistol from where I'd laid it beside me. I looked around and saw Beck jump on the back of a horse being ridden by one of his own men. He threw the man from the saddle and headed for me again. It's tricky shootin' at a man who is shootin' back, particular with a pistol that weighs near five pounds. It's even worse when the man's mounted. I cranked off three shots and killed the horse he was riding. When he hit the ground, I took another shot at him and missed again. I heard a yell and the attackers turned as one man and went back in the direction they'd come from. Beck was up behind one of the retreating men, riding double. The man he'd thrown from the horse was still lying in a heap with his head at a strange angle from his body.

It was over as quick as it had started. The fighting hadn't taken more than three or four minutes, and six men were dead. Two of them had been with us. Leavy and Turner, the Kansas boys, had been on the side of the island that got hit first. Major Daly had a bullet burn along his arm, and one of the Chapmans had a flesh wound on top of his shoulder. Owen came over to me. I was shakin' like a sick kitten in a sudden rain.

"Sit down, boy,'fore you fall down. You hit?"

"No," I managed to stammer.

14

"See to your guns," the Major yelled. "They might decide to try again."

He needn't have told them. They were all former soldiers and saw to the loading of their guns as a matter of course. I looked over at Chunk Colbert. He had a grin on his face and was pouring powder into the cylinder of one of the three pistols he carried. I'd heard tell of guns that fired with ready-made cartridges, but none of this group had one. Most men carried extra pistols and cylinders, so they wouldn't have to stop and load during a fight.

"I got two of them," Colbert said, "and the kid got one. Who got the other?"

I got ready to protest, but Colbert held up his hand. "The one on the ground over there is yours, kid," he said, pointing toward the man lying on his back. "I saw you nail him when Falcon Beck was comin' at you on the horse."

The shot I'd missed Beck with had killed the man behind him.

"Who killed this other one?" Earl, the younger Chapman, demanded.

"His neck is broke, Earl. He was thrown from his horse," Owen said quiet-like. Earl looked disappointed and turned away. I went to the bushes and lost what was left of last night's stew. I'd never been in a shootin' fight before. Fact, I hadn't been in much of any kind of fight before, much less killed a man. Owen came over to me.

"It's not bad to get sick over killin', Matt. I've seen too many men that killin' comes easy to. Colbert's like that. He's taken to keepin' score of late. I've killed men, Matt, but I'm not proud of it. When you start to find glory in the killin', something goes dead inside of you."

He got up and walked back toward the camp. He didn't need to worry. My number one thought was getting shut of Kansas and headin' back for the green of the farm. The last two days I'd had all the fightin' I wanted for the rest of my life.

I went back to the camp feeling empty and scared.

"Who had the watch?" Major Daly had the men together near the dead fire and asked the question.

"I did," Colbert replied.

"Why the hell didn't we have some warning? We are on an island. There was only one direction they could come at us. Everyone who had the watch during the night was appraised of that fact. Why didn't we have some warning, Colbert?"

The Major's voice had dropped ominously low, and Colbert

replied, ''I just didn't hear them, Major.'' There was a trace of whine in his voice.

''That's the truth as far as it goes, Chunk. The truth is that you didn't hear them because you were asleep. I came awake and looked over in time to see them sneaking in. I fired the first shot. I also saw you. You were asleep.''

''So what if I was,'' Colbert sneered. ''I ain't in the army no more, and I don't answer to you just because you appointed yourself leader. I never did cotton to riding with Rebs and Indians anyway.'' His last statement hung like a church bell peal on a frosty Sunday morning.

''Pack your gear and get out, Colbert. You cost the lives of two good men that asked nothing more than to turn over Kansas sod again. Now they're going to be under it, and the fault is yours.'' The Major said the last as he was turning away. Colbert grabbed for the pistol in his holster, his intent perfectly clear. A shot rang out, and Colbert's pistol fell from his hand. A perfect, round hole had been drilled right through his palm, and his pistol was smashed. Owen stood off to one side with his Navy smokin' in his hand.

''Get out, Chunk, before I decide to correct the fact that I missed shootin' you in the heart where I was aimin'.'' Owen said it with the same quiet fierceness that the Major had used.

Colbert turned on his heel holding his bleeding hand, threw his stuff together, got his horse saddled, and rode out to the east.

We buried Leavy and Turner first, with the Major reading some mighty fine verses from the good book. We moved them to the top of a knoll where the view took in a lot of Kansas river country. Then we buried the other men on the island where they had fallen. The Major said ashes to ashes over them, and we gathered up our camp.

''We're down to a six-man force,'' the Major remarked as he swung aboard his horse. He had included me in his count, and I swelled up a little bit. ''Anyone have any suggestions about a course of action?'' he asked, looking at Owen. ''Captain, comments?''

''No, Major. I'm along for the ride,'' Owen replied.

Major Daly looked out across the plain and sat dead still on his horse. ''It's not worth it, men. I fought nearly five years for an ideal that is dead. That same ideal killed enough Sons of the South that it will take generations to recover. I fought with them to protect their homes. I fought so I could keep my home. My wife is dead, my house is being lived in by scum, my horses have been stolen, and my dreams smashed. I am living in hate, and it will kill us all. Two very fine men died this morning. My farm is no longer worth the fight.''

"Major, sir?" The Major turned his horse toward Kiowa, who had spoken. "May I share with you an idea that came to me a few days ago?"

Now, I was plum taken back. It was the first words I had heard the Indian speak since I had joined. Most of the Indians I had heard talk, mostly grunted. This man spoke with words that could have graced a scholar's mouth, and with an English accent yet.

"Of course, you may. We are all equal in this endeavor," the Major replied.

"You are our leader, not only by right of former rank, but also because you have been informally chosen by us. You have come to the conclusion that recovering your farm is not worth what it may cost you, or us. I recommend that we move west, at least as far as Junction City, and look for work. If we stay together, pool our resources, and watch for opportunity, we may come to an enterprise that will reward us. Perhaps we shall all have farms, or better yet, a ranchero, as the Mexicans call their large holdings. They are combination farms and livestock industries that require several men to work. We may all find homes."

Owen glanced over at me and my slack jaw. I had never heard anyone speak like Kiowa, not even the teacher in our one-room school back home.

"Oxford. Class of fifty-eight. He was the foster son of an English trader to the Kiowa. He made only one request to his foster father: An English education. He got it," Owen explained to me. "Don't be fooled by his fancy talk. His gettin' educated didn't affect his fightin' ability none." The Kiowa smiled at me.

"Don't you believe it, Matthew. I'm a kind and gentle man."

The Major ran his hand over his face then turned toward us. "It sounds like a plausible plan, what do the rest of you think?"

"We'll follow you, Major," the older Chapman promptly replied.

"I'm in, what about you, Matt?" Owen turned toward me.

"I was thinkin' strongly on the farm, Owen," I replied. "What if one of the other boys show up, or Pa? They won't know where we got off to." I looked away as I said it, already feeling like a traitor.

"That's fine, Matt. Stay along the river 'til she hits the big

muddy one. Then a little north and east is home. There's plenty
of game, so you should make out good 'til you get there. You
got money?'' he asked.

I nodded my head.

"Okay, and if things don't work out for us, I'll be along home
as well," he smiled at me.

I knew he wouldn't. Our little hill farm wasn't near big enough
for him. Owen was goin' to make big tracks on the western land,
no question. He had qualities that other men were drawn to, a
presence that spoke of knowledge and honesty.

"I'll see you at home one of these days, Matt."

I nodded my head, not daring to try and speak past the lump
in my throat. They reined their horses around and moved off the
crest of the hill toward the west. They stopped once, as a body,
and raised their arms to me in a farewell salute.

What was I doin'? Ridin' off from me were some of the finest
men I'd ever met. They were what I wanted to be. Owen was
the only kin I knew I had left. I lifted my rifle and fired a shot
into the air. Firin' the old Sharps was near as dangerous for the
man doin' the firin' as it was for what he was aimin' at. I held
it well away from me when I pulled the trigger. They pulled up
and looked back toward me to see if there was trouble. I kicked
ol' Buck in the side, and we ambled down to where they waited.
They all had grins on their faces. I realized that the farm wasn't
big enough for me anymore either. That was one of the reasons
I'd left. Here I was, a farm boy just down from the hills, riding
a mule into whatever the future held. But I was an O'Malley, and
there had always been O'Malleys on the edge of great new lands.
Pa told often about some of the family that went before us and
they had always been men and women to reckon with. My future
lay west with these men.

I reached behind me and pulled a small hide bag from my belt.
I tossed it to the Major. It clinked when he caught it.

"There's two hundred in gold coin, Major. A hundred of it is
Owen's and a hundred mine. It's rent from the farm, money I
made while everyone was gone, and some family money left by
Pa when he took out. It will give us a start."

"That it will, son," the Major beamed at me. "Right here,
men, is where we begin. Let's collect and count what we have
together."

Everyone dismounted and tossed their coins into the blanket
the Major had laid out. It came to just over four hundred dollars.

"It doesn't seem fair that the O'Malleys have contributed more than the rest. How can we make it fair?" The Major asked.

Before a reply could be made, Owen spoke up, "It is fair, Major. If everyone pulls an equal load, then we will all share equally. I know the Chapmans are better farmers than I am, but I have things that I can do better than they. It's the same with all of us. We all have special abilities that will contribute to the whole. It is fair."

"Well spoken, Captain, and a point well taken. Unless someone objects, we will make Captain O'Malley custodian of our funds." Everyone spoke in agreement, and the partnership was formed. Six belted, booted, strong men (I counted myself), and we were going places. As soon as we got to wherever we were headin', I was going to ask the partnership for a different rifle. I'd near set my shirt on fire with the Sharps.

Junction City wasn't much. Eastern Kansas hadn't been a lot different than what I was used to at home, but Junction City lay right on the edge of the Great Plains. I never seen so much of nothin' in my whole life. Nothin' but grass and buffalo—or bison to some folks—to the west of us, and a few hardscrabble farmers along the creeks. Junction City was trying hard to be a city, but simply bein' called a city don't count for much. The army fort that lay close by the town supported most of the businesses, and the railroad had made an impact. The early May day we got to Junction City it was raining, and had been for most of the night before. The streets were ankle-deep in mud, and it was hard work for mule teams to pull the big freight wagons down the street. It was a depressing sight. It sure didn't make a fella feel that this was the end of the rainbow with its pot of gold.

"I got us a house at the end of town for five-dollars-a-month rent," Owen remarked, "and Kiowa got a job teachin' school already."

The two of them had been gone most of two hours getting the lay of the land as the Major had called it.

"Wasn't there some objection to having an Indian teach school here?" the Major asked.

We all knew how folks on the frontier felt about Indians. Most of the time it was undeclared war with the various tribes. Hate festered on both sides.

"There was one fella on the board who objected, but the president also owns the only saloon, and he's a crusty man who's been places and seen things 'fore he got here. He told the objector that if he didn't like it he could grab up his kids and move the hell out of town. He also remarked that a classical college education was more important than color of skin be it white, green, or purple. I think it also helped that he has eight kids of his own, and all school age,'' Owen replied.

"He is an astute individual, and a man of some influence in the community,'' Kiowa added. "He indicated that my education was better than the teacher's they had last year. He had graduated from the fourth grade. They had been paying him forty dollars a month, so they are paying me fifty due to my qualifications and at the insistence of the saloon keeper.'' He looked quite pleased, as well he should. Fifty dollars a month was a princely sum when you considered that a man could build a house for fifty dollars.

"Okay, men, let's get down to our new house and get settled,'' the Major said.

We moved down the street with Owen and Kiowa leading the way. The rain had slowed to a drizzle and my mule's hooves made sucking noises in the mud each time he picked them up. A few minutes later Owen was pointing proudly at our new home. It reminded me of the rest of Junction City. It was squat, gray, and ugly with walls and roof all made of cut sod taken directly from the surrounding prairie. It had one redeeming feature: it was large, and the stable around back near the creek was equally large. I think Owen was the only one that truly liked it, but then he was the one who found it.

"This will do just fine, Captain. It is nice and big, and this winter when the blizzards come we will appreciate how tight the sod is fitted. Sod houses are quite warm in the winter,'' the Major remarked as he stepped through the door. I felt better about it already. I surely hated bein' cold, and I had heard that the plains had some real rippers for winter storms.

We turned to and cleaned the house the rest of the day. By nightfall the place was shined up, and the Major had a big ham on the stove and bread in the oven. I hadn't tasted any pig since I'd left home, and no cured meat since Pa left.

"Matt, I heard a man talkin' in the saloon today about needing help over at the railroad. I think they're loading and unloading freights and need people who aren't scared to work,'' Owen commented as we dug into the ham. I wasn't surprised that Owen had been in the saloon. Saloons had a reputation of bein' bad places, but the truth was that they were clearing houses for information in these western towns, although fights did have a tendency to happen pretty regular in them.

"I'll check first thing in the morning. Where is the office?" I asked.

"I don't know for sure, but if you go to the tracks and follow them one way or the other, you should come up with something. The town just isn't all that big," he replied smiling at me. I nodded around a chunk of ham. The Chapmans weren't back yet. They'd left to go to the land office and check on homesteading. The Homestead Act, passed by Congress in 1862, said that every man at least twenty-one years old could squat on 160 acres of ground. If he made improvements, the land became his in five years for no charge. The Chapman boys were farmers; that's where their hearts were, and that was what they were best at.

They came stomping in when we were just about done eating. Beaming as they smelled the ham and fresh-baked bread, they took off their muddy shoes at the door. The floor was dirt, but it was hard-packed and we'd swept it clean.

"I think we got a good deal working," Earl remarked. "The man at the land office said we'd be in good shape homesteading. Plenty of prime spots left along the creeks, but he thought we might be better off to buy out a man named Clausen who has a proved up homestead on the Republican River. It's about three miles north of town, has a house and a small barn on it."

"The price is three hundred dollars, and he'll throw in the mules plus a few implements," David added. "Seems his wife is lonely for the city they come from, and Clausen has a chance to take over a company his daddy owns. Only thing holding him here is his place."

"That will just about wipe out our cash," the Major said. "What do the rest of you think?"

"I say to go for it if we can get a crop out of it this year," Owen said.

"I agree," said Kiowa.

They all looked at me. "What kind of crops grow here?" I asked.

"That's one of the good things about this deal. He already has about sixty acres planted to soft wheat. We should get a crop off sometime in August or early September," Earl replied.

"I say to do it," I agreed.

"It does sound like a good deal. What is the rest of the acreage like?" the Major asked.

"About twenty acres are waste because of the river. Another forty is broken out and lying fallow, and the remaining is still native grass. We'd like to harrow and plant alfalfa on the forty that's broken," Earl replied.

"We seem to be in concert on this, so Captain O'Malley will provide you with the funds in the morning," the Major remarked.

We helped clean up after the Chapmans finished eating, and then went outside so some of the men could have an evening pipe of tobacco. I didn't smoke, but I enjoyed the smell of the pungent mix. It reminded me of Pa. The sky had cleared and the evening stars were out. The men about me talked quiet and easy of things that mattered to them. The future, their dreams, their families both lost and still living. I wondered what my future held. I looked down at the scar on my arm and knew there was one thing I had to do. It was a violent, restless time, and my experiences showed me that a man had to be strong to make his own way. I wanted to make my own way.

"Matthew." I jumped as the Major spoke my name. "Go unroll my blanket. There's something there that I've been saving for just the right person."

I got up and went inside to the Major's bunk. His blanket roll was at the foot of his bed, and I carefully unrolled it. Lying there gleaming in the dim light was a Henry repeating rifle. I carried it outside and walked up to the Major. "Are you sure, sir?" I asked.

"Certainly I'm sure. I took it from a battlefield near the end of the war. I haven't found a use for it, since I prefer my own Spencer. I noticed that your Sharps carbine is like most of the breed. It leaks so much powder gas past the breech that it nearly sets you on fire to shoot it. I think you can retire it now."

"Thank you, sir," I said, which didn't seem like near enough. He nodded his head and turned and started talking to Kiowa. I walked back to where I'd been sitting beside Owen.

"It's a .44 rimfire," Owen said. "She holds sixteen shots back to back in that tube under the barrel. The Major told me earlier that he was going to give it to you. It's fully loaded now, and later you can get a box of cartridges for it at the mercantile."

I simply nodded, afraid to try and speak. It was the best thing anyone had ever given me, and it wasn't even Christmas.

I turned in an hour later and went to sleep with the Henry beside me in the bed.

I woke in the morning, jumped out of bed, grabbed a chunk

of cold ham, stashed the Henry under my blanket, and headed for the railroad track. I followed it a ways and came to a clap-board building that said "office" over the door. I walked in and stood at the counter until a bald-headed man seated behind a desk noticed me.

"What can I do for you, boy?" he asked me.

"I heard you were hiring men to load freight cars," I replied.

"You heard right. You're big and it looks like you have strength in your arms and chest. You'll need it. Pay is dollar a day until you prove yourself, then you go up to dollar and a half. The foreman of the work crew is up the line about a quarter of a mile. Report to him." He turned back to the papers on his desk, and I walked out the door and started up the tracks. I got to where a crew of men was unloading cut lumber from a flat car and approached a man who was standing off to one side giving di-rections.

"Are you the foreman?" I asked.

"Yeah, whatdaya want?" he said without looking at me.

"The man at the office said you'd put me to work," I re-sponded.

He turned to look at me then, looked back at the crew. "Hey Wedge," he yelled at a monster of a man who was throwing big armfuls of lumber over the side of the car. "We got us another greenie." Wedge jumped down from the car and started striding toward me. "There's only one requirement before you go to work here. You got to whip Wedge, or at least give it a good try. He's never been beat in any kind of fight, and his favorite is free-for-all with or without knives. He's real partial to biting off ears." The foreman grinned a rotten-toothed smile at me, and the ground seemed to shake as Wedge walked toward me. It just didn't seem that life was going to be simple no matter what I did.

Chapter Three

I had no chance. No chance at all. Wedge was all of three hundred pounds, and while some of it was fat, his arms bulged and rippled with muscle. He outweighed me by at least a hundred pounds. His face looked like it had been carved out of a slab of granite, and each of his hands was as big as the ham we had for supper the night before. I'd a notion that if all I lost was an ear I was going to be lucky. While I was watching Wedge walk toward me, I heard a horse walk up from behind.

"You boys don't need to worry this pup. I'm going to kill him for you." I turned to face the man who had come up from behind. It was Chunk Colbert, and he was holding a gun on me with his left hand. His right hand was still in a bandage.

"Who the hell are you, mister?" the foreman asked

"My name is Colbert. Chunk Colbert. Mark the name well 'cause you'll be hearing it a lot. I had trouble with this kid and the people he rides with. I'm going to kill them all startin' with him."

Wedge had kept on comin' and walked past me right up to Colbert with a crooked smile on his scarred face.

"Mister, we don't take to folks messin' with our friends. This man works with us and that makes him one of us," Wedge said in a surprisingly melodious voice.

Colbert started to shift the gun toward Wedge and suddenly found himself on the ground wondering how he got there. Wedge threw me Colbert's pistol, which I caught in the air, and then bodily picked Chunk up and threw him over his standing horse. The ground was still muddy, and Colbert landed with a nasty sounding squish.

"Watch him, Wedge," I yelled. "He always carries more than one pistol." I didn't know which one of them was worse, but I

24

knew that Colbert planned to kill me, and Wedge was just going to beat me up a little.

"Well, boy, if he ups with another short gun and points it at me, I expect you to kill him," Wedge said over his shoulder. He walked around Colbert's horse. We heard a few blows, and a second later Chunk came screaming over the saddle again. The would-be killer lay in a wheezing lump in the mud. Wedge came around the horse again and leaned over Colbert.

"Mister, I want you to always remember what I'm about to tell you. We don't hold to people who come into our town and pull down short guns on other folks who don't have guns. It just don't seem fair. I'm goin' to let you leave town if you promise you'll never come back." As Wedge leaned over him Colbert mumbled something through his swollen lips.

Wedge nodded. "That's fine, mister, and so you always remember your promise I'm going to give you a little reminder." He reached down to Colbert's right ear and deftly ripped it off his head. Colbert was still screaming as Wedge picked him up and placed him gently on his horse. Wedge slapped the horse on the rump, and it trotted out toward the open prairie. He turned toward me. It wasn't a good feeling I had in the pit of my stomach.

"I'm sorry you had to see that, boy. It's a hard land we live in and that man would've surely killed you," he said in his strange voice. "We have this little thing that we do on all new men we hire. Casey tells 'em this big, mean story about me and I start walkin' in on 'em. If they holds their ground and don't wet their pants then it means they got sand. That means they be worth workin' with. If they run, then we don't want 'em. It looked to me like you weren't runnin', and your pants are dry." He smiled at me with his giant mouth and clapped me on the back so hard I near lost my air. He guided me over to the flat car and started showin' me what was expected. No one talked. We didn't have the energy to spare.

It was brutal, hard work, and by the noon meal I was fair tuckered out. Without thinking, I had shoved Chunk's gun down in the back of my belt. I went to the shade of a cottonwood and pulled a cold ham sandwich from my canvas bag. The ham was nearly as good now as it had been the night before. My hands were sore and my muscles were protesting the work I'd done during the morning. I sat down and Colbert's gun poked me. I pulled it out and looked it over. It wasn't the Rootes Colt I'd seen him working with but an army .44 Colt with a solid frame, and it looked near new. It weighed about half what the Dragoon of Pa's did, and had a nice feel. If I ever saw Chunk Colbert again, I'd give it back to him, or else what it shot if he came lookin'.

We ate and then went back to work. I never sweated so much in my life, and by quittin' time I was wobble-legged. Wedge come over to me as I climbed out of a slab-side freight that had been full of coal.

"You put in a good day, kid. We respect them that work. I'll call you by name now if you have one." I could tell that this was a display of friendship, and also a show of respect.

"My name's Matt O'Malley."

Wedge got a funny look on his face. "You have kin that fought in the war?"

"Yeah, I had three brothers that were with the Union and my Pa got in there somewhere."

"One of those brothers named Danny?"

"Yep, he's the oldest. How do you know Danny?"

"I was a guard at Andersonville for a spell. He's the only man that come close to whippin' me with bare hands. He would have beaten me if he'd been eatin' anything besides coarse ground corn. He just plain run out of steam before he could finish the job. He gave me these scars on my face. He was a handy man with his fists, and a good man for all of that. I managed to slip him some greens before I got sent up to the real war."

My heart was pounding in my chest. "How long ago was that, Wedge?" I asked.

"That would have been about the summer of sixty-four I 'spect. You know what happened to him? I'd sure like to try him again."

"We haven't had a word on him since the war started," I replied.

"Wal, maybe somethin' will turn up on him one of these days. See ya tomorrow," Wedge said as he turned to go.

Two years ago. Danny had been alive two years ago.

I got to the house just in time to set and eat. The Major had traded a dried-apple pie for a hind quarter of venison and had it cooked to perfection, although as hungry as I was, a wet boot might have tasted pretty good. I told my partners what had happened during the day, and we agreed that we'd best watch for Colbert. He was still dangerous even if he was missing a gun and an ear. The Chapmans had bought the farm north of town and were moving out the next day. They were in a fair sweat to get started. The warm food, hard work, and the drone of their voices worked like a tonic on me, and before I had even finished eating, I found my face fallin' over in my food. I was tired and my muscles were sore.

"You best get to the rack, Matt, 'fore you choke to death on that deer." Owen laughed.

I nodded, shuffled over to my bed, and crawled under the blanket with my Henry. Colbert's gun poked me in the back again so I pulled it out and slid it under the bed. What a day I'd had. As I was drifting off to sleep, I heard the Major tell Owen that he'd gotten a job as a cook at a local restaurant. His ability to bake fruit pies and bread, not to mention donuts, had been the deciding factor in his favor. Owen remarked that he was tending bar at the saloon, but that was only temporary. He had his eye on something else. I drifted out about then and didn't hear the rest of his plans.

Morning came way too early and with it came the worst pain I'd ever had. I was sore in muscles I didn't know I owned. I couldn't get out of bed by sittin' up. I had to roll out onto the floor and then push myself up with my arms. I hobbled outside and washed up, getting a little looser as I moved. Kiowa came up from the creek with a couple of nice sized fish and a smile.

"Are you a little sore this morning, Matthew?" He laughed as I groaned out an answer. "After you wash up and come in the house, I have something for you." He walked in the door with me following shortly after.

"Here's something I'm sure you can use." He tossed me a pair of gloves. "They are made from the hide of an elk that I shot some years ago. From the looks of your hands you'd better wear them until you get toughened up."

"I can't take these, Kiowa. The work I'm doin' will wear them out in a few weeks."

"There's more elk hide around, Matt, and making another pair will give me something to do on long winter evenings," he said.

"Well, my hands are sore, and maybe I can get an elk before winter. Wedge told me yesterday that there are still some around in the creek bottoms. I'll help you work up the hide, Kiowa." I paused not knowing what else to say. "How was teachin' school yesterday?" I asked.

"It was fine, except I have a young lout of about fifteen who thinks he is too good to be in my school, and certainly too good to be taught by an Indian. How would you deal with him if you were me, Matthew?''

I thought for a minute as I worked my way around half of one of the Major's pies. ''I reckon if I was you I'd tell this lout that if he didn't turn to and work during school, I'd be wearing his hair on my belt.''

Kiowa broke into great whoops of laughter that woke the rest of the household. Every time he'd just about get settled down, he'd think of what I said and then bust out again. Pretty soon I could tell he was losin' control of his facilities, and he bolted out the door to the privy. I could hear his laughter echo in the outhouse. I hadn't thought it was all that funny, in fact, I'd been plumb serious. I bade goodbye to the rest of the guys and started limp-walkin' toward work with my lunch in my bag. By the time I got to the line, I had loosened up and was ready to go.

The rest of the week was like that. Work from can see to can't see, eat, go to bed, get up, and start over again. By the third day most of the soreness was gone, and I began to enjoy the work and the easy friendship of the people I worked with. By the second week Wedge had started comin' round the house after we'd eaten, and as I got to know him I realized that he was a surprisingly gentle-mannered man. He didn't have many friends (something about the way he jerked ears off people's heads made them steer away from him), and I think he warmed up to me 'cause I was the only man on the crew that could stay with his workin' speed at least part of the day. He respected work and did enough for two men most times. I'd had him repeat his story about Danny to Owen, and Owen and Wedge struck up a warm comradeship.

One night as we were sitting out front of the soddie after supper, Owen and Wedge got to talkin'.

''Wedge, you have a particular pretty voice. You wouldn't happen to sing, would you?'' Owen asked. Now pretty isn't the word that I would use for any part of Wedge, but he did have a nice speaking voice.

''Yeah, I love to sing. Matter o' fact I used to sing to the boys in the regiment quite a bit.''

''Do you happen to know 'Shue la Rue'?'' Owen asked.

''Sure I do,'' and with that Wedge started singing the lullaby with the most beautiful baritone voice I'd ever heard. Owen chimed in with a close harmony tenor, and I mean to tell ya it was the prettiest music I'd ever heard. I got goose bumps up and down my arms and my eyes even got a little misty. They sang all five verses and when they quit the echo carried down the creek and faded away.

"Gosh, Owen," Wedge said in a hushed voice, "We did that right good."

"You're welcome at our fire any time, Wedge," the Major remarked. "Anyone who can sing like that has to be kin to angels."

"Come to think on it, I believe there were some angels back a few generations on my ma's side," Wedge said with his crooked smile. Kiowa got tickled and near swallowed his pipe.

"Come on, Matt. Walk me part way to my house," Wedge said as the skeeters started buzzing around our heads. He'd never asked me to do that before, and I was right curious what was on his mind.

"Matt," he said after we'd walked a ways. "Your brother, Owen, has been paying some attention to my sister Patricia. I was a mite upset about it to start until I found out he was kin of yours. I wasn't real happy either when I found out he was a bartender. I started comin' over to see what manner of man he was, and I got to say that I like Owen O'Malley. I like him fine."

"I didn't know you had a sister, Wedge," I told him. I was some stung 'cause I thought he'd been comin over to spend time with me.

"Yep, Pat was a nurse during the war. Our folks died from cholera while we were gone, so's all we got left is each other. She's workin' for Doc Seals as his nurse now."

"I'm glad you like Owen, Wedge," I said. "I think he's a fine man, and I can promise you that he's honest and honorable."

"I figured he was, but I wanted to check him out myself. Pat is plumb taken with him, and I wouldn't want her man to be mean to her."

"Owen's not mean at all, Wedge. He's a fighter, but there's nothing mean in him," I remarked. I wondered how Owen would have looked with only one ear if Wedge hadn't liked him.

"I believe ya, Matt. Don't tell no one what we talked about. If Pat knew I'd been checkin' up on Owen, she'd get cross with me."

We walked a ways farther and then parted.

I walked back hopin' that Owen wasn't the kind of man that dallied around with women. I didn't want to have to fight Wedge, and I might have to if Wedge took a dislike to my brother. Us

O'Malleys always took up each others' fights. Second thought, if Owen was playin' light with Wedge's sister, maybe I'd let Wedge hurt him just a little 'fore I stepped in.

When I got back to the house, everyone was inside involved in a partnership confabulation.

"Pull up a seat, Matt, and tell us what ya think," Owen said as I came in. "The saloonkeeper wants to build a bigger saloon with some rooms to rent on a second story. He wants to sell us the old one."

"Our plan is to buy the old one, leave the bar and tables in, clean up, do some painting, and make a combination restaurant and saloon. We are hoping the rough element will go to the new saloon for drinking and fighting, and come to ours for meals, a good quality drink, and cultivated conversation," the Major added.

"What's the price of the old saloon?" I asked, trying to be practical.

"He's asking five hundred dollars for the building and some of the stock, so we wouldn't have to completely restock. We want to keep some of the finer spirits that he has, and let him take the rough brew. We are hoping to draw customers with more refined tastes," the Major replied. He clasped his hands in front of him, and I could see he was excited with the plannin'.

"Is that a good price?" I asked, feelin' ignorant but truly curious.

"We think it's a little high, but he won't talk down any," Owen said as he stood up and walked over to the window.

"How we gonna pay for it if we decide to buy it?" I asked. I knew our cash reserve was down to near a hundred dollars.

"The man says he will take a hundred now and a hundred a month until she's paid for. If we don't buy another thing for that four months, we can just make it," Owen explained.

"Well, it sounds like a gamble to me, but if we don't take a chance now and then, I don't see us getting anywhere," I responded.

Kiowa hadn't said anything, but as I spoke he looked up. "I have the opportunity to do some night tutoring with five or six of my students. That will help us with grocery money," he said.

"The garden out at the Chapmans' will be producing soon," the Major added. "We can eat some out of that. We can supplement with some buffalo if Matt can get the time to hunt. Meat won't keep long in this weather, but we can have some hump meat once a week or so. I hate killin' a critter and then only using a little bit of it, but as many of the shaggy cows as there are, I can't see us hurting the population much."

"It sounds like if we make some sacrifices we can just make the payments and keep body and soul together," Owen remarked. "I'll take the hundred to him in the morning before someone else beats us to it. I got something else to say while we're all together." Owen looked around the table at us before he continued. "I started seeing a girl." You could have heard a mouse break wind it got so quiet. "Her name is Patricia O'Brien, and she's a nurse for the Doc. I like her a lot and I plan on courtin' her if none of you have an objection." He was near breathless when he finished.

"Why would any of us object, Owen?" the Major asked.

"Well, we are partners, and I figure we should discuss near everything. I felt like I needed your approval 'fore I started courtin'," Owen replied.

"Well, I think I can speak for the entire group when I tell you we heartily approve, Captain," the Major said.

"Patricia O'Brien," I said partly to myself. "Ya know that's Wedge's last name. I wonder if they are relation?"

"What are you thinkin, Matt?" Owen exploded as he turned away from the window. "Look at Wedge. I mean he's a nice guy, but he sure ain't no vision of loveliness. Patricia is the prettiest thing that has graced this part of the world. Why I bet their families ain't even from the same part of Ireland."

I ducked my head so Owen couldn't see my smile. I'd told Wedge I wouldn't talk, but it was all I could do to keep from telling Owen the truth. It sounded like Owen's ears were safe from Patricia O'Brien's singin', ear rippin' brother anyhow. He sounded serious about her.

We bought the saloon, and named it the Rainbow City,'cause we hoped that it would have a pot of gold in it. Owen talked the owner down to four hundred and fifty dollars. Savin' that fifty bucks was mighty important to us. The railroad work stayed steady, and I got my increase the next month. Owen and Patricia became quite an item around town. She was popular and Owen, with his winnin' ways and smile, was approved by most of the townspeople. Wedge became a fixture at our soddie after supper and sometimes, if the Major invited him, he came early and ate with us. The man could surely eat, but he always brought something with him for the meal. Him and Owen sang most every evening and 'fore long folks were takin' their evenin' walks down our way so they could hear the singin'. It caused a little stir with Owen when he found out that Wedge and Patricia were brother and sister, but he didn't mind it much either. Every once in a while Wedge would take me down along the creek and show me some of the finer points of fist fightin'. There were times when we went at it hot and heavy. He was bigger than me, but I had speed to burn and could get inside on him. He showed me how a jab got to the target faster than a long punch, and he showed me other things not quite so refined. I learned that an elbow could deliver a stronger blow than a closed fist, and that folks just had a natural aversion to havin' their ears ripped off.

When I wasn't workin' with Wedge on my fist fightin', I was drawin' the army Colt from a cut-down holster. I fit the holster to a belt and slung it down lower on my leg without goin' through the belt loops. The gun came more natural to my hand that way. I had been gifted with speed, and my eyes and my hands had always worked together well. I knew that I was faster now than Colbert had been when I'd last seen him. I hoped I wouldn't need my new skills, but it was a hard land and Junction City had a cuttin' or shootin' most every week. I wanted to be prepared for the worst, but I wasn't huntin' trouble either; leastways if it wasn't named Falcon Beck. I figured that it wouldn't be long 'fore I could start huntin' Beck and have some chance of livin' through it when I found him.

Junction City was changin' fast. Folks were movin' out from the East to find farms, and a lot of them were using Junction City as a jumpin' off spot. Rainbow City was busy from the time it opened 'til it closed. I knew we were makin' money. Kiowa had thirty-five students in his class and was teaching six grades. Some of the bigger boys was givin' him a hard time, so he took to wearin' a big knife and a real hair wig that he'd sent for from St. Lou in his belt. That fetched him some respect,'cause they weren't quite sure if it was a joke or not. The Methodists put up a clapboard, white-painted church with a bell.

The Chapmans got the alfalfa planted just in time for a gentle two-inch rain to make it sprout, and their garden was puttin' out so much produce that they were makin' trips to town to sell the extra.

The summer got hot and then hotter still, with some of the rip-snortin'est thunderstorms a body ever seen. Lightning hit a cottonwood behind the soddie on the creek and dropped off a limb that was near as big as a regular tree. We heard tell that a twister had ripped through 'bout eight miles north of us, killed a passel of buffalo, and tore up a good stretch of trees along the river. But the highlight of the summer came when the Methodist preacher and a contingent of Methodist ladies came down to the soddie one evening.

"Mister O'Malley and Mister O'Brien," the little preacher said, "we would be honored if you would grace us with a couple of hymns come next Sunday."

Owen and Wedge had just finished singing an Irish ballad about a highwayman and a lost love that sent him on his path of crime. I was sure the Methodists had heard part of it, and it had been real purty. Owen looked surprised, but Wedge looked stricken. I knew by some of the language that Wedge used on the job that he wasn't a regular churchgoer. I could see things goin' through his head like a sharp saw through green wood. How could he tell the preacher no without being condemned straight to hell?

"We'd be proud to, preacher," Owen had replied with grace. I thought Wedge was goin' to be sick, but he nodded his head. I never seen anybody that green in my whole life. I had to go around back so they wouldn't see me grinnin'. When I come back 'round, I heard the Major tellin' Owen that he thought it was a gallant gesture them singin' in church, and he promised that the partnership would be there in force to support them. He looked right at me when he said it.

Come Sunday we dressed in the best we had, and Kiowa surprised us all with a natty black suit he'd stashed somewhere. He cut quite a figure, as did Owen in his fancy clothes. I didn't have a suit, so I wore by best shirt and put a saddle soap shine on my boots. I felt like I was goin' to a funeral with my hair slicked back with possum grease. We heard the bell sounding church time, so we headed up the street. It was hotter than blue blazes and sweat started on me like I'd been throwin' lumber all day. I felt better some when I saw Wedge. He was stuffed into a suit that might have fit him good when he was twelve, and sweat was pourin' off him. He had Pat on his arm, but he turned her over to Owen as we walked up to them.

"Owen, I just don't think this is a good idea," Wedge wheezed as they walked up the steps. Wedge had to duck his head as we walked in the door.

We took a spot right up front and waited for the service to

begin. The little preacher stood up to the podium, raised his arms, and said "Let us pray." Did we ever. That little feller made up for bein' short by bein' the best pray-er in the territory. It was terrible close in the church, and I even saw a little drop of sweat roll off the end of Pat's nose. I was some shocked. I didn't know girls sweated, not even a little bit. When the preacher got done prayin' he motioned Owen and Wedge up on the platform. He introduced them to the congregation and announced the hymn they were goin' to sing. The pump organ started breathin' as the lady pedaled and a surprisin' loud blast came out of the darn thing. I jumped, but tried to make it look like it was a crease in the back of my britches that made me move. The organ lady giggled a little, then settled into makin' some music. The boys put their hearts into the hymn and lookin' around you could see that folks were plumb pleased with the music. The preacher started preachin' again, and I truly thought that it was never goin' to get over.

The only good thing that came out of the whole mess was a mouse that kept pokin' his head out from under the pump organ. I calculated that mouse was the deafest critter that ever lived, else he couldn't have lived where he did. I kept hopin' that he'd crawl up the organ lady's leg and then we'd have some action. I got so entertained that I near missed all the preachin'. Finally I heard an amen from the preacher man. Owen and Wedge got up to sing folks out the door, and I headed out to get a breath of air. I walked down the steps just as a breeze rattled the cottonwood leaves and cooled the sweat on my back. I heard some horses comin' up the street and as I turned to see who it was, I looked right into the face of Falcon Beck, and I weren't wearin' a gun.

Chapter Four

He didn't recognize me, or else he just plain didn't see me. I was walkin' down the steps with a lot of folks, in a hurry to get out of the church, and he didn't look very long. I'd changed some since he'd last seen me too. I was probably an inch taller, and the railroad work had added beef to my shoulders, chest, and arms. He looked us over for a moment and then looked back down the road he had come in on. He swung his horse around and headed up main street, joining some other men in front of the new saloon. Since Junction City had got religion, the saloon-keeper had taken to closin' on Sunday mornings 'til church was out. He didn't figure it was right to have shootin's during church services.

"You look like you've seen a ghost, Matt. What's the trouble?" the Major asked as he came up to me.

"You got a gun on you, Major?" I asked.

"Why, no. I haven't been carrying a gun lately and particularly not to church," he replied.

"Let's go back inside and get the other men with us. Falcon Beck just looked over the church crowd, and he's ridin' with a passel of rough-lookin' people." I said it low enough so it wasn't overheard by the folks around us.

The Major didn't question. He turned on his heel and walked back into the church.

"Owen, Kiowa," he spoke to them as they came down the aisle. "Matthew has brought a problem to my attention. I suggest we go out the back window and walk the creek down to the house instead of going down the street." They didn't ask any questions either. They just followed the Major out the window and down the creek.

"What's the problem, Major?" Owen finally asked.

"Matthew," he said as he looked over at me.

35

"I went out the front door and near walked into Falcon Beck. He was lookin' over the church crowd, but didn't recognize me. They stopped down by the new saloon."

"Do you think they are looking for us, or is it just chance that they came this way?" Kiowa asked. "They surely wouldn't still be looking for us. We pose no threat to them now."

"They may not've come lookin' for us, but it won't take them long to find out we're here," Owen said.

"No, you're right there, Captain," the Major added. "We have become quite prominent here in Junction City, and if they stay, they will surely come against us. Falcon Beck is not one to forgive a grudge, regardless if we pose a threat or not."

"Well, I ain't runnin' this time, Major," I said with a quiet fierceness that surprised even me.

"Easy, Matthew," the Major said. "I'm not suggesting we turn and run. We have avoided this fight as best we could, and we will continue to try and avoid it. However, if they come against us, we will have to make a fight. There is no question that this time we are in the right, and if we live through a confrontation, we will have popular support behind us. There is no law here, so we must see to ourselves."

"I have a concern, Major," Kiowa said. "The Chapmans are out on the river farm with no knowledge that they may be in danger. I'm sure they are alert because of the trouble with the Cheyenne, but we should warn them of Beck."

"Yes, you're quite right, Kiowa," the Major agreed. "Matt, when we get to the house, saddle my horse and ride out there. They don't need to come in, but they should be warned quickly. The saloonkeeper has no reason to know the trouble we've had, so he will probably tell Beck all of our affairs if inquiry is made."

"Yes sir, Major," I replied. I'd never been in the military, but I could see that these men worked together like a well-oiled machine when trouble came. They'd seen enough trouble to last them a lifetime, yet here it was again.

I changed clothes as soon as we hit the soddie, grabbed the Henry, and belted on my army Colt. Then I went around back to the stable and saddled the Major's horse. I still had my old buck mule, but I needed a quick trip, which no cursedness like a mule will give you if he takes the notion. I was 'bout due for a real horse. People still looked at me funny when I rode down Main Street on the mule. The Major's horse was a Morgan, and big for the breed. He wasn't red and he wasn't brown, but somewhere in between. I bounced into the saddle and headed north like there was supper waitin'.

I got to the river farm in good time, but the Chapmans weren't at the house. I started lookin' about for a sign and found a fresh wagon track goin' up river. I followed it, and about an hour later I came up with the boys just as they finished loadin' the meat from two buffalo onto the wagon. After I explained the situation to them they unhitched the team and rode bareback to the farm. They tied the horses to the corral and went into the house to fetch guns. I got down from the Morgan, and went over to the horse trough where I hand pumped some fresh water and took a cold drink from a deep well. Then I rinsed my face, slicked back my hair, and put on my hat. I'd taken to wearin' a Union cavalry hat Owen had gotten for me. It kept the sun and rain off my face better than a regular felt hat.

"Well, ain't he purty, now boys?" a coarse voice said behind me. I turned around slowly and they were sittin' their horses lookin' at me. Six men had come for us from Beck's group. I recognized the one that had spoken as one of the men that had been with Beck durin' the raid on the island.

"We found out by accident that you boys were in town," he said with his voice loud enough to be heard in town. "We had us a little woman trouble back East, and the local folks decided to run us out. We left, but we took some of their women with us, and we killed us a few farmers along the way. Beck has the rest of your troop treed back in town, so he sent us out to kill some more farmers. We figured since we were passin' through we might as well take care of some unfinished business."

I guess he expected me to do some talkin', maybe even beg for my life, but O'Malleys don't take too well to bein' pushed into corners. Pa always told us boys that there was a time for fightin' and a time for talkin'. Time for talkin' was past. I shucked my army Colt out of the holster and shot the big talker through the second button on his greasy shirt. It blew him backwards out of the saddle. One of the Chapmans had opened a window and cut loose with a Colt revolving shotgun. The range wasn't over thirty yards, and he emptied two saddles with one shot.

Things got a bit confused after that. Horses started rearing, and the men that had been shot with the shotgun weren't dead and were mighty noisy. I triggered another shot at a man ridin' toward me and missed. He didn't have a gun out and seemed intent on ridin' me over, but most horses have a real aversion to strikin' people, so his horse laid on the brakes just as he got to me. The man unloaded from the saddle and fell at my feet. I kicked him under the chin, and he stayed put. There was shootin' all around me, and the dust was so thick I could barely see.

Suddenly, the noise quit, and I could hear a horse runnin' full out. I walked out of the cloud of dust and watched a man ridin' as hard as he could back toward town. I had picked up my Henry, and the man made one mistake. He stopped to take a shot at the house. He never got it off. My .44 took him through the throat just as he was drawin' a bead. He fell off the horse and lay quiet. The horse came back into the yard to stand with the others. Six men were down and four of them were dead. The man I'd kicked was still out, but alive. One of the two that had been shot with the shotgun was dead. The buckshot intended for marauding Cheyenne had done for a crook just as well. The other man was tore up bad, but would probably make it. One of the Chapmans had been using a '55 Union musket he'd picked up somewhere, and the giant ball had taken another man through the gut. He wouldn't be killin' any more farmers.

I jumped on the Morgan and gathered the reins. "One of you stay here with the shotgun and watch the farm. The other grab one of these horses and come with me. It sounds like the rest of the partnership may be in trouble." They didn't say a word, just moved to obey. Earl already had the shotgun and David was astride one of the dead men's horses. We lit out for town at a sprint. The Morgan loved to run, and he loved to fight. Darndest thing about military horses. Some of them seemed to have a nose for battle, and some of them always tried to dodge a fight just like some men. We stopped just before we came in sight of the soddie. We were screened by willows along the creek bank, which we tied our horses to.

We could hear shooting, which came to us as single shots with an occasional flurry. Someone was still alive at the house.

"You come up from the back at the stable. I'll circle and come up behind Beck and his mob." David nodded agreement and moved away from me. I took a wide circle out into the prairie and came in on the street south of Beck's position. I started movin' up the street keepin' to the cover of the store fronts. I had my Henry in my hand and my army Colt lay snug against my leg. I had an anger on me, and I wasn't goin' to show mercy to nobody. They'd come askin' for it, and I was goin' to make sure some of them got it.

I got close. I got real close. I could see the house well, and I figured I was an easy rifle shot from it. A man came over the top of the soddie roof with a torch in his hand. He was goin' to try and fire the house. He just didn't make it. I shot him right through the chest, and he fell in front of the front door. There was a yell and a tremendous crash of gunfire. I had a tree between me and them, but they had no cover from me. Their cover had been to the other side, protected from the soddie. I emptied the Henry, watching as men started going for their horses. There was a tremendous blast, and I saw a man lifted out of the saddle like he'd been hit with a club. That would be David and his musket.

The firing picked up from the house, and Beck's men started to scatter. I drew the army Colt and rolled five shots off so fast they sounded near like one. I saw a man go down and get up with blood on his thigh. Another went down and didn't move. I pulled the cylinder out of the Colt and dropped it as it scalded my hand. I had another cylinder in my back pocket and slid it into place. Then I holstered the Colt and saw to loadin' the Henry.

A horse galloped by and pulled up sharply. When I looked up there was Falcon Beck leveling a pistol at me. He splintered the stock of the Henry, knocking it from my hand. I drew the Colt, and I saw shock register on his face. He had no idea I could load my hand so fast. I triggered a shot and burned his face with the ball. He turned his horse and ran. He flat ran until he was out of sight. I was so surprised that I didn't even think to shoot him.

It was over. The door to the house came open, and the Major and Owen came out with guns in their hands. David came around the side of the stable carrying his musket. It might be slow to load, but when he shot them they stayed shot no matter where he hit 'em.

"You okay, Matt?" Owen yelled out to me. I raised my hand to show them I was fine and noticed blood on me. I took a closer look and realized I had several large splinters buried in my hand from the Henry. I leaned over and picked up my empty cylinder and my poor rifle. The stock was a goner. I heard footsteps comin' down the street, and turned to face them. There were about ten townsmen walkin' toward me, and they were armed to the teeth. Wedge was in the front. "You all right, Matt?" he

asked me when he got up close and saw the blood on my arm
and hand.

"I'm fine, Wedge, but I didn't see Kiowa come out of the
house with the others," I remarked.

"Damn," the saloonkeeper exclaimed. "If they hurt our
schoolteacher, we're goin' to get up a posse and run them renegades' til we catch 'em, and then hang them from the nearest
telegraph pole."

Trees were scarce on the plains, and telegraph poles often
served double duty.

We walked toward the house with men droppin' off here and
there to check renegades that were lyin' around. We didn't want
to get shot in the back, and some of the townsfolk were humane
enough to make sure that even Beck's rabble got medical attention if they were still breathin'. I didn't care much. They'd come
at us wishin' for a fight. They deserved what they got.

"Where's Kiowa?" I asked as soon as we got near.

"He took one through the upper chest at the first volley. He
is in pain, but it doesn't look like it touched anything vital," the
Major responded.

"I'll be the judge of that," Doc said as he pushed his way
through the massed men in front of the door. "Get out of my
way, so I can tend to him."

I followed the doctor into the room.

"Boy, you look mighty pale for a redskin." The doctor smiled
at Kiowa. Kiowa grinned back, but it turned into a grimace. The
wound looked bad, but I was no judge. I went back into the
sunlight, and someone grabbed me. "Matthew O'Malley, you sit
right here and let me dig some of those splinters out of you."
Patty O'Brien had hold of me, and she was most intent on diggin'
the wood out of my hide. I sat down in the shade, and she started
workin' on me, as Owen stood by and watched. She was wonderful gentle, and it was the first time I could ever remember a
woman doin' for me,'cept for Ma when I was little. It was kind
of nice.

"We're even, Matthew," Owen said to me in his quiet voice.
I looked up at him some confused. "I saved you from Falcon
Beck once, and now you saved me. I reckon that makes us even."

"He ran, Owen. He flat ran out on the fight. It was a close
thing between us, and it might've gone either way, but he ran
out."

Owen nodded his head. "I got this rotten feelin' that we still haven't seen the last of Falcon Beck.'' He looked down the road where Beck, and what was left of his men, had gone. It was evening and the locusts started singing down in the trees on the creek like nothing much had happened. I could still smell powder smoke and death on the small breeze. When Pat finished I thanked her, then David and I went down to the creek and retrieved our horses from the willows.

"Tell everybody that I went back out to the farm, would you, Matt?'' David said as he swung aboard the horse. "You might come out after a while with word of what they want us to do with the two live ones we got out there.''

"All right, David. You take care. There may still be some of them around.''

I walked the Morgan back to the stable and rubbed him down. I'd used him hard and he needed the attention, besides I didn't want any part of the post battle celebration. Human critters are like that. They fight and if they win they have to brag it up. None of the partnership would, but I knew the store clerks would whoop it up like they done most the fightin'. I could hear them, and I wanted no part of it. A man does what he has to do and then gets on with life. There's not much time for celebratin' death although we Irish are famous for it.

"Matt, you want some supper?'' Owen had come out to the stable as dark settled in.

"No, I'm not feelin' hungry. I guess David told you we got jumped out at the farm by some of Beck's men?''

"Yeah, and from the sounds of it they barely even got a shot off. Your speed with a short gun caught 'em fully by surprise.'' Owen had kind of snickered at me when I'd been practicing down by the creek as if it were child's play. I had felt kind of foolish when he'd watched, but he wasn't laughing now.

"Well, when we left the farm, there were still two of them alive. David wants to know what to do with 'em.''

"I don't really know, Matt. Why don't you go out and bring them back to town, and we'll have a confab on it. While you're at it, David says we got six new horses out of the deal. Why don't you pick the best of the lot and leave Buck out at the farm. That mule would rather pull a wagon than be rode anyway.''

Owen left the stable, and I moved over to Buck's stall. He bared his teeth to me like always, and I had to knee him in the gut to pull up the cinch. I was goin' to miss him, but only a little. A horse would be nice.

"David, Earl?" I hollered as I rode into the farmyard. It was dark and quiet. No one answered my hail. I heard the barn door open with a squall, and I was off my mule and down on one knee with the Colt in my hand.

"That you, Matt?" Earl's voice echoed through the still night. I holstered the Colt and walked toward the younger Chapman. "Where's David?" I asked.

"We got those two skunks locked in a closet in the house. He has the shotgun and is standing guard over them. What you want to do with them?"

"Owen said for me to bring them back to town, and we'd have a talk on it. What do you and David think we should do?"

"I think we ought let them go. I've seen enough killin' to last me forever, but I bet there's some town folk will want to string them up to a tree. We be part of the town, and it's like they attacked the whole blame town when they took us on. I reckon they's gonna be storekeepers wantin' to string them up as an example to other crooks," Earl replied.

That notion hadn't occurred to me, but Earl was some older than me and had seen a lot more of the world. What he said made sense.

"I'll tell the partnership what you said, Earl. You and David are a big part of our team. David feel the same?"

"Yep. He's like me. They's been enough killin'."

We went into the house, and Earl lit a lamp. The place was neat and tidy, not at all what I expected from two men livin' together. David came in from one of the bedrooms with the Colt shotgun in the crook of his arm.

"Owen wants me to bring them to town, David." He nodded and went back into the room. He came back a few minutes later with Beck's men in front of the shotgun.

"They ain't for tryin' nothin', Matt. That one still has a hide full of buckshot, and the other one has a broken jaw," David remarked.

Lookin' at the outlaws up close made me almost feel sorry for them. Almost. We walked them outside and helped them onto a couple of the captured horses, then tied their hands to the pommel of their saddles.

"Owen said for me to pick out one of the horses and leave Buck out here with you," I remarked to David. "Which of the six do you think is the best?"

"There's a black with a small white blaze on his forehead in the corral. He has a deep trunk, which means stayin' power, and he has a lot of muscle. You ain't no little boy, Matt. You need a big animal under you. I'd say you and the black are suited,'' he replied. ''You watch these boys, and I'll put your saddle on him.''

He came back into the yard a few minutes later leading a beautiful black horse by my bridle. The horse walked right up to me and nuzzled my shoulder. He was a big horse, but still had the look of speed. I was taken by him as soon as I saw him. I swung up into the saddle and took the lead rope on the two other horses from Earl.

''You boys take care, and keep watchin' for Cheyenne. They be just up the river a mite, and they may decide to come and give you a visit,'' I said with a smile.

''Hell, Matthew. The Cheyenne would be an easy chore after what we faced today.'' Earl grinned back. I rode off toward town thinkin' how the Chapmans were the salt of the earth. They were good men who only wanted to be good farmers if folks would give them half a chance.

Owen and the Major must have heard me cross the creek,'cause they were at the stable when I rode in.

''Any trouble, Matt?'' the Major asked as I stepped out of the saddle and he took the lead rope from me.

''Nope. I don't think they're feelin' too spry,'' I replied. ''We best have the Doc take a look at them 'fore we tuck them away.''

''He's still in the cabin tending Kiowa. Seems as though the bullet didn't hit anything vital, but it tore a big track and broke his shoulder. The Doc's watchin' over him for awhile tonight,'' Owen replied.

''That's a beautiful animal, Matt,'' the Major commented as we stabled the animals. ''I've seen that brand before. In fact, I've seen that horse before. It belonged to General Herm Smith, a neighbor of mine back in eastern Kansas. This was his battle horse for the last year of the war. He fought for the Union and has a reputation as a hard man. A mighty hard man. His hand was against us during our late difficulties back there, but I want no man to ever accuse us of stealing horses. I suppose Beck and his band of thieves stole it from Smith's pasture.''

I was some upset. I'd really taken to the black and he to me. I knew I couldn't keep him.

''I reckon tomorrow we'd best send the general a telegram and let him know we got his horse out here," I remarked. "If him and the black were together durin' the war, he'll want him back."

"I'm afraid it's the only thing to do, Matt. We'll look over the other horses we captured. Perhaps you can find something suitable among them." He turned toward the front of the house showing the two bandits the path around the side.

I stood for a minute lookin' at the black as he chewed on some oats I'd slipped him. He was a beautiful animal. I should've known it was too good to be true. I walked up the path and stepped into the soddie. Wedge was there, as was the Doc and Pat. The Doc was lookin' over Beck's men.

"It's a funny thing," Doc commented. "These are the only survivors of the raid. The attackers that were left behind here in town were either all dead or died soon after the fight."

"They had some wounded that rode out with the rest," I said remembering the man I'd hit in the leg.

"Yes, that makes sense," Doc replied. "They certainly wouldn't have wanted to stay in town considering the way people are feeling here. I am afraid that I will fix these men up simply to be healthy when they are hanged."

I walked back to the kitchen and slapped together a sandwich with fresh bread. The Major always found time to feed us. He said it was a lesson of the war that would always stay with him. A man with a full belly is a happy man, most times.

As I sat on the edge of my bed watchin' Doc tend Kiowa, I thought about the day we'd had. After a while I kicked off my boots and laid back.

When I woke, it was mornin' and the birds were singin' down at the creek; I must've been more tired than I'd thought. I got up, took off my gun belt, and walked outside to the pump. I pumped water into the basin, and washed up back by the stable where we always did so we didn't make mud close to the house. I finished washin' and looked at the big black horse standing quiet in the stall. I opened the door and backed him out by his halter. He nuzzled me for a treat, which I didn't have, and then wickered at me softly. I tied him off to the corral and slapped my blanket and saddle on him. I slipped the bridle between his teeth and swung up on his back. The general surely wouldn't object if I exercised his horse.

I rode down through town and out east on the main road. The black had an easy gait and was a real comfort to ride. I didn't run him, just kept him to a brisk pace 'til he broke a good sweat.

I turned around and started walkin' him back toward town to cool him off. Soon enough I heard horses comin' up the road from the east and turned in my saddle. They weren't outlaws. In fact, they rode as if they were a cavalry troop, but in civilian clothes. I pulled off to the side to let them pass, and turned my face back toward town. The men caught up with me and about half of them swept on by. Suddenly, they whirled their mounts around, and with the men behind me, they had me neatly boxed.

"Son, I reckon we're going to have to hang you. That's my horse you're riding, and the man that stole him also killed my daughter. We're going to hang you slow. There won't be any breaking your neck. We're going to let your feet barely touch the ground, and finally you're going to get tired and hang yourself. It may take two days or maybe even three, but finally you're going to choke yourself to death." There was barely controlled rage behind the general's voice, and I knew he meant what he said. It didn't sound like a very nice way to die. I was at least three miles out from town, and there were cottonwoods a lot closer than town was. I hadn't told anyone where I was going, and I hadn't worn my gun. I swore that if I lived through this, I'd never make that mistake again.

Chapter Five

"General, I can explain," I started to remark.

"Shut your mouth, boy. No sense in making things worse by trying to lie. Take him and gag him," he said to the men behind me. Rough hands grabbed me from the black horse, and a rag was stuffed into my mouth. Another rag was tied around my head to keep me from spittin' the gag out. They tied my hands behind me with a piece of rawhide, then lifted me back onto the black horse. We turned off the road and headed directly for the river. We stopped under a cottonwood with big branches and one of the men threw a new rope over a low branch. A loop was made in the end. I was taken from the horse again, and stood on the ground. The loop was thrown over my head, and the slack taken out until I was on my toes.

"That's good, men. That's just right. If the rope stretches any, I want the slack taken out again. I want him on his toes," the general said.

I felt tears of frustration start in my eyes, and the general saw them.

"Try and be a man, son. You felt you were a man when you stole my horse and killed my sweet girl, so act like one now."

The arches in my feet were already hurtin', and I knew I wouldn't last two or three days. It was one of those times when I wished I wasn't so big. The general turned away from me and walked over to where one of the men was puttin' together a fire.

"He's one of Beck's, or he wouldn't know that I'd been a general. Besides, he was riding my horse, Sin. It's certain he was there when . . ." His voice trailed off, and he looked over at me, then away.

"I remember the night that horse was born. It was the first year of the war. I was home on a short leave from the army and my mare foaled. I saw him while he was still wet, and one of

46

my grooms remarked that he was blacker than sin. The name stuck to him. I've never owned a better horse." He moved to the other side of the fire. "It's because of that horse I'm still alive. He saved my life more than once in battle." The general became quiet and looked into the fire. At least I knew the name of the horse that got me hung.

The slowest hour I'd ever known passed by, and my calves began to cramp. I surely wasn't going to last the day. My neck was chafed, and I could hardly catch a breath, what with the rope and the gag.

"General." One of the men strode up to the fire and kicked an ember back into the pit. "There's a big company of men coming up from the direction of town."

"Thank you, Sergeant. Tell the men to stand by their guns and get Bradford to take hold of the rope 'round the boy's neck. If these men are here for this murdering bastard, and a fight commences, I want Bradford to raise him off the ground. No matter what happens to me, I want him hung." The General spat into the fire, and then turned toward me. "You're going to hang, boy. You're going to die for what you did."

I wasn't real encouraged by his words, but I was sure hopin' that the people comin' from town were friends of mine.

They rode up in a cloud of dust, and the Major stepped down from his Morgan.

"General Smith, I would advise you to let Matthew O'Malley down. You have obviously made a mistake."

The dust had cleared, and I could see near thirty men with guns had come out with the Major. It was purely heart warmin' to know I had that many friends. I only wished the Major would hurry along with it. My legs were tired, and the guy holding on to the rope had me as high on my toes as I could go.

"I have not made a mistake, Daly. I caught this young man riding a stolen horse. My stolen horse. I was in Kansas City when Beck hit my place. He stole all my riding stock, and killed my daughter and three of my hands. I am obligated to hang all of Beck's men I catch, the same as I will Beck when we come upon him." The General strode toward Major Daly as he spoke.

"General," Owen spoke as he stepped down from his horse, "that's my brother you have at the end of that rope. He's not the man that stole your horse, nor was he with the men that stole the horse. He's been here, working every day, all summer long. He hasn't been out of town for more than a few hours anytime since we arrived in Junction City, and these men will swear to it.''

"What do I care what these men will swear to? As I recall, Daly was associating with a bunch of men who had the name of renegades before he left the eastern part of the state. Who might you be, sir?'' he said addressing Owen.

"My name is Owen O'Malley. I was riding with Major Daly, and we did have the name of renegades before we left. Beck and his political friends were the ones that attached that designation to us. We were fighting Beck and his men so that the Major and two other men, now dead, could recover their homes.''

The general took a step back from Owen who was obviously angry.

I was hopin' they'd quit discussin' Beck and remember that I was behind them with a man holdin' onto a rope that was makin' me 'bout seven feet tall.

"Owen O'Malley,'' the general repeated. "Captain Owen O'Malley?'' he asked.

"Yes, sir. I rode with you in three separate engagements as second in command of your cavalry,'' Owen replied.

The general looked surprised, and the Major stepped up close to him as Owen quit talkin'.

"Herm, we might have fought for different sides during the war, but before that we were good neighbors. We were friends. I've helped you put up hay, and we've drunk from the same dipper at my well. You know that I'm an honest man. I'm telling you that you have the wrong man,'' the Major spoke quietly and directly to the general. "I know you're bitter. I know you're a hard and unforgiving man, but these men with me are ready to fight to save Matt's life, and your men are seasoned fighters. Let's not compound your mistake with the deaths of these good men that stand with us.'' The Major was pleading, and it finally got to the general.

"Let him down, Bradford,'' the general said as he turned toward me.

Bradford let some slack in the rope and then went to where it was tied around the base of the tree and untied it. I fell onto my back as he dropped the rope. Hands untied me and took out the gag. Owen was standing beside me, talkin', but I wasn't listening. I was still trying to drag deep breaths of sweet Kansas air into my lungs. There was a buzz of voices from all of the men; then it got still, and I heard the General talking to the Major.

"They killed my beautiful girl, Bob. They killed my Amy," he said. He was crying as he said it, and the Major had his arm around the general's shoulders, talking to him in a hushed tone. They walked off together into the trees. Two warriors that understood each other's pain. Two old friends.

"Okay, men," Owen spoke loud enough for everyone to hear. "Let's help the general's men get saddled and take 'em into town. We got to tell them exactly what happened here with Beck, and it's best done at Rainbow City." People started moving around, glad for something to do. It was a strange thing for them to see the general cry, particular those who had ridden with him for years.

"Good grief, Matt. You were near a goner," Wedge said as he lifted me to my feet. "I saw you ridin' that black horse out of town and figured you'd be right back. When you didn't show for work, I went over to Rainbow City and told Owen I had a bad feelin'. We rang the church bell and got these men together. I thought Beck's men had come back and taken you. We almost took to shootin' when we seen you strung up, but the Major recognized Herm Smith and knew what must've of happened. You're damn lucky that Smith wanted to kill you slow, else we'd have been an hour too late."

I tried to speak, but all I did was croak. My throat was bruised, and my talk box wasn't workin'.

"Owen," the big man spoke to my brother, "I'm takin' Matt back in to see the doc. We'll see you in town." Owen raised his arm to show that he'd heard. Wedge picked me off my feet and sat me in my own saddle on the back of the horse that had near gotten me killed. I wasn't feelin' too kindly toward the horse, but I was in no shape to argue either.

Wedge turned toward one of the general's men. "Tell your boss that he can pick this horse up in town." He didn't wait for an answer, and after watchin' Wedge sit me on the horse like I was a baby, the man wasn't inclined to offer comment.

"Your vocal cords are bruised, so I would recommend you not try to talk for a couple of days," Doc said when he looked at me. "It appears that's all the damage done, other than the raw spot on your neck. You'll heal fine."

"Can you get home, Matt?" Wedge asked me after Doc had taken care of my neck. "I want to go over to the restaurant and find out what's goin' on."

"I'll get him home," Doc commented. "I need to look in on Kiowa anyhow."

We walked out to the rail, and I climbed onto Sin's back. My legs were terrible sore, and my disposition wasn't real pleasant either. We rode down to the soddie, took my saddle off Sin, and tied him to the top rail on the corral. I left him out 'cause I figured the Major would be givin' him back to General Smith.

Doc went in the house, and I was left alone with the horse.

I stroked the black horse's velvety nose, and he rubbed against my shoulder. I didn't know if a man could have love at first sight for a horse, but I was sure taken to that black gelding.

I went in the house, got my gun belt, and laid down on my bed. I lay the Colt right beside me. I swore then and there that never for the rest of my life would I be caught without a gun. It might have gotten me killed this morning, but it also might have been a little harder to take me prisoner. I went to sleep thinkin' on how close I'd come to dyin'.

"Matt, if you can eat, dinner's ready." Owen had hold of my shoulder. I was powerful hungry, but it felt like my throat was near swollen shut. I rolled out of bed and managed to take a sip of water, and then a drink. It hurt bad to swallow, so I settled for a warm beer while the rest of the men ate the noon meal.

"That general, he's sure a sudden kind, ain't he?" Wedge asked no one in particular.

"Well, it didn't take him long to dispense justice, for sure," the Major replied.

Owen moved his plate back and turned toward me. "General Smith heard our story about Beck. We brought out the two men that you captured at the river farm yesterday, and he questioned them. Turns out that the big man you shot is the one that stole the General's horses. He was the one ridin' the black. It was him and Beck that killed Smith's daughter." Owen scooted back from the table and stood up. "We had a trial for 'em. There wasn't any of the general's men on the jury, only townsmen. We heard testimony from the general regarding the crimes back East, and then we heard testimony about what took place here yesterday. The jury found them guilty, and the general hung 'em. It was as fair as it could be, and satisfied most everybody except the outlaws." Owen moved toward the front door. "I thought you ought to know that things have been set right with the general, and he wants to see you this evening. He feels right sorry about what happened."

Owen left for Rainbow City. I had a sick feelin' down in my gut. I never did like the thought of hangin' men, even bad men, but I really hated it now.

"Darndest thing," the Major said. "Herm Smith and I were neighbors and friends before the war, and deadly enemies after. He was one of the political people that put Beck in a position of superficial correctness with the confiscation of lands, mine among them. It sure fired backwards on him, and now I feel sorry for the man. He actually invited me to come home with him. He said he'd help me put my place in order." The Major moved toward the front door to follow Owen back to work. "He told me that Beck burned my house before he left. I think that when the house burnt so did the bridge that would take me back there." He walked on out the door.

"You know, Matt," Wedge looked toward me and got up from the table, "I'm sure glad I'm a simple man. These high, fast thinkers sure make life complicated." He gave me that crooked grin of his, and I felt some better. "I'm goin' down to the railroad yard, but you're off for the rest of today. I'll see you tonight."

Doc came in from outside. "I have to get back to the office. Patricia will be expecting me back this afternoon. Kiowa is doing as well as can be expected, and I'm going to keep him doped for a couple days. Try not to wake him except for light meals and some water." Doc walked up to me and looked me over. "You look like hell, but if you can drink warm beer, I expect you'll live." He smiled at me and went out the door.

I followed him and untied Sin. I took the big horse over to the trough and let him water before I tied him back. I went down to the stable and got a currycomb and a piece of sacking. I spent a couple of hours goin' over his coat until he shined. He liked the attention, and I needed somethin' to do.

When I finished, I looked down the street and saw a man walkin' toward the house. I slipped the thong from the hammer of my gun, which held it in the holster, and waited. It was General Smith and he was walkin' slow. He came up to me and looked at the black horse. "He's a beautiful animal," he commented. "I guess you heard this morning when I told one of my men about this horse. He means a lot to me." The general cleared his throat. "May we sit in the shade a moment, Matthew?" he asked.

I pointed toward the benches by the corral, and we walked over to them and sat.

The general cleared his throat again and looked right in my

face. "It's not easy for me to say I'm sorry, Matthew. It's never been easy for me, and I haven't done it more than two or three times in my whole life." He took a swing at a horsefly that landed on his arm and continued. "I'm not going to offer you any excuses, or beg for understanding. I am simply going to say that I was wrong, and I am sorry." He looked like an old bitter man to me with the heart near gone out of him, and I wasn't feelin' like makin' his chore any easier for him. He owed me.

"I'm not goin' to tell you that I understand, General," I managed to croak. "I know you've had a hard time, and I know what it is to lose someone you love." I stopped for a minute and swallowed. It hurt like hell. "I feel sorry for you. I think your bitterness will be the death of you and probably some of your men. If I'd had my gun on this morning, we'd probably both be dead right now."

He nodded his head. "Yes, Captain O'Malley told me that you were very impressive yesterday during the fight with Beck and his men." He stood and turned away from me and looked toward town. "Matthew, you're young and have your life before you. What you said about me may be right, but I have learned one thing today. I can make mistakes. I can be wrong. I was wrong about you, and I was wrong about Bob Daly. I'm going back home, Matthew. I am done with Beck. I had it in my mind to chase him to the ends of the earth and make him pay. Bob Daly made me realize that hate is more deadly for the person that carries it than it is for the man that is hated. I said that for you, Matt. You hate me now for what I did, and Owen told me that you took a blood oath to kill Beck. I don't blame you, but you must get it out of your system, not for my sake or Beck's, but for your own." The general walked over to Sin and untied him from the corral, then walked back toward me. I felt a lump come up in my throat. I was goin' to miss that big horse.

"Matt, I'm going home. People like Beck always do the same things and somehow, somewhere he is going to pay the price. I want to thank you for killing the big man who was riding my horse. At least one of the men that killed my daughter has been brought to justice." He stopped for a minute and blinked back some tears. "I want you to have a special gift from me. Something that will partially make up for my mistake and reward you for your part in the battle with Beck's men." He reached up and swiped at a tear that had fallen down his cheek. "I want you to have Sin. I won't take no for an answer, and to show you I am sincere I have the bill of sale already drawn and signed."

Well, that did it. I wasn't mad at the general anymore for hangin' me. In fact, I was feelin' right friendly toward him. He handed me the tie rope and stuck out his right hand for me to shake. I took it and held it a moment. "Thanks, General. I promise to take good care of him."

"I know you will, son. God bless you, and I hope to see you again." With that, he turned away from me and walked back up the street. I watched him go and could feel what the Major had felt. I guess he'd call it compassion. The black stomped his foot, and I looked at him, then at the bill of sale in my hand. Sin was really mine. No more mules. I was ridin' in style from now on.

The afternoon sun was burning down, and it was so still that there wasn't even a rustle from the cottonwood leaves along the creek. It was so blamed hot that the flies didn't even want to fly. I needed to move. I wasn't accustomed to sittin' on my bottom end for more than a short spell at a time, so I decided to saddle my new horse and go up to the rail line.

I grabbed my saddle and five minutes later I was ridin' up the street. I got near where the main road came into town from the east and looked out over the prairie. Comin' up the road, almost in town, were three wagons loaded with pilgrims. There was startin' to be quite a few immigrants. They were comin' through, headin' for places they hoped to homestead on the Kansas flatland along the rivers and creeks. These looked a little more prosperous than some I'd seen. The horses were better fed, the wagons painted, and the folks were wearing store-bought clothes instead of homespun. They came on into town, their horses' hooves sounding loud in the still of the summer afternoon.

I sat on my black horse, interested in the manner of people they might be. They weren't normal movers; they looked like people who'd left something behind, and had grand hopes for the future. As they pulled past me, I touched my hat brim to the ladies. Ladies they were, three of them, wearing sunbonnets and long dresses. As the last wagon went past, I caught a glimpse of red hair under a blue bonnet. I fell in behind them and followed them up Main Street until they stopped at Rainbow City. I stepped the black around them and dismounted, intending to walk in ahead of them.

"Would you help me down, please?" She had a voice like an angel, and when I reached my hand up to help her down, I looked

her full in the face. You could have knocked me over with a
feather. I'd never seen anyone so beautiful.

"Are you going to help me, or simply stare?'' she asked.

I lifted her down and realized that she was quite the figure of
a woman although she couldn't be any older than me.

"You can let me go now. I can walk by myself.'' I realized
that I still had my hands on her waist, and I quickly backed away.
Her hair was red, but not fire red. It was a softer red, and it
framed a perfect face with pert green eyes.

"Lad, can you tell me how to find the Clausen farm?'' I nearly
jumped when the man spoke to me. I turned to face him and
realized that this had to be the father of the girl I'd just helped
down.

"I'm sorry, sir. I didn't hear you,'' I croaked.

"We're looking for the Clausen farm. It seems he has a pat-
ented farm for sale somewhere just north of town along the river.
Might ye know where it is?'' he asked again.

Clausen, Clausen, where had I heard that name? The Chapmans and the river farm. We bought it from a man named Clausen.

"Yes, sir, I know where it is, but you're too late. The farm
has been sold,'' I replied.

He looked disappointed. "He told me that he'd hold it for me,
but I was afraid if someone came along with money he'd sell her
out from under me.'' His Irish brogue spoke of being born on
the Emerald Isle. "Can ye tell me, lad, who was the man that
bought her?''

"He's right inside here, at the bar.'' I wasn't about to tell him
I might also bear a responsibility for his disappointment.

"My name is Angus Turbech, lately of Ohio, and this fair thing
ye helped from the wagon is my first daughter, Ara.'' He waved
toward the other two wagons. "Yonder is my first son, Brian,
my second daughter, Una, and my wife, Grania. Named for a
pirate she was, on her mother's side.'' He laughed when he said
the last, and the lovely woman that was his wife glared at him.

"I am Matthew O'Malley, sir, lately of Pennsylvania, but now
of Kansas.''

"Ah, I thought ye had the look of the Irish about ye, lad.
Introduce me to this man that bought me farm.'' He moved toward the doors of Rainbow City, and then stopped and turned as
Brian jumped down from his wagon. "Brian, stay here with the
girls and keep an eye out. I'll be back in a minute. Ara, see to

your mother. She may have need of you.'' The girl moved away from her wagon with exquisite grace. I went in the door with Angus, but I was lookin' over my shoulder. There'd been girls before, but they'd been country girls. Ara Turbech was something completely different.

We walked up to the bar, and Angus asked Owen, ''My good man, do ye happen to have a drap of the Irish that's kept in a bottle? It been a long dry trip, what with the wife ridin' close with me in the wagon. She doesn't hold with bottled Irish, but a shot would clear the dust from me throat.''

Owen looked at me as he got a bottle of Irish whiskey from under the bar.

''Angus Turbech, this is Owen O'Malley,'' I said, presenting him to my brother. The father of the girl I loved was about to find out that I was a party to buyin' the farm that he'd come all the way from Ohio to own. He probably wasn't goin' to take too kindly, me askin' him if I could court his daughter. I wondered if he owned a shotgun.

Chapter Six

"I'm sorry, Mr. Turbech, but we have a legal deed to the Clausen farm. In fact, two of our people are living there now, and we have a wheat harvest about to begin," Owen said.

"Oh, I believe ye, lad. The O'Malleys of Clew Bay have always been a good honest lot, and ye have the look of the O'Malley clan about ye." Turbech was takin' the news of his loss pretty well. "Me wife is an O'Malley, back aways, and in fact was named for the matriarch of the clan. Grania, or Grace in the English, was her name, and she was a pirate. She commanded over two hundred men, had three castles, and a wealth of ships. But, that's another story." Angus paused a moment, leaned back, and looked into the mirror over the bar.

"It's a story that we've heard before," Owen said. "Pa used to tell us about one of our ancestors named Grace that was a pirate."

"Well, 'tis a true story, lad, and no mistake. You are surely related to my wife." He took a drink from his glass and sighed. "The Clausen farm, 'tis a disappointment, but I'm not unprepared. I knew he was all afire to move. I have me a brother west of here. Some little village called Abilene. He's written and spoken of the virtues of the place. In fact, the very name was taken from the good book and means 'beautiful area of the plains,' translated, or so my brother says. He was always a little top-heavy with blarney, but a good eye for land he has. We'll move that direction and see what is offered."

"I am truly sorry, Mr. Turbech," Owen said kindly. "The bottled Irish is on the house."

"I thank ye, sir, most kindly," Turbech responded. "I wonder if ye could direct me to a good camping spot with water and a dab of shade?"

"I think you would be comfortable down at the creek near our house. We've had some trouble here in town of late, and there are rough men that come over from the army fort. We could offer you safety, and yet it is private. Matthew will show you the way," Owen said, pointing at me.

I jumped when I heard my name called. I'd managed to station myself close to a window where I could see Ara standing in the shade of her father's wagon. Turbech stood and walked toward the door.

"Mr. Turbech," Owen said, and Turbech paused for a moment. "Would you honor us with the company of yourself and your family at supper tonight, here at Rainbow City? The Major has fixed roast wild turkey, and we have the dining room separate from the saloon, so your women will be welcome."

We had built a partition between the saloon area and the dining room just for the purpose of making women feel comfortable. Saloons were nearly sole domains of the men; women just weren't welcome.

"Would be a pleasure and a most welcome treat for the family, O'Malley. The women would relish a change from their own cookin', and I thank ye." He turned and walked out the door. I was close behind him.

"Into the wagons, Turbechs," Angus hollered. "Matthew O'Malley will show us to a camp, and it's supper tonight at Rainbow City with the O'Malley clan."

"What of the farm, Angus?" his wife quietly asked.

"It is as we feared. Clausen sold it out, but it went to your O'Malley kin, woman. Put a smile on your pretty face and come tomorrow we head for the beautiful place in the plains just like the good book says." Angus had a big smile on his face. I was really starting to like him. He hid his disappointment well, so his family would more easily accept the fact that they had to go on west. Go on west! My gosh, I'd just met her, and they were headin' out in the morning.

"Mr. O'Malley, can you give me a hand up, please?" There was that beautiful voice again. I could listen to it all day. I walked over to Ara and helped her onto the wagon seat. I caught a glimpse of trim ankle as she made the step, and it set my heart to beatin' something fierce. My face felt like it was on fire, and I turned to my horse, untied him, and mounted. I rode to the front wagon where Angus had situated himself next to his wife.

"If you'll follow me, Mr. Turbech . . ." I motioned to him and then rode slowly ahead. I took them to a low bank on our side of the creek and upstream about a hundred yards. They parked the wagons in nearly a triangle with a place for a fire pit in the middle. Ara handled the lines of her team like a professional driver, but most farm girls could drive a team. It wasn't many girls that could handle a team from Ohio to Kansas, though, and it put her up another notch in my book. I tied my black to a willow close at hand, and turned toward Ara's wagon. I was too slow. Her father lifted her down, and she stirred around helping set up the Turbech camp. I felt mostly in the way, so after a few minutes I excused myself and took Sin up to the stable. I went in the house and looked in the mirror by the back door.

"Who you tryin' to fool, O'Malley?" I said to the image lookin' back at me. "That girl is the prettiest thing that ever come down the pike, and you're about the ugliest. You don't stand a chance."

"Don't sell yourself short, Matt."

I nearly jumped out of my boots. I'd forgotten Kiowa was laid up and still home. I turned toward him so embarrassed that I could have crawled through a crack in the floor.

"You must think me an awful fool talkin' to myself in the mirror," I said to him.

"Not if there is a woman on your mind, Matthew. A woman can make a man do strange things. I've heard full-grown men talking to themselves in the outhouse over a woman. At least you were talking to the mirror." He chuckled and then gasped with pain. "Don't make me laugh, Matt. It really hurts when I laugh."

"You got to promise that you won't say nothin' to Owen or the rest of the guys about me talkin' to the mirror over a girl." I had him now. I'd get him to laughin' and cause him real pain.

"How can you ask me to keep that quiet, Matt? I can hear Wedge now. Why, he'd go into hysterics," Kiowa replied.

"I mean it, Kiowa. If you say a word about it to anyone I'm gonna make you think that bullet wound is four times bigger than it is. I know how ticklish you are on the bottoms of your feet, and you're in no shape to fight me off." I had to keep him quiet. If the rest of the guys found out I'd been moonin' over a girl, I'd never live it down.

"It's not fair, Matthew, but I'll be quiet. I just couldn't stand the laughing right now. I meant what I said, by the way. Don't sell yourself short. You would be quite a catch for some young woman."

I couldn't tell if he was funnin' or not, but I didn't think he was, and I got embarrassed all over again.

"You need anything?" I asked him quiet-like. He still looked mighty sick.

"No, Matt, but thanks. Doc left some medicine here if the pain gets too bad, but I'd prefer not to use it. It puts me out, and I hate not being in control. I sleep a lot without it anyway."

A small knock sounded at the door. I didn't remember ever hearin' anyone knock on our door before. They mostly just tracked right on in. The door wasn't even closed 'cause of the heat. I walked over and looked out.

"Mr. O'Malley," Ara said, nearly in my face, "my father was wondering if you had some oats to spare. He would gladly pay you for them. We ran out a few days ago, and the teams work much better with some grain in them."

Well, I didn't know whether to spit or go blind. Instead I stuttered.

"You . . . You . . . You bet we do." I just couldn't get it to come out. "We have an extra fifty-pound bag in the stable. I'll bring them down to your camp."

"Thank you. I'll tell my father," she replied as she turned and walked back toward her camp. I watched her a few minutes and then lit out the back door like my shirttail was on fire.

"Be careful the mirror, Matthew. Don't slam the door and break it. You won't have anybody left to talk to," Kiowa said as I rushed by.

Damned Indian wasn't half sick enough.

I grabbed the sack of oats, hoisted them on my shoulder, and walked upstream to the Turbech camp.

"Ah, Matthew me lad, thanks be to ye. I ran out of grain a few days ago, and I forgot to get some when we were in town. I hate to hook up a wagon just to go to the livery," Angus said as I dropped the bag on the ground.

"That's okay, Mr. Turbech. We've plenty. You can settle with Owen tonight at supper," I replied.

I was lookin' past him, tryin' to catch a glimpse of Ara.

"If it's Ara ye be lookin' for, she and Una went down to the creek," Angus said with a half smile.

My face flamed up again. I stammered my thanks to him and walked over the low bank.

"Do you think he always wears a gun, Ara?" Una was talkin', and I could hear them plain.

"Father says that everyone wears a gun out here. I think it is a barbarian custom, and I doubt that he wears it all the time. I would imagine he carries it more to create an impression than for the fact that he might have to use it."

Well, it was plain to see that Ara had a few things to learn, but if she stayed in the country she'd change her views.

"Did you see how blue his eyes were, Ara? And how big his arms are? Why, he lifted you as if you were a feather." Una sighed and moved slightly. I couldn't see them because of a screen of willows, but I could hear them clear.

"Will you kiss him, Ara?"

"Good grief, Una. We are here but for a few days. I will hardly get to know him well enough for a kiss in that time. Besides, what makes you think I even like Matthew O'Malley?"

"You like him all right. It shows every time you look at him." I heard water splash, and Una squealed. Good grief, gosh almighty, and little woodpeckers. I had to get. They was talkin' about me, and if I showed up now, they'd know I heard. I was already mortified to the point of dyin', and I'd come to the conclusion that guns, horses, and fightin' were a whole lot simpler than girls. I tried to back-step but came right down on a cottonwood branch that popped like a gunshot. There was no help for it. I stepped on it again and then thrashed around in the willows so they'd think I'd just come over the bank.

"Goodness, Mr. O'Malley, I surely thought we were being attacked by outlaws," Ara said with her hand near her throat.

"I'm sorry," I managed to stammer. "I guess I got caught up in the brush."

"I have to get back and finish helping mother set up camp," Una said. She stood and moved up the bank.

"Una . . ." Ara began, but Una was already through the willows.

We stood for a moment lookin' at each other, then Ara held out her arm. "I wonder if you would be so kind as to escort me out onto the prairie, Mr. O'Malley. I saw some lovely yellow flowers not far across the creek, but Father said that I must have an escort before I could pick some."

"I'd be honored, Ara, and call me, Matt, please."

"Okay, Matt. You'll have to carry me across the creek, so I don't get my shoes and skirts wet."

She put her arms around my neck, and I scooped her up in my arms. The creek was only about four steps wide, and I was wishin' it was wider, more like the river. Her hair was against my face, and her breath was gentle on my neck. I was near to pass out, my heart was goin' so fast. I set her on her feet easy like, on the other side. It seemed that she held on a little longer than needful, but I wasn't complainin'. She took my arm and pointed to a patch of sunflowers on top a small, short knoll.

"What are they called, Matt?" she asked me as we walked up to the flowers. "We've seen them a lot since we came onto the prairie. They are so bright, and they add so much color to the grass."

"Well, white men call them sunflowers 'cause they follow the sun's path from east to west during the day. Their faces are always lookin' up at the sun. The Kiowa Indians call them *ho-son-a,* which means 'lookin' at you,' and the Pawnee call them *kirik tara kata,* or 'yellow eyes,' " I told her. "If you pick them, they'll sure make your hands sticky."

"Maybe it's best we don't pick them then, but leave them here where they belong, Matt. How did you get to know so much about them?"

"I reckon I always thought they added color to the country, and I asked one of my friends about 'em. I picked some once, and they surely got my hands sticky. I decided, like you, that maybe they was best left where they brighten up the whole world, and not just my corner of it."

She looked up at me with a little wonder in her eyes. I guess I'd talked too much, and said some things I'd never said out loud. What kind of man talks about flowers anyhow?

"We best get back, Ara. It's not really fittin' that we stay out here alone too long. Your Pa will be askin' questions of me."

"My father trusts me, Matthew, but you are right, of course. Thank you for bringing me out, and thank you for telling me about the sunflowers."

We walked back slow, her arm on mine, and I carried her over the creek again. We walked into the camp, and Ara turned to helping her Ma and sister. I helped Brian and Angus picket the horses, then returned to the soddie. I sat down on the bench out front and looked toward the Turbech camp. Brian Turbech came up from the creek and sat down beside me.

"I heard Mother tell my father that she thought you were plumb taken with Ara." He didn't beat around the bush.

"I reckon it's true enough, Brian. Only I don't want you sayin' anything around your family. I'm not a fittin' man for the likes of your sister. I'm uneducated, quick to fight, and just plain stubborn. I have no refinement at all, and not much future. I got nothin' to offer Ara." I paused a minute and looked down toward her camp again. "I'm goin' to be more, one of these days, Brian. I know I am. I'm goin' to be somethin', and I'm goin' places. Only, I never made no plans for a girl. I don't know if she'll wait long enough for me to get to where I'm goin'."

"I bet she would, Matt." he said.

We sat quiet for a while and then started talkin' stuff that was important. Guns, horses, Indians, and food.

Supper was a nice affair and it was pleasant to have womenfolk around. The Major outdone himself, and I ate enough for two people. Brian and I sat together, and as soon as the pie was down, we left out. I knew it wasn't fittin' to try and spend time with Ara after dark set in, but there was nothin' said I couldn't make friends with her brother.

They took out early in the morning for Abilene, and I watched them go. I'd finally worked up courage to ask Angus if I could come over and help get them set up. I knew there'd be a cabin to build, a well to dig, and a ton of other work. He'd told me that another pair of hands was always welcome. I saw Ara stand and wave, and then they were swallowed up in the dust of the road west. I reckoned Abilene was 'bout a half day's ride from where I stood. I was goin' to beat a regular path over there 'til my horse knew the way home without me havin' to turn a rein.

I went to work with my mind makin' dreams about my life ahead. I had no right to think after a girl like Ara, only I couldn't help it. She was stuck there like a burr in a horse's tail.

I looked down at the scar on my arm. I had no right to think about a girl at all.

Time moved along fast. The Chapmans had us all come out for a few days late in August and help bring in the harvest. The wheat did good, makin' about thirty bushel to the acre, and we already had a market for it. As soon as we got the wagons to town, the man who bought it loaded it on a covered rail car. He paid us cash money, and the Chapmans were proud of their accomplishment, and rightly so. The money was added to our total, which as gettin' pretty big. Kiowa and I donated most of every penny we made, and Rainbow City was really bringin' it in.

The first frost came, and the cottonwoods turned yellow. The Chapmans brought their fall vegetables to town and surprised even us with a big harvest of potatoes, keepin' only enough out for seed. The days were gettin' shorter, and the ducks were flyin' overhead. We put in a stock of food for ourselves and smoked some venison for the restaurant. We cut firewood until we had it stacked to the roof all the way around the house in double rows. The Major had hired a cook for Rainbow City who turned out to be near as good as the Major. It gave the Major a little more time for doin' things. Kiowa healed up right good. He found out that he'd become a local hero with near everyone, but particular with the kids he was teachin'.

The railroad made it to Abilene in October, and the Turbechs had ridden it back for a visit. We had a fine time. Brian and I hunted, and Ara, Una, and I went out to the sunflower patch. They'd been frosted, but there was a little color left. Ara and I spent time walkin' along the creek. We talked about what we wanted from life, and she surprised me by kissin' me flush on the cheek when I'd told her I thought she was a fine woman. Angus hadn't filed on a homestead yet. He planned on waitin' 'til spring. They were all livin' with his brother, who had a good-sized, cottonwood log house with a loft. Angus had found a natural spring of good water, and the land around it was creek bottom. It was next to his brother's place, so it was convenient for both of them to share work. I hadn't kept my promise to beat a path to Abilene. There was just too much work to get done.

I practiced with my handgun near every day, and I had gotten the stock on my Henry fixed. I'd kept the old one to remind me how close I'd come. The new stock was made from a chunk of dark walnut that had been cut locally from a stump. It was a piece of beautiful burl, and I rubbed it with oil every day until it was smooth as glass. Wedge and I kept workin' at my bare-handed fightin' skills, and I was givin' him a real run for his money. Sin put on a winter coat, and looked pretty rough, though he was a marvel to ride. He seemed to know exactly where I wanted to go and about how fast I wanted to get there.

Winter came on with a three-day blizzard during the first part of November that heaped snow against the north side of the sod-die. The Major had been right about the sod house. It was probably the warmest house in town. I could see we laid up too much firewood, but we could always use it the next year. We had a four-day blow over Thanksgivin' and another howler the first week of December. There was so much snow that rail traffic was down to only those trains that had to run. The end of the tracks became Junction City again. They didn't bother clearin' the tracks to Abilene, and I was some disappointed. I'd planned on goin' over to Abilene for Christmas, but I knew it was foolish to try and ride over.

There wasn't much freight to unload, but what came in Wedge and I unloaded. The railroad had let everyone else go. Rainbow City became the most important place in town. The men swapped lies, guns and horses on the saloon side while the ladies drank tea and talked about the men on the eatin' side.

Patty and Owen became topics of conversation in Junction City when he gave her an engagement ring for Christmas. I was plumb happy for both of them. They seemed like a matched pair, and I could see that they'd pull fine in double harness. I got a new Montana mackinaw coat for Christmas from the partnership, and Wedge got me a new belt knife. It was a fine blade made with imported steel from Spain. I knew it had been expensive, and I appreciated it. It held a razor edge for a long time.

January came with more snow and February was the same, although toward the end of the month there were some days that reminded me that there would be springtime, if I lived long enough. I was so sick of seein' snow and feelin' cold that I could near start screamin' every time I saw a new flake float down.

March came in with winds that a body could hardly stand up in. There was no way to keep a hat on your head without tyin' it down, and weak branches in the cottonwoods ended up on the ground. But the winds grew warmer, and the snow started makin' its way to the creeks and rivers. Pretty soon it was so muddy that you lost your boots if you tried to cross the street. There was no way to manage a wagon in the mess, and so traffic was near at a standstill. Toward April it started dryin' out, and the Chapmans came to town for the first time since just after Christmas. They looked a little gaunted up, but otherwise had wintered pretty good. They already had ten acres of potatoes in, and they planned on workin' the wheat ground right soon. The spring flowers started bloomin', and a man had the feelin' that he might just make it after all.

Patty and Owen had decided April fifteenth was a good time to get married, and the whole town was gettin' set for the party. April fifteenth seemed like a particular good day to me, too. It was my birthday.

As the weather cleared, people started comin' in on the trains. Pretty soon we didn't know most of the people walkin' the

streets, and with new people came new problems. The shootin'
and fightin' started again, but none in Rainbow City. The word
seemed to get passed around that Owen and the Major wouldn't
stand for no trouble. It also helped that the new marshal was
partial to Rainbow City and spent a good deal of his free time
there.

The fifteenth came bright and warm with the meadowlarks singin' loud and long across the creek. The saloon side of Rainbow
City was cleared of tables, and the bar was shut down. The Methodist ladies put up all kinds of decorations, and a little sawdust
was laid down on the floor for those that wanted dancin'. Patty
and Owen were bein' married in the church, but the reception
was bein' held at Rainbow City.

The Turbechs came in on the mornin' train from Abilene, and
Ara was dressed in her finest long dress. Brian had a suit on and
looked 'bout as uncomfortable as a fella can get. Angus told
Owen that he had a world of work to do on his new place, but
there was no way he'd miss a marryin', or a buryin' for that
matter.

Owen had asked me to be his best man, and even though I had
expected it, I was still honored. The partnership had sprung for
new suits for everybody, which cost near a hundred dollars. They
had been ordered in from Chicago, and the new tailor had fitted
them. He'd had a hard time with mine. I was built like a bull
through the shoulders, but had no waist or hips to speak of. My
thighs were big, and he had a hard time findin' enough material
to keep my pants decent. The coats were black and long over the
waist. When we got all dressed, I had to say we were the finest
lookin' partnership in Kansas, and maybe the world. As we got
ready to go over to the church, I almost decided to leave my gun
at home, but I remembered the promise I'd made to myself. I
belted the Colt on and fastened my coat over it. It showed a little,
but not bad.

We headed down the street toward the church, laughin' and
givin' Owen a hard time. The Turbechs met us part way, and Ara
took my arm just like it was a natural thing to do.

"Good grief. Would ya look at what's comin'," Owen remarked.

It was Wedge, and he had a new suit on. It was a fancy swal-
low-tailed thing with tails that hung down his backside.

"Wedge, you look almost dignified," Kiowa said as we got
up to him.

"I hope that means somethin' good, Kiowa. I'd hate to have to relieve ya of an ear 'fore we went into the church." He had that crooked smile of his on. He looked as close to elegant as a bull moose in formal dress.

The church was full, and there were a lot of people standin' outside. Patty wasn't there yet. We'd been told that we'd have to go stand up front, and then she'd come in when the organ lady started playin' the music.

I stood to the left of Owen, and the Major stood next to me. The Turbechs got the front pew, bein' friends of the family. The little preacher was standing in front of us and was just plumb full of hisself. The organ started wheezing, and I looked back to see Patty comin' up the steps. Man, she was beautiful in her white dress and veil. I just couldn't imagine how her and Wedge came from the same set of parents. She stood right up next to Owen, and the preacher cleared his throat.

"Dearly beloved, we are gathered here today to join this man and woman in the holy bonds of matrimony." His voice squeaked a little, but it didn't slow him down none. I figured a marryin' would take at least as long as a sermon, but 'fore I knew it Owen was kissin' Patty full on the lips. We turned around, I took Ara by the arm and headed down the aisle at near a gallop. We stepped out into the bright sun ahead of Owen and Patty. People made a path and started throwin' rice and wheat as they came out. We stayed ahead of the newlyweds and got to the end of the people. We stopped and waited for them to catch up. Owen was smilin' big and held Patty close by. He wasn't 'bout to let her go. People were millin' around shakin' hands, laughin', clappin' backs, and generally havin' a good time.

All of a sudden it got so quiet I looked around. There were two hard lookin' men with guns tied low. They looked like trouble. I unfastened my coat and took the thong from my gun hammer.

"Owen O'Malley, Falcon Beck wants to give you a weddin' present," the man on the left said. I threw Ara behind me and heard her gasp. The man's hand went down for the gun on his leg, and I shot him twice. A bullet whipped by my side, and I turned slightly toward the other man. I fired three times as fast as I could, in a panic that Ara, Owen, or Patty would get hit. When the smoke cleared, both men were down and dead in the dust of the street. It was mortal quiet. I turned around to see if everyone was all right. Ara stood with her hand over her mouth, and a look of shock on her face. She looked at me as if she didn't know me, then turned toward her father. It was April fifteenth. It was my seventeenth birthday, and I had just killed numbers five and six.

Chapter Seven

"She told Angus that if you would have waited and tried to talk to the men, there wouldn't have been a shooting," Kiowa said to me. "Angus tried to reason with her, but she wouldn't listen. A part of her rationale was that the marshall was only a few steps behind you, and he is paid to protect people."

It was the day after the weddin'. We had just gotten home from an inquest that had been held in the Rainbow City. Folks in Junction City still didn't appreciate would-be badmen tryin' to kill their citizens, particularly when they'd just got married. The jury had voted unanimously, and noisily, that the shooting had been self-defense. Ara had left on the train back to Abilene without a word to me. I felt like the heart had gone out of me, and there was a big empty feelin' in my stomach. Kiowa and I were at the house alone.

"What do you think, Kiowa? Should I have waited?" I asked him.

"You couldn't have waited, Matt. Those men were intent on killing. There is no question that you did what was necessary." He paused for a moment and turned to look out the window. "Matthew, you have uncommon gifts. Gifts of speed and uncanny coordination. The speed with which you draw a pistol is almost freakish, and I have never seen anyone who is a better shot." He turned back toward me and walked up close. "Those gifts make you a very dangerous man. You must always make sure that you use those gifts in doing what is right. You have shown that you have judgment, perhaps a maturity beyond your years. You must constantly guard against being too fast." He stopped for a minute.

"How can you be too fast?" I asked him.

"What I mean is that someday, in some circumstance, you are going to have the opportunity to either avoid a confrontation, or resolve an adversarial situation without using your gun. You will have a chance, perhaps many chances, to save lives by use of your judgment and good sense, rather than a gun." His voice got quiet, and he took me gently by the arm. "If you kill the wrong man, it will haunt you always. You have, to this point, used your gun to protect yourself, your property, your friends. Make sure that you assess every situation and use your gun only as a last resort. Your judgments will have to be split-second, and you will live with the consequences of your decisions for the rest of your life. You must promise to always try to use your head."

I felt sick and scared. I knew what he meant and it scared me.

"I promise, Kiowa. I'll always try and think things through."

He nodded and walked out the door toward town. I'd hated the fact that we'd had a shootin' on Owen's weddin' day, but it hadn't stopped the party. The reception had gone over in a big way. I hadn't attended. Somehow it hadn't seemed like I ought to go. I stayed back in the stable with my horse until near bedtime. I kept remembering the way Ara had looked at me. It made me feel alone and useless.

After Kiowa left, I went down to the rail yard and started to work unloadin' some ear corn from a short-sided car. I always thought best when I was workin, only today I didn't want to think. I let my muscles take over and tried to blank my mind. After a couple hours, I had a strange feelin', and I looked up to see a man on a mouse-colored horse watchin' me. I sat down the shovel and slipped the thong from my gun. Considerin' what had happened of recent, I wasn't too trustin' of folks, particular strangers.

"Hello," he said, lookin' up at me. "I wonder if you could give me some information, and directions?"

"I will if I can, mister," I replied. "Stand there a minute, and I'll come down." I went over the backside of the car so as not to offer my back to him as I climbed down. I walked around the car, and he had gotten down from his horse.

"My name is Joseph McCoy," he said in a friendly voice. "I'm just in from Illinois, and I am looking for the owner of this particular piece of ground." He pointed to a large, flat, cleared area of land that was adjacent to the railroad and just south. The cleared area was probably about twenty acres.

"I don't rightly know, Mr. McCoy, but the foreman is up the line about ten cars, and he might have some idea," I replied.

"Thank you. I don't believe that I caught your name, sir," he said.

"I ain't a sir. I'm just plain ole Matt O'Malley, late of Pennsylvania, but now of Kansas."

"Well, plain old Matt O'Malley," Mr. McCoy said, laughing, "at least you're not an arrogant rube as I have found some of the western men to be. Can you recommend a good eating place?"

"There's only one place worth eatin' at in Junction City, and that's the Rainbow City right there on Main Street," I said pointing up town.

"Thank you, Matt. Perhaps I'll see you again while I'm in town," he said.

"Might be, Mr. McCoy. I get around some, and the town ain't real big."

He swung up on his horse, tipped his hat to me, and rode up to where Wedge and the foreman were breakin' in some new help. I went back to unloadin' corn, wonderin' why the man was interested in an empty piece of ground. I soon forgot him and the rest of the day went fast. Come quittin' time I felt some better about myself, and Wedge and I walked over to Rainbow City. We'd taken to eatin' our meals at the restaurant. It was doin' so much business that the Major couldn't get home to cook. Besides, it didn't seem fair that he should cook all day, then come home and cook for us.

We walked in and realized that the restaurant side was near full. Wedge found a single seat at a table with a bunch of boys that worked the eastbound Kansas Pacific train. I spotted a seat near the window. The one other man sitting at the table had his back to me, and I didn't recognize the set of his shoulders. He turned as if he felt me lookin' and waved me over. It was Mr. McCoy.

"Have a seat, Matt. In fact, I'll buy your supper," he said as I walked up.

"Thanks, but there's no need to, Mr. McCoy. I eat here free," I replied.

He got a puzzled look on his face. "I own a part of this place. My brother runs the saloon on the other side, and one of my partners runs the eatin' house," I explained.

"I'm finding out that things are not always as they appear," he said, laughing. "I would never have dreamed you were a partner in Rainbow City when I saw you unloading a freight car today. I guess that also explains why you recommended this as the best place to eat in town."

"Oh no, it really is the best place to eat in town." I smiled back at him. "Did you find out who owns that piece of ground?"

"Yes, as a matter of fact, I did. It belongs to the Kansas and Pacific Railroad. I would like to buy it, and they seem somewhat interested in selling it, but their price is much too high. I also • have another problem with the K and P. I presented my idea to them with a view to using them as a primary shipper. The executive I spoke with not only didn't think it was a good idea, he laughed at me. I'm afraid I got angry and called him a few names. He's also the man I would have to deal with on this land, and I won't give him the satisfaction of getting any of my money," he responded to my question.

The waitress came over and took my order. The decision wasn't hard to make, since the only thing on the blackboard menu was buffalo steak. I wanted to ask Mr. McCoy, in the worst way, why he wanted twenty acres of no-count land next to the railroad, but I had learned one thing about the West. Folks didn't ask questions of a man. His business was his own until he volunteered to tell ya otherwise. He must have seen the curiosity on me.

"I suppose you must be interested in why I want that particular piece of ground when there is all the land a man could want lying unused all around Junction City. I want it because of the way it lies next to the railroad, close to town, and yet not in town." He went quiet as our meals came, and then started talking again around buffalo hump steak. "I must ask you not to say anything, Matt, about what I am going to tell you. You seem like an honest man, and I am usually a good judge of character. In fact, I would like to have your opinion on the whole idea I have been working on."

I was some flattered by his inclination to believe me an honest man.

"I am a cattle dealer by trade," he continued. "Last year my brothers and I were in Sedalia, Missouri, and bought some wild-looking, long-horned cattle from some fellas who had driven them up from Texas. They encountered all kinds of hardships on the way, not the least of which were the Missouri farmers shooting at them as they came north. They made it with about four hundred head. I paid them twenty dollars a head for their stock. They had lost at least half of their original herd in the drive north, but they told me they still made a clear profit of more than one

thousand dollars a man. The drive had taken them three months.
They felt it was a pretty good paycheck, and my company didn't
do so bad either. We turned around and sold the herd for thirty-
two dollars a head." He stopped for a moment to finish off his
steak and take a drink of coffee.

"Those Texas boys told me that some folks estimated there
were nearly four million head of wild cattle in Texas. During the
Civil War, the cattle bred like rabbits, and there was no market,
or men to market them for that matter."

The waitress brought us pie and refilled our cups. I was beginnin' to wonder where McCoy's conversation was goin', or if
it was ever goin' to end. I was tired, but I didn't want to be rude.
I sat up straight and looked interested.

"Those boys told me that they could buy all the cows in the
country down there for three or four dollars a head. It doesn't
take much math to figure that if you can get them north and east,
you stand to make a lot of money. That's what I want that land
for, Matt."

I must've looked a little blank, because he went on and explained.

"Here's the problem. There are four million cattle in Texas.
There are tons of people hungry for meat in the East. I propose
to get them together. In short, I want to establish a market
whereat the Southern drover and Northern buyer would meet on
equal footing, and both be undisturbed by mobs or swindling
thieves. There are some real obstacles to the completion of my
plan. First, there is a gang of Jayhawkers, or at least there was
last year, who demand a tribute of ten cents a head to allow the
cattle to pass across the Kansas/Oklahoma border. Second, the
farmers in eastern Kansas and western Missouri, where the most
westerly stockyards are now, don't want the Texas cattle coming
through at all. They are afraid that the southern cattle will infect
their stock with Spanish Fever. The fear of fever is so bad that
the governor of Kansas has even been persuaded to put up a
quarantine line, and no Texas cattle are allowed east of it." He
stopped for a moment to catch his breath and scooted back away
from the table a little.

"That means that the location I finally settle on has to be at
least as far west as Junction City. I want that vacant land out
there to build a stockyard from which I can ship Texas cattle to
the East. If I can swing it, my company stands to make a fortune.
I already have a contract with the Hannibal and St. Joe Railroad

to ship the cattle, but I haven't secured a good place to ship from.''

The lights came on. I could see exactly what he was gettin' at, and suddenly it made a lot of sense. It didn't take much pencil pushin' to see the enormous potential for profit, but it was a gamble.

''How do you plan on gettin' the word around down in Texas that you have a place ready for them to drive to?'' I asked.

McCoy looked sharply at me. ''That's a good question, Matt, and one that I will have to consider. I have finally come to the conclusion that my brothers and I cannot undertake the whole endeavor by ourselves. We need some people with us that we can trust, that have good ideas, and that have some money to invest.''

''Mr. McCoy, your plan sounds like something my brother and the rest of our partnership might be interested in. I surely am. I wonder if you would come home with me and explain your plan to the other men of my partnership?''

''I'd be delighted to, Matt. I must go to the hotel and see to a room first. If you can give me directions to your house, I'll arrange to come over later this evening,'' he said.

''You won't find a room at the hotel, Mr. McCoy. It's been full since the weather turned nice. We have room at the soddie, if you don't mind bedding down with a bunch of bachelors,'' I replied. Owen and Patty had taken a set of rooms over Rainbow City in which to live and that left an extra bed in the house.

''All right, Matt. If you don't think your friends will mind, I'd appreciate a place to stay,'' he agreed.

I gave him directions to the house, and he headed to the livery to get his stuff. I went over to the saloon to ask Owen if he could meet with us at the soddie. I didn't tell him the nature of the meeting, only that the partnership needed to have a confab. He had hired another bartender, so he could spend more time with Patty, so the meeting presented no particular problem for him or the Major, who also had an extra cook. Owen agreed to tell the Major, and I headed home.

Mr. McCoy arrived a short time after the partnership was gathered and was warmly greeted by the rest of the partners. He wasted no time in presenting his plan. I saw excitement come in the Major's eyes as McCoy's story unfolded. He certainly saw the potential. I wasn't so sure about Kiowa and Owen.

''. . . and that's what I'm doing here, gentlemen. I attempted to buy the land next to the railroad here in Junction City, but the price is too high. I have decided to go on west and check for land adjacent to the railroad in Solomon City and Salina," McCoy finished up.

It was quiet a moment, and then the Major spoke to McCoy.

"Sir, I wonder if you would be so kind as to go out and have a smoke while we discuss this situation. I don't want to appear rude, but I am afraid our discussion would be hampered with you here."

"Of course, I completely understand. I saw a comfortable looking bench outside, and the evening is nice," McCoy said as he got up and went to the door. He closed the door quietly behind him.

"What do you think, Kiowa?" the Major asked.

"I am somewhat skeptical. Not particularly about Mr. Mc-Coy's concept, but his ability to get the Texas people to come to his location. I don't know if the market actually exists. In fact, we don't know Mr. McCoy, for that matter. He doesn't come across as a crook, but what if he is simply raising money for the purpose of absconding with it? I am not against the partnerships' participating, but there should be some way for us to safeguard our investment." The big Indian had brought up some issues I hadn't even thought about, and he had some good points. What did we know about McCoy?

"I agree with Kiowa completely," Owen added. "I don't want to offend Mr. McCoy, but we have worked too hard for the money we have accumulated to risk it unnecessarily. I also think that we should not commit all of our resources, initially."

"How much cash money do we have available, Owen?" the Major asked with a thoughtful look on his face.

"We have a little over five thousand dollars in hard money," Owen responded immediately.

"Okay, I propose that we dedicate one half of our available money to McCoy's project," the Major said. "I served with some of the men from Texas during the war. I know the cattle are there, and I know that if those Texas boys have decided to bring cattle to a northern market, they will flat do it. I think McCoy's idea will make us money and hasten us toward our goal of having our own place."

"I don't disagree, Major, but shouldn't we confer with the Chapman boys? And what about some kind of a safeguard for our investment?" Kiowa asked.

"The Chapmans told me some time ago that if an investment came up that needed immediate action, they would go along with the majority vote. I think we can go ahead with their blessing if we can come to an arrangement. We won't do it, of course, unless we are all in agreement," The Major said.

"I think I can help with the safeguard for our money," I said. "I'll go with Mr. McCoy and make sure that things roll along. I'm plumb sick of shovelin' corn, and I need a change. Besides, if we are goin' to end up with our own ranch, we have to have someone who knows cow critters. I 'spect I can learn a lot from Mr. McCoy, not to mention the Texas stockmen." As I said it, I realized I really meant it. It would mean leaving my friends and the town I'd gotten accustomed to that had actually become home. But I did need a change. I wasn't makin' much progress on the end of a shovel.

The partners were quiet for a few minutes, and then Owen spoke up. "I think it's a great plan, and Matt has a point. None of us know much about cattle. I actually trust McCoy, but I'll feel better with Matt watchin' what's goin' on."

"I will vote yes with the rest, given this set of circumstances," Kiowa agreed.

The Major got up and opened the front door. "Mr. McCoy, we have arrived at a decision if you would come back in please."

McCoy came back in and took his chair. "What a beautiful evening," he commented.

"We have decided to participate with you, Mr. McCoy, but we have some conditions," the Major informed him. A troubled look came over McCoy's face. "We will hazard twenty-five hundred dollars with your project on the condition that you explain exactly how the money will be used, and what return we can expect. Also we want to include one of our members as a companion to you, specifically during the initial phase of the operation. This condition is designed to safeguard our investment."

The cattle buyer looked thoughtful for a moment and then spoke, "The sum of money you want to invest doubles the available funding from my company, so the percentage share would naturally be fifty-fifty for both partnerships. The return would, of course, be on total profits and payable after the first full year of operation." He paused a moment and then continued, "I have made no provision to have someone with me, although I see your point of safeguarding your contribution. Who would you prefer to send?" he asked.

''Matthew was the man we had elected to go with you, unless you object to him,'' the Major responded.

A large smile came over McCoy's face. ''He would be my choice if I had the option. I will be carrying a large sum of money, and I have been told around town that Matt is good with a gun, and very smart. I think we may need all of his talents before we execute our plan. Gentlemen, shall we shake as partners in this new adventure?'' He rose to his feet. We shook hands all around, and with that handshake my life dramatically changed.

Chapter Eight

"I get the distinct impression that we are not wanted here, Matthew," Joe McCoy said to me as we got back to the hotel room in Salina. It was the end of May, and we were lookin' for a suitable spot to set our dream in motion.

"I think you're readin' the sign about right, Joe. They have less use for our idea here than they had in Solomon City," I agreed. "Fact, these guys were downright rude about it."

"I think there is still a chance for us here in Salina, but we're going to have to offer them some incentive to swing the vote our way," he said.

"I 'spose that's the way business is done, but it seems like we've given up enough to the railroad without buyin' off the folks here. We've already committed to building a hotel to get the contract from the railroad. I'd think that would be a nice carrot for one of these towns," I said.

"Not really, if you think about it. A hotel, particularly one with a restaurant and saloon, will operate in competition to many of the businessmen we met with today," McCoy disagreed. "Besides, these boys want to put a little of our silver into their own pockets."

"I guess that's what rubs me a little. I feel like they're tryin' to make us pay for the privilege of comin' to town, and even if we are goin' to operate in competition, the increase in business will offset the losses they may have due to another business comin' in," I commented.

"Greed, Matthew. Good, old human greed. It is one of the driving forces of our system, unfortunately." Joe walked over to the window and threw it open, letting in a small summer breeze. "Well, perhaps we will resolve the issue at the meeting tomorrow." He walked away from the window and looked in the mirror.

"I can't wear this shirt again tomorrow, Matt. Can you believe that my bag ended up in Abilene with all my clean clothes?"

"I believe it. I mean we are talkin' about the Kansas and Pacific," I replied. "We can take the train over in the morning, get your bag, and still be back here for the meeting in the afternoon."

"Yes, I suppose you're right. I had planned to do a bit more campaigning for our cause before the meeting, but perhaps a train ride will accomplish as much good. The politics are pretty negative, and my backdoor discussions might hurt us more than they help." He ran his hand through his hair and turned away from the mirror. "Do you want a drink, Matt?"

"I don't drink much, Joe, but I'll tag along if you want to go down to the saloon. I could use somethin' to eat, and I think they had some stew in a pot," I replied.

We went to the door, and I turned to look at our room as we left. There was nothing of value since we were carrying our money, split between us, in money belts. My Henry was in my hand, and my army Colt was on my leg. I wasn't lookin' for trouble, but trouble seemed to have a way of seekin' me out. Besides, I wasn't takin' any chances of bein' robbed. This section of Kansas seemed to have more than its fair share of rough characters.

We walked down the stairs and out onto the boardwalk that fronted the street; three doors south was the saloon. Joe ordered stew and a drink. I ordered stew and a beer.

"This is really ideal country for our plan, Matt. There is a lot of flatland, and the grass is wonderful. I think the river is accessible in a number of places for both crossing and watering herds. There are almost no farmers here yet, so we won't be bothering anyone to speak of."

"You're botherin' me, mister, and I surely hate to be bothered."

I looked over at the bar and the man that had spoken. I saw trouble. He was a large, unwashed man with a big mustache and a gun tied low. He had a partner standing beside him with a wicked grin on his face, and he also carried a gun.

"Ignore them, Matt. I really want to avoid trouble," Joe said quietly.

Our stew was served up, and I watched the two men from the corner of my eye. A few minutes passed, and I saw the man with the face hair start walkin' toward our table. I remembered the promise I'd made to Kiowa. I didn't want to kill these men, and since we were tryin' to make a deal for land in this town, it didn't seem fittin' that I should kill some of 'em.

"You must not have heard me, greenhorn. I said you were botherin' me, and I don't like being bothered. I want you to drag your ass and your wet-eared kid out of this saloon. I want you to do it right now."

He directed his comments to Joe, dismissing me as a kid and nothing to worry about. The big man was leanin' against our table with both hands flat on top. He smelled like he didn't know what water was. His face was greasy, as was his hair. His hat was tipped back on his head, and big sweat circles made rings under his arms.

"Mister, all we want to do is eat our stew, have a quiet drink, and enjoy the summer evening. We ain't askin' for trouble," I said.

He burst out laughin' and blew spit on me with the explosion. "Ain't you a dandy, now. Why I'm just plum takin' with you, sweetheart." He snorted his nose, hacked it into his mouth, and spit it into my stew bowl. "Eat that, kid, and maybe you can grow up to be just like me."

Well, I tried to avoid it. I surely did. I mean I had spoken with a soft voice and turned the other cheek. I had my Henry between my knees, but my hand went to the knife in my belt. I drew it like a flash of summer lightnin' and stuck it through the big man's right hand that lay flat on the table. I stabbed with power lent from anger and fear, and pinned him solid to the table. In the same motion, with the other hand, I pulled my rifle up and stuck it flush under his chin with the hammer on full cock.

"You twitch, mister, and I'm goin' to make the pain quit in your hand by blowin' your head off." I looked behind Mr. Face Hair at the other man. He had a nasty, pasty look on his face. I could see he was more than a little surprised. "Smiley, come over here, I got somethin' to say to you, and come easy with your gun hand where I can see it. I'd hate to have to squeeze off a shot under your buddy's chin 'cause you didn't think."

The other man shuffled over.

"I want you to get me and Mr. McCoy another bowl of stew, and I want you to pay for it, please." Pa always told me I should say please when askin' for somethin'. He was big on manners. "I want you to put it on that other table over there 'cause the smell of this here critter is 'bout more than I can stand. It's 'nough to kill my appetite."

I turned my attention back to Face Hair. "Mister, all we wanted to do was eat our supper and be left alone. I set great store by my food, and it gets me all upset to have my supper disturbed. Mr. McCoy and I are goin' over to that table and eat our meal. You're goin' to stand right here and not pay no attention to us until we're done eatin'. When I get done, I'll come over and take my knife back, and you can have your hand back. If you try and deviate any from them ground rules, I'm sure goin' to kill you, and I just plain don't want too. I got promises to keep."

I pulled my rifle barrel from under his chin, and it left a little red, round mark. I backed over to where Smiley had put our new bowls of stew. Face Hair was white as a new bleached sheet, and great drops of sweat were fallin' from his nose onto the table. I turned to my bowl and ate my stew, but Joe was a little slow. He acted like he didn't feel too good, and I reckoned the whole incident had left him a little shaky. The stew was good, and I had a second bowl and another beer, takin' my time to enjoy every bite and swallow. I looked up from my supper to see the big front windows lined with folks lookin' in. Seems the word got around the streets pretty fast. I finally finished supper and moved back from the table.

"Joe, if you want to go ahead back to the room, I'll be there right quick," I said to McCoy.

He got up without a word and left the saloon. I walked over to Face Hair. Smiley had taken a chair at the table where Face Hair was pinned, and was lookin' with fascination at my Spanish steel stuck through the man's hand. He wasn't bleedin' much, but he was surely sweatin'.

"Boys, Mr. McCoy and me are goin' to be in town for a few days. If I see you again, I'm just natural goin' to suspect that you're huntin' me, and I'm goin' to start shootin'. I most always hit what I aim at. I'd suggest that you stay out of sight until we leave out."

I reached down and, with some difficulty, pulled my knife out of the table and Face Hair's hand. He slumped against the table and then fell on the floor holding his hand and groanin'. I wiped my blade on his shirt and put it back in the sheath. Then I turned my back to them and walked out the door. Folks made way for me, and one man stopped me as I got to the hotel.

"Do you know who that man is?" he asked me. "The one you stuck to the table?"

"No, sir, I don't," I replied.

"His name is Macon Beck. He's a sure-thing killer that folks say always shoots from ambush and never takes a chance. He also never misses."

"He wouldn't be kin to Falcon Beck, would he?" I asked the man.

"I think he does have a younger brother named Falcon. Macon has been in prison for the last three years and just got out. He's a bad man to tangle with, and hangs with a rough string," the man volunteered. "I sure admire the way you handled that situation in there, Mr. O'Malley. You could have just as easy killed him, but you didn't."

"How do you know my name?" I asked.

" 'Bout everybody from Junction City out to Hays City knows who you are, O'Malley. You got the name of a real fightin' man here in Kansas." He waved as he walked away from me.

Great. I'd just made a killin' enemy of the brother of the one man in the whole territory who was probably huntin' me. Oh well, I guess I kept it in the family anyway. One thing I wasn't huntin' was a reputation. I kept hearin' talk of Wes Hardin, Ben Thompson, Bill Longley, and other of the Texas boys that were buildin' reputations as gunmen. I didn't want that followin' me around.

I started walkin' up the stairs to the hotel toward our room. At least I'd kept my promise to Kiowa. I'd thought the situation through and avoided a killin', at least for now. I had a notion I was goin' to see Macon Beck again. I walked in the door, and Joe met me as it swung open.

"Matt, you probably just did more to improve our chances of locating here in Salina than I would have done in a month of politicking." Joe was elated. "I must have had a half dozen men speak to me as I walked to the hotel. Everyone hates a bully, and it seems that Macon Beck has been making life miserable for folks here in Salina the last week. He's been pushing people around, started two or three fights, and threatened practically everyone that he saw. He's been walking hard-heeled since he got here. They really admired the way you handled him, and you didn't even get out of your chair." He stopped for a moment to catch his breath. "I must say that I was a little shocked at how fast it happened, but I think you handled the situation admirably."

"I don't like bullies either, Joe, and he was plum set on makin' trouble for us. If we'd have turned tail and run, they wouldn't give us the time of day at that meetin' tomorrow. They wouldn't have even let us in the room. The main thing, though, was just like I told him. I set store by my supper, and I was hungry. I just wanted to eat in peace." I went over to my bed and lay down with my hands behind my head. "You got anything to read, Joe?" I asked.

"Why, as a matter of fact, I bought a copy of Scott this afternoon at the mercantile," he said, holding up a rather large book. "It was the only book that they had in the store, and I picked up a couple of Kansas City newspapers in the lobby of the hotel. Which would you prefer?"

"Well, Kiowa is always tellin' me I ought to read good books, so if you don't mind, I'll try and read this Scott gent," I replied.

He handed me the book, and I sat there a minute judgin' the weight of it. If a good book was measured by what it weighed, then this one ought to be a winner. I pulled one of the lamps over close to me on the chest of drawers and turned it up for more light. I opened the book and started trying to read it. I reckon I read as good as most folks and better than some. Pa made sure that we went to school regular, and he was right particular 'bout us readin' at home. Like I said, I reckon I read as good as most folks, but I read the first five pages of that Scott fella probably ten times. There was a lot of words jammed in close, and a man had to study on them to make any kind of sense. It was like a real thick beefsteak that come off a twenty-year-old bull. You chewed on the words for a while, spit 'em out, turned 'em over, then chewed on 'em some more.

I done that for a while and 'fore I knowed it my eyes were near as heavy as the book. I even went to sleep and dropped the book on my forehead. It raised a lump and made me see stars. I figured it was time for me to get to bed. Joe was already there.

Morning came before I was ready. Joe was up, washed and shaved before I'd quit snorin'. I washed up, and we headed out the door.

Meadowlarks seem to think summer mornings are made for singin', and they were really gettin' after it as we loaded on the train. We'd decided to go to Abilene and pick up Joe's bag, which had been left off there by mistake. He needed a clean shirt, and I wanted to see the town for a couple of reasons. We'd come by there a few days earlier, but it'd been dark, and I hadn't seen anything. The Kansas Pacific engine huffed, puffed, bellered and shook. It took us near three hours to get where we was goin'. It probably wouldn't have taken all that long if we hadn't had to wait for a large herd of buffalo that blocked the tracks.

I was some disappointed when we got there. There wasn't a station, just a wooden platform, and the town was a collection of about a dozen squatty log cabins made of cottonwood logs taken from beside the Smoky Hill River. I saw only one roof that even had shingles, the rest were all dirt roofs. It was a small, mean, poor place that we'd come to. Joe's bag was sittin' at the end of the platform with some other stuff that had been left off. It was a wonder it was still there.

"Let's go down to the town, Matt," Joe said to me. "The train back for Salina doesn't leave 'til late afternoon."

"She don't look like much to me, Joe," I said, pointing toward the collection of log huts. "I bet they don't even have a saloon."

"You can't mean that, Matt. I've never seen a town that didn't have a saloon, or at least something that passed for one," he replied.

He picked up his bag, and we walked down a cleared lane that must have passed for a street. Actually, it was more a wagon track then street. We got up close to the cabins and a speckled dog came out and yapped once, then turned around and laid down. Guess he figured there wasn't much to protect. Wasn't worth more than a couple barks, and I had to agree with him. We found a door standin' open on a two-room cabin, and I looked in.

"You were right, Joe. Here it is, with a mirror and everything," I said turnin' around to grin at him.

We walked in, and I realized that no one else was in the room.

"It's a poor excuse for a saloon, but I'd still think there'd be somebody around that passed for a bartender," Joe said as he looked around. I found a barrel of beer and a pair of glasses that looked almost clean. I ran myself a beer and then one for Joe. We sat down at one of the two tables. I had to admit that the beer was pretty good. It tasted like it was homemade, probably from potatoes. We sat there talkin' for a spell, and finally a man came in the door with an apron on that might have been white when it was new.

"Oh, didn't realize I had customers," he said. "I was out catchin' prairie dogs. The folks from back East really like them, and I sell 'em for a dollar a pair. We don't get many folks that stop through here, except on the stage, and I 'spose the train will kill that trade 'fore long. I got to make money where I can. Actually, I make more money on the prairie dogs than I do on the saloon trade. The folks that live here don't drink much, and the train don't stop every day." He lifted the apron up to his sweaty face and wiped it down. He folded the apron back over a belly that he could have hauled around in a wheelbarrow.

Joe had gotten up from the table and was standin' at the door lookin' out.

"You boys get what you want?" the fat man asked me.

"Yep, and the money is there on the bar," I replied. The fat man scooped up the coins and made as if he was wipin' down the bar.

"Matt, come here a moment," Joe said.

I got up and walked over to the door. I could see excitement on his face.

"What do you see out there?" he asked me.

"Nothin'," I replied. "A whole lot of nothin."

"Exactly, Matthew. There is nothing. There are no people, no farms, and no businesses. There is nothing but grass, water, flat ground, and a railroad line," he said excitedly.

"You're right, Joe. It meets all of our needs." I saw immediately what he was gettin' at.

Joe turned around to the bartender. "Who owns this stretch of ground between here and the railroad tracks?" he asked.

"That would be Tim Hersey. He owns most all the land around us here, not that he's proud of it, but he calls it his townsite."

"Where would I find Mr. Hersey?" Joe asked the fat man.

"If you stand your ground and have another beer, he'll be in here in about a quarter hour. He comes up every day at the same time to see what the news is. His place is down on Mud Creek 'bout a long stone's throw south of here."

The bartender drew us both another beer, and a few minutes later a tall, slender man with an intense look about him came in through the door.

"Let me have some of that vile brew you call beer, Colten," he said as he got to the bar. The fat man drew another beer and handed it over to the man. He turned around and looked at us curiously.

"These boys seem to want to talk to you, Tim," the bartender said, pointin' at us. "Somethin' about buyin' ground."

He walked over to our table and pulled out a chair. "I'm Tim Hersey. Can I do something for you fellas?" he said to us.

"Who owns the stretch of territory from here to the railroad?"
Joe didn't waste time.

"I reckon I do," Hersey replied.

"Would you sell it?" Joe asked.

"I might if the price was right," the tall man said.

Joe laid out the plan for Hersey and didn't hide nothin' or pull
any punches. He told Hersey that in a town where the barkeeper
sold prairie dogs to make grocery money he figured the land
ought to come a little easier than Junction City, Salina, or one of
the other bigger towns. Joe told him the whole plan from top to
bottom, and then started dickerin' for the ground. He might've
saved us money if he'd just out and bought it, but I knew he
figured that might cause hard feelin's later when Hersey found
out what was goin' on. When Joe finished, we was proud owners
of a nice, flat stretch of ground that we hoped would soon be
stock pens. We bought the whole dern place, except for a small
patch of townsite that Tim kept out for speculation. We paid him
twenty-four hundred dollars.

We shook hands all around, with the barkeeper included, for
good luck. Hersey went out the door and down to his cabin on
Mud Creek. We started walkin' toward the railroad, lookin' over
our new land as we went.

"It's nearly perfect, Matt. We have plenty of room for the
stock pens, a barn, and the hotel. The country all around is perfect
for holding cattle." Joe was enthusiastic about our purchase.

"I think we're on our way, Joe. Let's get back to Salina and
gather our horses and other gear. Then we can get back here and
start buildin'." I was rarin' to get started. We'd taken our horses
to Salina on a stock car when we'd rode the train over. I wanted
to get back to my horse, Sin. I was payin' fifty cents a day to
have him taken care of at the livery, but I liked doin' it myself.

"You go and get our stuff, Matt, would you? I want to send
a telegraph to the Kansas Pacific. I saw three big piles of railroad
ties just off the landing platform. I want to buy them for posts
for the pens. From what I've seen of these Texas longhorns,
we're going to have to have extremely strong pens. I also want
to contact a man I know that runs a sawmill at Lenexa. We're
goin' to need sawn lumber, and I'm also going to telegraph my
brothers and have them come up from Springfield. We're going
to need help. I'm going to get hold of some more lumber in
Hannibal, Missouri. . . ." He walked back toward the town talkin'
to himself. I watched him go, knowin' full well that Joe McCoy

was a man who was seein' his dream come to pass, and a large part of it had been done, and would be done, by good, old-fashioned work.

I'd learned something from Joseph McCoy. I'd learned that a man could be a sky-lookin' dreamer, and still make those dreams come to pass by havin' a will to work for them. I'd seen people who had the dreams, but laid back and never turned a hand to make 'em happen. I figured to have a ranch, with the rest of the partnership, somewhere in a big green valley with a fast runnin' river and grass that was butt deep to a tall horse. I knew if I kept workin toward that dream, I'd make it happen.

I heard the afternoon train comin', and I hurried up the dusty wagon track toward the platform. The train just wasn't used to stoppin' at Abilene, and sometimes they completely forgot it. I wanted to be where the engineer could see me. I wanted to get the horses and get back to Abilene as fast as I could. Joe would be needin' help. I might not be much of a thinker, but I was pretty good at work that called for muscle. We had the pens to build, and then we had to get goin' on the hotel. We'd told the railroad that we'd build a hotel for the cattle buyers and the cattlemen to meet in. Joe and I figured that it had to be pretty fancy, just so's the boys from the East would feel at home, and the boss boys from Texas would have somethin' to look forward to after three months on the trail. Joe wanted to decorate it Southern rich-style, and still have all the fixin's of the big hotels back East. I had to agree it sounded like a good idea, even if it would be expensive. We'd decided to call it the Drover's Cottage. It was a right fancy name, and we was proud of thinkin' of it.

The whistle blew on the Kansas Pacific train again as she got close. I could see the coal smoke belchin' from her stack, and the rails started to hum from her drivers. She pulled in slow and vented steam as she pulled up to the platform. I started to swing up without even lookin' at the car door.

"Excuse me. We would like to get off, please," a woman's voice said. I stepped back and looked up right into the eyes of Ara Turbech.

Chapter Nine

Ara refused my offer to help her down; then she walked right past and hardly looked at me. I helped Una down and then Mrs. Turbech. Brian and Angus came after with the baggage.

"Matthew, me lad, how have you been?" Angus asked me.

"I've been fine, Mr. Turbech." I noticed he was wearing a short gun in his belt. I bet that made Ara mad, seein' her Pa packin' a gun. "You been on a trip?" I asked the obvious, mostly to get a conversation started.

"Yep, we went up to Kansas City. I bought a sod plow and other things that we needed. We were all feelin' the need fer a wee bit of entertainment after bein' here in Abilene for so long without any. We took in a couple of plays and listened to some fat lady sing in a foreign language," Angus said with his tongue in his cheek. Brian laughed behind his dad.

I helped them with the baggage, and then I noticed a man had pulled up to the platform with a big wagon and a couple of ridin' horses tied behind.

"That's me brother, Matthew, and a fine man he is. He told us the truth about this fair land. I love our homestead, and the ground is deep, rich, and sweet."

We walked over to the wagon. I could have told they were brothers even without havin' it pointed out.

"Me name is Dillen Turbech, Mr. O'Malley," the man in the wagon said after Angus told him my name. "I am pleased to meet you. Angus and the family set great store by you and your kin."

"Well, I know at least some of the family is friendly, but there's one that don't have much use for me," I replied glancing toward where Ara stood with Una at the end of the platform.

"Aye, I heard the story and a sad thing it is. Ara has read too many books, and her ideals get in the way of practicality. She

87

will learn. 'Tis a hard land we've come to, and not all the men are gentlemen.'' Dillen got down from the wagon, and we all walked over to a closed boxcar. We opened the door, and there stood a plow with a steel blade.

"This is the implement that will open these western lands," Angus said to no one in particular.

We got hold of the plow and wrestled it into the wagon, then got together the rest of the baggage and loaded it.

"What are ye doing here, lad?" Angus asked me as we stepped back from the wagon.

"Well, I guess you'd say that I'm part owner of Abilene," I replied. "Me and a Scotsman named McCoy just bought all the ground from here down to Mud Creek. We plan on shippin' Texas cattle out of here."

"Well, lad, I told me woman that you'd make your mark on the world, and here you are ownin' your own town, although I'd not brag on it lookin' at it from here." He laughed as did I. "Would ye have some work for a good, sturdy lad? Me Brian boy would like some wage work. We be busy out at the farms, but it pays little. He has some needs that require hard money."

"We need good help badly, Mr. Turbech, and I'd be proud to have Brian. I know he can work 'cause he's had the best teacher in the world." I meant what I said. I knew the Turbecks were workers.

"Aye, ye be an O'Malley, lad. I can tell by the blarney that flows from your tongue like honey. If ye'll have him, then I'll leave off his stuff and he can stay with you, at least for a spell of time. Come harvest I'll have need of him, but he knows that, and if ye are going to be here in town, I will be seein' the both of you regular. I can tell you when I have need of him," Angus smiled at me, and then walked over to the wagon. I could see Brian was excited, and he grabbed his bag from among the others. He walked over to me as the rest of the family loaded into the wagon, except Angus who mounted one of the horses. He waved and they started down the road. I saw Ara look back at me and then turn back toward the front. I had that big pain right under my heart. It was a girl pain, except the way Ara was actin' the pain should have been where I sit down.

The train whistle blew, and I could hear the boiler makin' steam to head down the track. The crew had been good enough to give the Turbechs time to unload, but they had a schedule to keep.

"Back on the train, Brian. We have to go to Salina," I said.

He never said hey or nay, just went up the car steps and into the car. My stuff was still in Salina, since we really hadn't planned on buyin' Abilene when we came over.

The train shuddered a little, and then started moving with jerks and jolts.

"Thanks for takin' me on, Mr. O'Malley," Brian said as he settled into the seat across from me.

"My first name's not Mister, it's Matt, and you might not be thankin' me in a few days, Brian. We got a world of work to do, and not much time to do it. We'll pay you good, but you're goin' to earn every penny," I replied with a smile.

"I like hard work, Matt, and I reckon whatever you pay me will be plenty. I'm sick of the farm, and this looks like a chance to turn my hand to something that will be a change," he said.

"How'd you like the city?" I asked him, tryin' to make conversation.

"I don't like cities much. They're dirty, smelly, and crowded. There's places where the buildings are so close together they block out the sky. I figure any place you can't see the sky is a place where I'd rather not be," he said. I smiled and nodded my head. I knew what he meant.

"I guess the girls liked it better than me. They got some new clothes, and they attracted some attention when we went to the plays." He paused for a moment as if thinking and then continued. "I reckon you'll find out anyhow, so I'll tell you now. Ara stepped out with a man she'd met in Abilene, and who we saw again in Kansas City. I thought it was a little convenient that he showed up when he did, and so did Pap. She'd hear none of it and went out with him anyhow. He's a real slick dresser and talks even better than he dresses. I don't like the cut of him, and Pap really doesn't like him, but he's careful not to say anything. If he told Ara he didn't like the fella, then Ara would just natural have to have him. She's like that."

"I got no hold on Ara, Brian. She can go out with whoever she wants," I said with what I hoped sounded like sincerity. The pain under my heart had gotten worse, and my breath was comin' in little puffs.

"What's this guy's name, anyhow?" I asked Brian.

"I think it's Beck, but I disremember his first name. Seems like it was some kind of bird," he said, pushing his hat back and scratchin' his head.

"Falcon?" I asked.

"Yeah, that's it," Brian said. "Do you know him?"

I was seein' stars and having trouble catchin' my wind. I felt like I'd been belted in the gut. "Yeah, I know him. He's the skunk that paid those two men to kill Owen at his weddin'. He's one of my mortal enemies, and I reckon he'd try to kill me on sight."

"I thought I'd heard that name before," Brian remarked. "That's where I heard it. Those guys you shot said his name before the guns came out."

"It's the same man, Brian. He's a thief, and a killer, and those are just the nice things. He has a brother that just got out of prison that has cause not to like me too well either," I said, remembering Macon Beck's face as he fell on the floor of the saloon. What happened to Macon in Salina was the kind of thing that would follow a man wherever he went. I'd put him in a position where he near had to kill me just to be able to hold his head up again. Folks wouldn't laugh in his face, but there would be a lot of snickers behind his back.

I couldn't believe that Ara would be so stupid as to step out with Falcon Beck. I guess he was a fancy dresser, and a man like that would know the things to say that would turn a farm girl's head. I'd never found much to say to Ara, so I couldn't really blame her. I didn't look like much compared to Beck. I didn't dare speak up against Beck to her 'cause she'd just think it was me bein' jealous. It made me near sick to think on it. Brian went to sleep, and I sat quiet with my thoughts. I 'sposed if I shot Beck that wouldn't go over too big with Ara either. I might have a little trouble keepin' my promise to Kiowa where Falcon Beck was concerned. If he came against me, I might not mind shootin' him up just a little, or maybe a lot.

We pulled in to Salina 'bout supper time, and Brian and I went straight over to the hotel. I gathered up what little stuff we'd left in our room, and then went down to the front desk to settle up.

"Are you leavin' permanent, Mr. O'Malley?" the clerk asked. "Or are you still lookin' to buy ground here?" He wrote something in his book and continued talkin' before I had a chance to answer. "I know that since the incident last night at the saloon there are quite a few people that would like to see you and Mr. McCoy stick around. There's been some talk of havin' you as a lawman here in Salina."

He pushed my change over the counter and looked me in the face, expectin' an answer.

"McCoy and I bought some ground over at Abilene. I guess that's where we'll set up our operation," I replied. The clerk looked disappointed. "We didn't have to pay any bribes over there to get folks to have us. They seemed real excited by the idea." I was still a little burned that many of the Salina merchants had expected a pay-off under the table.

Brian picked up my bag, and we went out the door toward the livery. People stopped to stare and talk as we went by. After a while, Brian began to take notice.

"What's with these people over here, Matt? They act like we have the plague or something," he asked.

"I had a little difficulty with a gent in the saloon last night, and the word must have got around town." I didn't elaborate, and Brian didn't ask any more questions. We got to the stable, and the hostler was leanin' on a fork outside.

"I reckon we need to get the horses, mister. Did you get paid, or is there still somethin' owin'?" I asked.

"Nope, you're paid up, Mr. O'Malley. In fact, you got another day comin' on what's already paid," he said. He started twichin' his eyes toward the barn in a most unnatural way. "I really like takin' care of your black. He has a wonderful disposition for a horse that big." His eyes were still twitchin', and his head was startin' to get into the act. He was also talkin' louder than necessary. I was finally gettin' his message. I slipped the keeper thong off the hammer of my Colt. I figured there was someone in the barn waitin' on me, and he probably had a gun in his hand.

"Brian, you stay out here," I said to the boy. "I'll bring the horses, and you can help saddle out here." I wanted him out of the way of a stray bullet. Angus would be all fired mad if I got his only boy killed.

I went through the door low and immediately stepped off to the left and through an open door of an empty stall. It was nearly dark inside after standin' in the light outside, so I waited for my eyes to adjust. After a few minutes I could see better, and I looked over the stall wall. I saw a blossom of fire and heard the bullet hit the wall behind me. The man was using a rifle, and he was standin' near where my black was stabled. If he hurt my horse, I was goin' to do worse than kill him. I heard the sound of runnin' steps, and I moved to the stall door. I saw the man dodge into an empty stall, and I put a bullet 'bout where I expected him to be. A .44 ball will penetrate several inches of pine board, and the stall walls weren't several inches thick. I heard him screech and start thrashin' around. I wasn't goin' over to check him out just yet. I was green, but I wasn't that green. Pretty soon the noise quit, and a weak voice came from the stall.

"You done for me, O'Malley. I'm dyin', and you played hell. Macon Beck will be huntin' your scalp," the man said.

"It looks to me like he's already huntin', but he sends coyotes to do his work for him," I replied.

"He couldn't handle a gun 'cause of his hand, so he asked me to take you out for him," he replied.

"Well, I'm just as sorry as I can be that you're shot, but you come a beggin' for it." I really wasn't all that sorry. "Throw your rifle out in the alleyway where I can see it, and then your short gun. If you hold out on me, I'm goin' to help you along toward dyin' quicker."

A Spencer came out into the alley between the stalls, and then a pistol followed. I'd already started ghostin' over to the stall the man was in. I stuck my head in quick and took a look. I'd sure hit him, and I just bet he did think he was goin' to die. I'd put that .44 ball right through his hind pocket on the right side. It had gone through the wall first, so the soft lead had spread out a little. It dug a pretty deep canal from side to side. He was groanin' and carryin' on somethin awful.

"Matt?" Brian yelled in the door.

"I'm okay, Brian. Run over and get the doc," I yelled back. The man looked a little familiar, and then I placed him. It was Smiley. The man that had been with Beck the night before. He groaned a little louder. He wasn't goin' to die, but I bet before he healed all the way up he was goin' to wish I'd killed him.

The doc came in the livery, and I moved back and pointed. The doc managed a chuckle when he saw the wound, and then regained his composure. "Have some men bring a door over, and we'll carry him over to my office. He won't be able to walk." Several men had pushed in behind the doc, and a couple moved to do his biddin'. They came back in a minute with a door. Doc had used my knife and cut Smiley's pants off. They slid the door under him, with him face down, and four men lifted it.

"Doc, you're not goin' to take me out there like this are you?" Smiley whined.

"I have to get you over to my office so I can fix that wound. This is the only way." The doc turned and winked at me.

They carried him out the livery door with his butt shinin' toward the sky like a full moon. The hostler had already told several people that Smiley had been waitin' for me in the barn, so there was a fair crowd gathered outside. I heard one man laugh, and then it became a general, loud swelling of hoots and belly laughs. Smiley would sure have to leave the country, only he was goin' to have to take the train 'cause it'd be a spell 'fore he sat a horse.

Brian and I got the two horses saddled and put our bedrolls up behind the saddles. I put my small bag on the saddle horn, and Brian did the same with his. As we were gettin' ready to go, I kept a close watch on the people that stood around us. I'd made a few enemies here and yon, and I didn't want any of them sneakin' up on me. I also slipped the livery hostler a five-dollar tip for givin' me a warnin'. The Spencer and the Navy Colt that Smiley had thrown out I gave to Brian. He didn't have a gun yet, and it just didn't seem fittin' to me. He knew how to shoot 'cause he'd used his dad's weapons for years, he just didn't have his own. I felt like when Smiley had tried to shoot me with them, he flat forfeited them.

"O'Malley, the hotel clerk says your goin' to leave us in favor of Abilene," a man I recognized as the banker said.

"Yes, sir, that's right. We bought some ground over there, and we're settin' up shop," I replied.

"Luck to you, son, and if you get sick of Abilene, come on back. You've made some friends here in Salina, and there's been talk of asking you to take the city marshal's job. We don't have one, and we've stood in need of a good lawman a number of times. We're peace lovin' folks and would like to have an officer who could impress the 'sporting crowd' that the title 'peace officer' has a special meaning here in Salina." Several people spoke in agreement with the banker.

"I surely appreciate that, and it's nice to know that I'm wanted someplace. When we get things settled in Abilene, I'll come back over for a visit," I told them.

"You do that, O'Malley, and we'll look forward to it," the banker said.

I reined my horse around, and we headed out of town east toward Abilene. I knew we wouldn't make it with dark settin' in already, but I wanted to get out of Salina. I calculated that there was no reason askin' for more trouble. We rode an hour down the road 'til the moon was up, then we made camp under a nice stand of cottonwoods that stood by an unnamed creek.

It was a beautiful night with a big, yellow prairie moon hanging low in the sky. The cottonwoods rustled and rattled with a small summer breeze, and an owl was trillin' up the creek. I realized that I'd come to love the big, flat open spaces of Kansas. It had become my home, at least for now.

"What do you want to end up bein'?" Brian asked me after we'd had some beans and coffee. The question caught me by surprise, and I had to study on it.

"I reckon I'm not right sure, only I know I want to be the best at whatever I do," I responded. "Out here a man is judged on how he does the job, no matter what it is. If you turn your hand to somethin', then it ought to be worth the effort to do it the best you can. I suppose I want to be a rancher, but I'm not sure that's what I want to end up doin' forever."

"I want to read for the law," Brian said after we'd been quiet a spell. "Pa says I got a natural gift for both readin' and talkin', so he calculates I'm a natural for law. He bought me a big, black book by some man named Blackstone when we were in Kansas City. I read some of it, and the man makes the law sound like a noble profession." Brian was quiet a minute, and we listened to the cottonwood log crackin' in the fire. "Pa told me that there is a world of opportunity for a man with education and particular for law readers."

"Your Pa is right, Brian. As time goes on, the western land is goin' to have need of men of education, scholars, if you will. The men that will eventually form the governments in the new land will have to know how the law works. We'll have need of honest men who know the law. There's plenty of the dishonest kind who say they know law, but when it gets right down to the bottom line, they'll all wash out. People have a way of recognizing insincerity, or those that would use government for their own ends. Always be honest, Brian." I sounded like a Sunday preacher, but I meant what I said.

We talked about things men will talk about around a fire, and then we rolled up in the blankets. I listened to a coyote out over the grass a long ways out, and one answered closer in and on the other side. I went to sleep with their song in my ears.

My horse pawed the ground and snorted. I was out of the blankets and behind a log with my gun in my hand. It looked like it was maybe a half hour before dawn. There was a little light in the east, and the moon was down. I heard a footstep and then a stick breakin' back in the dark under the trees. Then I heard hoofbeats comin' in hard from the north and west. I grabbed my Henry and I saw Brian had the Spencer. We both got behind trees and waited for the riders. They rode right into our camp without a hail or much warnin'. Now, most times a man will stand out a ways from a camp and call out that he was friendly. Those that didn't most generally were thought to be unfriendly, and usually got shot. I knew they could see the camp 'cause the fire was still burnin' a little. One gent rode right over my blankets, his horse stompin' them into the ground.

"Do you see him anywhere?" a man yelled from out in the dark. There were three men on horses in our camp, and I could only guess at how many more there were out on the grass.

"I don't see nothin', boss, 'cept some blankets and the fire," one of the men in our camp replied. I was glad that we'd put our horses back up the creek just a little ways.

"Mister, I have a Henry rifle pointed right at your stomach. I am in no good mood since you woke me from a sound sleep, and your horse just stepped on my blankets. I have 'bout two thirds of a notion to kill you just 'cause you got me mad," I said to the man that had done the talkin'. He was closest to me, and I talked in a quiet voice that didn't carry to the other men.

"I want you to get down from that horse and lead him off my bed. Then I want you to shake my blankets out and put my bed in order. You get that done, then we'll talk, and if you try to get the horse between you and me, I'll kill him, then you. Now do it," I ordered. The man did what I'd told him, and the other men that sat on the horses started lookin' at him real curious.

"What the hell are you doin', Pike?" one of them asked.

"I got a man here with a rifle on me that wants his bed shaken out and cleaned up. I reckon I'll do just as he says 'cause he sounds mad," the man replied.

"The rest of you get down and do the same thing with the other bed," I said in a little louder voice. One of them started reachin' down for his short gun. "Mister, I can see you plain as day the way you're sittin' on the other side of the fire, and if you touch that pistol, I'm sure goin' to shoot Mr. Pike," I told him. His hand came away like his gun was hot, and he dismounted. They shook out our blankets and laid our beds out nice and pretty, then stood by their horses.

"Now, gents, I want you to ride back out there where the rest of your party is, and do this thing right. If you want to come into my camp, you holler first. Then I'll decide if I want you in. Tell the boss man that if he decides to come in with drawn guns, that suits me fine. We have good cover here, and some of you just ain't goin' to see the sun come up today. Now get!'' My voice had got pretty strong there at the end 'cause I hate bein' woke up by rude folks.

They stuck the spurs in and quick jumped out of our camp.

"Stay put, Brian. This ain't over yet," I said to the boy.

I was wonderin' what my black had heard that made him nervous, and I wondered about the footstep that I'd heard.

"Hello in the camp," a voice came from out on the grass. "Can we come in?"

"One of you can until I find out if you're friendly," I hollered back.

I heard a horse slow walkin' in, and it finally got into the small firelight where I could see the rider. He was a runty man with chaps on his legs and a rope on his saddle. I took him for a cattleman.

"'Light and set up to the fire," I told him. I stepped out from behind my tree. "Brian, you stay put with your rifle on this fella until we get things sorted out."

"I'm right sorry, O'Malley," the man started off. "We had us a little problem with an Injun, and we chased him over this direction."

"How do you know my name?" I asked him.

"My name's Brewer. Jason Brewer. I'm trail boss for an outfit from north of here, up in Nebraska country. We came down and picked up fifty head of breeders for our ranch, and we stopped just outside of Salina on the river there. I was in the saloon when you took care of Beck." He stopped and looked out toward the grassland. It was lighter now, and I could see six or eight men on horses against the sky. "Anyhow, we got these high-priced breeders from Missouri. We brought them as far as we could on the train and then started drivin' them. We caught an Injun skinnin' one of the young bulls out, and we took out after him. We killed his horse about five miles west of here, and then chased him some more. We lost him somewhere out in the grass, but I'm pretty sure that we got a couple of bullets into him. We saw your fire and thought it was him."

"Well, Mister Brewer, I'd think you'd know that any Indian

worth half his salt ain't goin' to stop and build a fire when he's bein' chased by a passel of people on horses. Anyhow, I ain't seen an Indian, and we've been here all night.'' I was kind of short with him. I knew that he was within his rights to shoot somebody takin' some of his beef, but I still didn't hold with chasin' a man down without he had a fair chance.

''Well, I reckon we'll just head on back toward the herd. Half the boys are still there, and we have to get on up the trail. Sorry again about your camp.'' I nodded my head at him as he mounted, and he rode out to where the rest of his crew was waitin'. He raised an arm, and then they rode off toward the west.

''Brian, did you hear anything before those men rode into our camp?'' I asked.

''Yeah, as a matter of fact, I heard somethin' thrashin' around back by the creek and beyond the horses.''

I started walkin' easy up toward our horses. It was fairly light now, and I could see pretty well under the trees. The horses were fine, and the black nuzzled me as I put my hand to his nose. I looked up the creek and could make out somethin' layin' half in the creek. I went on up slow and easy, a careful step at a time with the Henry right out in front. I got up to him and saw the blood. It was the Indian that Brewer had been chasin', and he wasn't goin' anywhere. I got up closer and rolled him over gentle. He had a fine, strong face, and was built good in the upper body. His shoulders were wide and his hips narrow, but I realized that he was short. Probably not over five-five or so. He had two bullet holes in him, and they looked mean. One was down about waist level and on the left side. The other was through his upper chest. He'd near bled out. I looked at his face again and was startled to see his eyes were open and bright.

''Don't worry none,'' I said. ''I'm not with those that shot you.'' I didn't know if he could understand me, but I kept the tone of my voice level and friendly. Brian came up behind me.

''He looks 'bout done in,'' Brian said.

''Yeah, he's in bad shape. We can't leave him here. I won't have it said that an O'Malley turned his back on a man in this kind of shape.''

The Indian opened his eyes again, then sighed.

What in the name of Irish gods was I goin' to do with a shot-up Indian that had been caught stealin' another man's stock? How did I get into these predicaments?

Chapter Ten

"Brian, I want you to get McCoy's horse and go get a buckboard from Colten in Abilene," I said to him. "We can't carry this man on horseback in this condition, and it's closer to Abilene than Salina. Tell Colten I'll stand good for the rig."

"Okay, Matt. It'll take me a little while 'cause the wagon will be slower, but I'll hurry every chance I get."

Brian grabbed the horse, got him saddled, and set off down the road. I moved the Indian back away from the creek and took off his blood-soaked shirt. The wounds looked bad, and I had no knowledge of what to do for them. I made him a bed with my blankets and heated some water. I bathed both of the wounds until they looked clean, and then tore up one of my clean shirts for bandages. Both of the bullets had gone clear through, so there were actually four wounds to treat. The Indian went to sleep— or passed out—after I had given him a little broth I'd made from shavin' jerky in boilin' water. I nodded off from time to time and jerked awake when I heard a horse comin' down the creek. I moved away from the Indian and back into my camp so as not to give away his position. It could be Brewer and his boys comin' back.

The man that rode up to my fire was a complete stranger. I slipped the keeper from my pistol.

"What can I do for you?" I asked in a friendly voice.

"You can give me that Indian you been takin' care of all mornin'," he said, and his voice wasn't near as friendly as mine.

"No, I don't reckon I can do that." There was no reason to play dumb. He'd obviously been watchin' me and knew that the wounded man was in my care. "You see, mister," I continued, "that Indian is in my camp, or near enough to count as bein' in my camp, and bein' here puts him under my protection. I'd sure

98

hate to have to fight you over him, but I will if you think it's worth it."

He gave a nasty laugh. "You take in a real spread of country don't you, kid? Well, I know who you are from the description that Macon Beck has been tellin' around, and I know you're real sudden when it comes to fightin'. That Indian is worth one hundred dollars to the SK ranch. They posted a reward for his body, and that's how I make my livin', by gatherin' in rewards. He ain't worth fightin' you over, but one of these days the Beck boys might make you worth enough to cause me reconsiderin'," he said as he rolled a cigarette. I wasn't lettin' down my guard 'cause I noticed that he did everything with his left hand and his mouth. He kept his right hand down near his pistol. If I let down just a little, I figured he'd try.

"Mister, you can have a go at me when you take the notion. I'm ready right now, or anytime for that matter," I said to him.

"No, O'Malley, you just ain't worth enough for me to take a chance on it just yet. You keep causin' the Becks trouble, though, and they'll make it worthwhile. There'll surely come a time, and when it does, I'll find you." He turned his horse sharply and kicked him into a gallop.

Seemed like I was buildin' a real passel of enemies, and I didn't even know some of their names.

A short time later I heard a rig clatterin' out on the road, and Brian came into sight. He had someone with him on the seat, and as they got closer I could tell it was Kiowa. They pulled up, and I had to admit I was powerful glad to see the big Indian. I missed the rest of the partnership. The easy talk and evenings at the soddie were things that had become a part of me.

"Well, Matthew. I'm glad to see you, boy," Kiowa said as they pulled up. "Brian tells me you've been keeping out of trouble. In fact, he says you have been so good you might start teaching Sunday School." He laughed out loud as he climbed down from the rig. Brian must've told him about my difficulties in Salina. He walked over to me and grabbed my hand. "I am glad to see you, Matt. Now what do you have here?"

"I got an Indian up the creek with two bullet holes clean through him. I cleaned up the wounds, but they look real bad to me." I stood back a moment and looked at Kiowa. I hadn't realized how much I'd missed him. "It's good to see you." I meant every word.

"Let's go up and take a look at your friend, and I'll catch you up on happenings in Junction City.'' We turned and walked up the creek. Brian watered the team on the wagon and followed us up.

"He's a Mountain Ute,'' Kiowa said as we got to where the wounded man lay. ''I wonder what he is doing here on the Plains. He is a long way from his home territory, and there can be nothing but danger for him here. The Plains Indians are enemies to the Utes, and have been for as long as tribal memories go back. They are some of the most respected and feared fighters that the Kiowa know.'' He started going over the Ute's wounds with gentle fingers. ''You did a good job, Matt. Now, I need you to go down in the creek bottom just below your camp. There is a plant there with a trumpet-shaped blue flower that stands about a yard tall. I will need a large piece of root. It is called tolache by the Indians and devil's trumpet by the white man. It helps to kill pain. Do not taste it, because it can cause strange visions.'' I knew the plants he was talkin' about. I'd seen them when we'd set up our camp.

"Brian,'' Kiowa spoke to the boy, ''I want you to go back up the road about a quarter of a mile. Do you remember seeing a patch of trees just under the brow of a hill that we passed?''

"No, sir, but I'll find it,'' Brian said.

"All right, you find it, and under the trees you will find a plant that is about a foot tall, has big leaves, and a small greenish-white flower. It is called goldenseal. I need all the roots that you can dig. I will grind the roots on a rock and apply them to his wounds. They will help the healing process begin.''

Brian hurried toward the wagon as I went down the creek to where the trumpet bush was. I used my knife and dug several large roots. Kiowa had selected a flat rock and ground the roots against it until he had a sizable pile. The Ute was still unconscious and had started groaning in his sleep.

"If he makes it through the night, he stands a chance of living,'' Kiowa said as he worked on his medicine. ''We cannot move him until at least tomorrow afternoon, and possibly not then.''

I went down to the other campsite and gathered up my stuff. If we were staying on the creek another night, we'd want the camp up where the wounded man lay. I took Sin off his picket pin and moved him up to a new patch of grass where I could see him from the new camp. Come night I'd move him in close. Brian came rattlin' back with his roots, and Kiowa continued to grind them and treat the wounds of the Ute. After he applied poultices of the combined roots, the Ute seemed to rest a little easier. As I watched Kiowa work, I thought maybe what he knew about medicine was ahead of all the high-toned stuff the town doctors did. They gave ya medicine, bled a man dry, and did all the stuff they'd learned in some far-off school, and right here on the plains were people that had been practicin' their own brand of medicine for generations. If we'd pay attention to them, they might just teach us somethin'.

"Well, I've done all I can for him now. I'll put on new applications of the poultices in a few hours," Kiowa said. He turned from the wounded man and sat down on a log I'd pulled into the camp. "Brian says you and McCoy have things moving with the cattle deal."

"Yep, I guess we do. We bought most of the town of Abilene, and I estimate that Joe has things movin' right along 'bout now. He was in a real fever when I left."

I told Kiowa the things that had happened since we'd last been together, and he had several questions that I tried to answer. We talked late into the afternoon, and when we'd finished, he went to tend the wounded Ute. When I finished building the campsite, I made a small cook-fire and stirred up some supper. It wasn't all that great, but nobody complained much.

"I guess I told you everything," Kiowa remarked, "except the most important news. I quit my teaching position, and I have come out to give you and Joe a hand at getting things operating. It appears that I am arriving just at the right time to be of some use." He stood up and put another small piece of wood on the fire. We'd probably let it burn down after a while, since we didn't want to advertise our position. "Owen and the Major have had an offer for Rainbow City. They are still negotiating, but I really expect them to sell shortly. We will realize something over eight thousand dollars in profit if they take the current offer, and I expect the buyer to go at least a thousand higher. As soon as they make the sale, they will join us in Abilene."

"Good grief, Kiowa. That's a lot of money." I was quiet, pondering what that much money meant to the partnership. A stick popped in the fire, and the Ute groaned in his troubled sleep. Brian had gone to bring the stock up close to the camp. "How much money will it take to get a ranch and stock it with breeders?" I asked Kiowa. I hoped that was still the aim of the partnership.

"I figure it will take about twenty thousand dollars. We won't have to spend much on land, but the breeders will cost us, and we have to take into account that we won't sell any beef for the first two years. That means we will be required to have operating money without any income for that time." He sat quiet for a moment and then continued, "If we were to sell the river farm and our interest in the McCoy venture, we would just about be ready to go. There are some problems, however. The Chapmans have become very attached to the river farm, and at my suggestion Owen and the Major have offered them the farm for their interest in the partnership. It is my belief that they would rather stay on the farm than to go on west. They are, after all, farmers not ranchers." Kiowa stood and walked over to where the Ute was becoming more restless. He was still in easy earshot.

"I don't think we could just up and pull out on Joe McCoy right now either, Kiowa. He's depending on us not only for the money, but for hands to help get the whole project rollin'. I sure hate thinkin' we might pull out of the deal," I said. I knew that Kiowa hadn't been entirely in favor of us putting money in McCoy's dream.

"No, of course we couldn't pull out at this point in the campaign. I wasn't suggesting that we should." He looked over the fire at me. "I still think we should go ahead with the project, only with a view to selling out to McCoy when we have completed construction and things are well on the way."

I nodded my head. That made sense to me, and I often wondered about the two brothers of McCoy. I kind of expected some kind of trouble with them. They were older than Joe, and from what he'd told me, they had little use for his dreams.

A small breeze sprung up, and the fire fluttered. Kiowa heated a little water to mix his roots with, then scattered the fire so it would go out. It was nearly full dark. The big moon came risin' and was a sultry red color that spoke of blood. Folks back in the hills had a sayin' 'bout a bloodred moon. Blood on the moon meant that death was close behind. I hoped it wasn't pointin' at me. Things were just beginnin' to get interestin', and I wasn't ready to check out just yet.

Mornin' came with low clouds and the threat of rain.

"I hate to move the Ute, but we have little shelter here, and it wouldn't do him any good to get a soaking," Kiowa said, looking at the sky. "I don't think it will rain until late this afternoon, but when it does, it is going to be a real dandy. We better load him and head for Abilene.''

Brian hitched the team to the buckboard, and I threw the saddle on my black. We had put a blanket under the wounded man, and we used it as a kind of stretcher to load him into the wagon. He was quite a load for the three of us, but we managed without jerkin' him around too bad. We had laid all of our extra blankets over most of a load of grass that we had stacked in the wagon to make a bed. He still wasn't conscious, but Kiowa said he was some improved. I'd have to take his word for it, 'cause he still looked pretty sick to me. We got loaded and started goin' up the road for home slow and easy. I rode the point knowin' that there was no good feelin' about the wounded man in the region. Few white men had sympathy for an Indian, and certainly not one that had a price on his head for killin' a beef.

We got to Abilene without incident, and McCoy was there to meet us at the saloon. ''I managed to secure a couple of the cabins for us to shelter in,'' he said without preamble. ''Colten told me that you were bringing in a wounded man, and I knew you'd want to get him out of sight from what Brian had said. They are located down near the creek, and the doors are open. You take the one you want, Matt. I'll take the other.''

''Thanks, Joe. I'll come back up when I get things settled in,'' I said, and motioned for Brain and Kiowa to follow me.

The cabins didn't amount to much, but then none of the buildings in Abilene amounted to much. They were small, dirt-floored, and dark, with only one window on the front. They stood side by side and were built exactly the same. I calculated that they were probably built by the same person. I looked in the one on the south and then the one on the north. The one on the south seemed to draw me, so I motioned for Brian to pull up to the door. We unloaded the Ute and lay him on one of the bunks built against the wall. As we sat him down, I noticed his eyes were open, and he was taking in everything around him. I wondered what he was thinkin'. Here he was, obviously in the camp of his enemies, and yet they had treated his wounds and given him a place of refuge. He watched Kiowa the most. I went back outside and looked up toward the railroad. I was truly surprised. Joe McCoy had hired a bunch of railroaders that had been laid off from the K and P, and they were puttin' up the stock pens as fast as ties could be set and lumber strung. He might be a dreamer, but he knew how to get things done.

"Brian, would you take the team and wagon back over to Colten's place?" I asked. "Here's a buck for the rent." I flipped him a silver dollar. "I'm goin' up the street and find McCoy."

"Sure, Matt," the boy responded. "What do you want me to do when I get the wagon taken care of?"

"Come back over here. I'll be back soon, and Kiowa may have need of you," I replied

He climbed aboard the wagon and drove over to Colten's place. I walked up to where Joe was overseein' the buildin' of the stock yard.

"You didn't wait for the grass to grow up under your feet, did you?" I asked the cattleman.

McCoy grinned at me, "I couldn't see wasting time when there was so much to do."

"What do you want me to do?" I asked.

McCoy turned away from the scene of activity and walked over to the rail landing platform. He sat down and pushed back his hat. "I was thinking about something you asked me, Matthew. You asked one time how we would get the word to the trail herds, and on into Texas, that we were up here buyin' cattle. Well, the only way I can figure it is that someone needs to head south and intercept some of the herds and redirect them to Abilene. I think you're the man for the job."

"How soon would you want me to leave?" I asked.

"I would think the sooner the better. I would assume that some of the herds are getting close to the Kansas-Oklahoma border. We have to turn them west as soon as we can. It's getting late in the season, and if we're going to recover any of our cost this year, we have to get those herds here. You get the cattle here, and I'll get the buyers here," he promised.

"I'll leave out in the mornin', Joe. Kiowa will be here to help you, and he said somethin' about the other men comin' over. Seems they have a buyer for Rainbow City," I told him.

"Wedge is comin' over on the mornin' train," McCoy said. "I hired him away from the railroad. I needed someone to be foreman of the construction crew, and he struck me as the man for the job. I didn't think you would mind."

"You couldn't find a better man for the job. He's not only good with men, but he's a first-rate carpenter." I stood up and looked at the crew puttin' together the stockyards. "Joe, I think you not only have to have the pens ready for cattle, but the hotel should be up as well. I may have trouble sellin' them the idea of a drive further west, and I'll need every hook that I can find to bait.''

"You give me twenty days, and I'll have the Drover's Cottage up and running, Matt. As fast as the yards are going up, I would think the hotel would go up rather quickly as well. I have the plans drawn and ready for a crew to commence on. I have more men coming in on the train with Wedge.''

"Okay, Joe. I'll see you with a herd as quick as I can get 'em here,'' I said.

We talked for a few more minutes, and then he went back over to the construction to correct a mistake on a gate. I walked down the street toward the saloon. Stepping into the darkened room, I stopped just inside the doorway to let my eyes adjust. I looked around the small room and realized there were more people in the two-table saloon now than there had been in all of Abilene when we bought it.

I walked over to the bar and stood beside Tim Hersey.

"Tim, do you know anyone in town that has rounds for my Henry rifle?'' I asked.

"I've got some over at my little store, O'Malley. If you want to come over later, I'll get them for you,'' he replied. He took a drink of Colten's homebrew and looked at me. "I hear you had some trouble over at Salina,'' he said.

"Yeah, a little. It didn't amount to much, and no one got killed,'' I replied.

"It may not have amounted to much, but there was a man in here asking for you. I don't think he was friendly. He mentioned a fight with his brother, and he said he should have taken care of the pup when he had the knife on him. That make any sense to you?''

"Yeah. That man was Falcon Beck. He had me at the point of a knife after I'd knocked him down in an eatin' house back East. My brother, Owen, convinced him that he didn't want to continue the fight, at least not there and then. He hates all of us, and most particular me,'' I told him. "Do you know if he is still in town?'' I asked.

"No, he went out to Turbech's place. Something about one of his girls,'' Tim said.

I felt my heart drop down about level with my belly button. I knew I couldn't match Beck for looks, or talkin' for that matter.

"Thanks, Tim. I reckon our paths won't cross this time. I'm headin' out for Oklahoma first thing in the mornin'.''

"You have a care, boy. Beck strikes me as a man that would follow you and make an issue of the problem somewhere out in the brush. He might do it from behind you," Tim warned.

"He surely would, Tim, only I'm not the same wet-eared kid that he went against the last time. I won't sell him short, though. I been hearin' things about him. Seems he killed a man over at Hays City in a stand-up fight, and the man he killed had a reputation of a bad man to tangle with. They say Beck's rattlesnake quick and 'bout as mean," I observed.

Tim nodded and moved to leave. "You come down and get those shells, Matt. You may have need of them." He walked out the door, and I can't say his partin' comment made me feel any better. I just couldn't stand the thought of Ara Turbech seein' the likes of Falcon Beck. My problem was that I not only didn't have the tools to compete for her, I didn't have the time either.

I left the saloon and went back to the cabin where Brian and Kiowa were tending the wounded Ute. Kiowa was bending over the Indian, and Brian was sittin' in a chair lookin' out the window up the street toward the construction.

"You guys be all right if I leave out in the mornin'?" I asked as a way of lettin' them know I was goin'. I explained my mission, and Kiowa walked over to where I stood in the doorway.

"You know we'll be fine here, Matthew. Wedge will be over tomorrow, according to what you have told us, and I expect Owen and the Major soon. It's you I am concerned about. You look like the weight of the world is riding on your shoulders," he said with concern in his voice.

I didn't know that I looked miserable enough for it to show on me. I couldn't fool Kiowa for long anyhow. "Falcon Beck is out to Turbech's seein' Ara," I said with some shortness.

"Ara won't disappoint you, Matt. She comes from good stock, and she has a good head on her shoulders. She will see what Beck is," the Indian said.

I looked over at Brian. "He's right, Matt. Ara is sometimes pigheaded and hard to talk sense to, but she'll see the truth about him," her brother assured me. I still felt like I had a rock in my gut, but there just wasn't much I could do about it.

"How's our friend?" I asked Kiowa, pointing at the Ute.

"Well, for one thing, I doubt very seriously that he is our friend. I would guess that he perceives our help as a show of weakness. If he were in our position he would have simply killed the enemy. The Utes in particular hate any show of feebleness, and have only contempt for those who show any sign of weakness. I think he is going to make it, and as soon as he gets better, we will have to watch him closely, or we may come up missing our hair," Kiowa said.

I could follow his line of thinkin', but it didn't make much sense to me. We had given the Ute his life. How could I make the Ute respect what we were doin'? I looked over at him. His eyes were open, and he was watchin' us while we talked. I walked over to him and on impulse spoke, "When you are well, we will fight, you and I. No weapons, just our hands, and I will win."

His eyes opened wider, and a smile split his face. "It will help me heal, white man. I wondered why you kept me alive, and now I know. We will fight, and I shall win. I may die at the hands of your friends after, but I will die with victory in my teeth."

I took a step back and turned toward Kiowa, who had a big smile on his face. "Well, Matt, you probably assured that he will live. He has something to live for, and now you have it to do," he said to me.

"I had no idea he could talk American," I remarked.

"I suspected that he might. The traders have spent much time among the Utes, and Old Bill Williams lived with them for several years, just as he did with the Kiowa. By the way, the Utes are great wrestlers and bare-handed fighters. You have taken on a load when you challenged him," Kiowa told me.

I looked back at the Ute, and then at Kiowa. "It will be a day or two before he's in shape for any kind of fight," I commented.

"Yes, but that day will surely come, Matthew. He is looking forward to it." I could see humor on the big Indian, and it irked me. Me and my big mouth. I walked out the door and went to my horse. I took off the saddle, rubbed him down, and gave him grain. I started packin' my bedroll for the trip. I heard a step behind me and turned to see Brian comin' up.

"Do you want me to go with you, Matthew? I'd sure admire ridin' along, and you could be ridin' into trouble," he said.

He spoke the truth, but somethin' that Pa always told us boys came to mind. A man who rides into trouble alone is always stronger than a man who rides with other men. He either depends on the other men for help, and they let him down, or they depend on him, and suddenly he is a leader with responsibility for the group. A man who is responsible only for hisself can make faster decisions and take quicker action. Ride alone.

"Thanks, Brian, but I reckon I'd best take the trail alone. I 'spect the men here are goin' to have need of you more than me," I said. He looked disappointed, and I knew how he felt. He helped me get my stuff together, and we walked over to Hersey's little store to get some supplies and ammunition. I got outfitted and went back to the cabin. It was comin' up evening, and I was ready to go. I had the itch on me to leave out. There wasn't much room in the cabin, and it would be too hot to sleep inside anyhow. I figured I might as well be on the trail south, so I said my good-byes and mounted Sin, heading out just as night was fallin'. The storm that Kiowa had promised earlier in the day had finally hit. It started with a rush of rain, but then settled in to a steady drizzle. I pulled my slicker from my saddlebag and slipped into it. The weather matched my mood perfectly.

As I went south on the road out of town, Falcon Beck was ridin' in from the north. Macon and fifteen hard-faced men rode in from the west. They met at Colten's, then walked hard-heeled around Abilene lookin' for a certain O'Malley. They didn't find me, and the word started goin' around that I had run. It surely must've looked like that to 'most everybody except the men who knew me. They knew I wasn't the kind to cut and run on a fight. Any kind of fight.

Chapter Eleven

The shot had knocked me from my horse, and I lay quiet in the Oklahoma oak brush with my Henry in my hand. I knew I was hit, but I didn't know how bad. The man that had shot me would surely come to make certain of a kill, and I counted on getting a shot at him. Sin had stepped in a shallow depression just as the shot had been fired. That step had saved my life. It felt like the bullet had hit me near the top of my shoulder, and without the step down, it would've taken me through the chest. The man in the brush couldn't have known he'd missed a killin' shot. This guy was a sure-thing killer. I'd fallen natural-like, and Sin had gone only a few steps from me. He was cropping ricegrass and looking at me from time to time. I was under some oak brush and in a slight depression. I was certain hurt, bad scared, and I didn't know if all my parts worked. I wouldn't know 'til I tried 'em.

Suddenly I heard a shot, and then another. I jumped involuntarily, but remained in my position wondering what the heck was goin' on. The shots hadn't sounded like a rifle or a pistol. They had more the hollow boom of a shotgun, and they hadn't hit anywhere near me. If it was the man that had shot me, he'd changed guns, and he was shootin' at somethin' else. Maybe he was tryin' to get a rise out of me, but I lay still and waited. After a while I heard a horse walkin' up slow, and my black blew through his nose. I had one leg cocked under me. I figured if everything was workin', I would push off with that leg and try to catch the would-be killer by surprise. The horse stopped, and I got ready. The killer would surely put another bullet in me before he got down.

"Feller, if ya ain't dead, I want ya to know that I ain't the one that shot ya. Him that shot ya is laying over in the brush lookin' at the sky, only he ain't seein' nothin'." The man talkin' to me had a low-pitched voice, and it was somehow familiar.

"I don't hold with bushwhackers or paid killers, and this gent was both," the man continued. "I knew this feller down in Texas, and he only worked if someone paid him 'nough to make it worth his while. I reckon if you're dead, this conversation is gonna be kind of one-sided. I also figure if you're dead, you got no more use for this black horse."

"You leave my horse alone." I rolled over and covered the man with my Henry. "I'm 'bliged that you kilt the man what shot me, but I got neck hung for that horse, and I'm partial to him." I realized that I didn't sound real sensible, but he shook me up some talkin' about takin' my horse. I looked up into the man's face. It was a handsome face on a fair-sized man. He also had a Greener double-barrel shotgun laid across the saddle. I knew him, but I couldn't place him. He was wearin' a store-bought blue shirt that was thin with wearin' and washin'. The left sleeve of his shirt was pinned up, and I realized that the man had lost an arm somewhere. He saw me lookin' at it.

"It was a close thing at Shiloh, but all the Rebs got was my arm. Us O'Malleys are dang hard to kill."

I drew in a sharp breath and let it out between my teeth.

"We heard you'd went down for good at Shiloh, Mike," I said.

His eyes narrowed, and he swung down from his horse. "Do I know ya, kid? You look familiar to me, but I can't place it," he said.

"We knew each other in Pennsylvania," I replied. "In fact, one time you and Danny stuck my head in the outhouse hole and nailed a fir strip over my neck so's I couldn't get out. Pa gave you a pretty good lickin' for that one."

"My God," he exploded. "You got to be Matt, only I'd never recognize ya now."

I moved to get up and the world started to spin. I fell flat on my face. Mike jumped from his horse and ran over to me.

"I'm sorry, boy. I plum forgot you'd been shot. Where ya hit?" he asked. I wasn't up to answerin' since I was seein' stars, then blackness set in.

My eyes were open, but it was still dark. I was wonderin' if I'd up and died, then I heard a night bird call, so I figured out that I wasn't dead. Night had set in while I'd been passed out. I turned my head toward a little sound and looked into a tiny, smokeless fire that Mike was workin' over. He looked up at me, "Ya finally awake, Matt? Ya had me some worried, boy." He stood up and came around the little fire. "Ya got a bullet groove across the top of your shoulder, and ya bled like ya was really shot. I cleaned it up and got a dressin' on it. I got pretty handy with field dressin' durin' the war, even one handed." He pushed another small stick of oak into the fire and continued. "I joined the calvary after I'd lost my arm, and seen a good bit of action astraddle a horse. You know what Pa always said, 'No sense quitin' the fight 'til it's over.' I followed that bit of wisdom and got mustered out at Fort Riley after things quieted down." I could tell he was talkin' to make me feel better, and maybe he was a mite worried about me.

"After the war I went to Texas with a couple of my partners, and we gathered a bunch of unbranded cattle. We threw in with a feller named Thompson that had some cows. He said he was heading north and east with 'em. We'd just crossed the border into the Nation when he said he was sick of the drive what with all the troubles, and sold his herd out to some Eastern boys. Me and my partners still got our cows, and we're still drivin', only now we're tryin' to make cowboys out of the city boys that bought the other part of the herd. It ain't an easy thing. We're shorthanded, and we're expecting trouble with the Jayhawkers 'bout any time."

"You don't have to go into Missouri, Mike," I remarked. "I know a place in Kansas where they're buyin' cattle, and it's west of the quarantine line. There's no marked trail after Wichita Village, but I can guide you in. There's good water and grass, so it should be an easy drive. How far's your herd from here?" I asked.

"I 'spect it's about five miles east and a little south from here," he replied. "My partners will be gettin' worried. I left out this mornin' looking for a renegade that's been takin' a beef now and again. I don't mind givin' a beef once in awhile fer eatin', but I 'spect this feller is tradin' beef for whiskey. I got sick of it, and told the rest of the boys I was goin' to have a polite talk with the renegade. He's been followin' us since we got into the Nation, and I calculated I could reason with him." Mike stood up and looked over in the general direction where the bush-whacker still lay. "I cut the sign of this here feller and figured it was the man I was huntin'. I came up on him just as he shot ya. He didn't realize that I was around 'cause he was concentra-

tin' on killin' ya. I watched him 'cause I'd thought maybe someone had been huntin' him, and he was defendin' hisself. Then I
recognized him and reckoned he was tryin' to kill somebody for
money. I fetched him with the Greener," Mike said, patting the
shotgun. It was sawed off both front and back, and he carried it
on a strap slung around his neck. He packed it in a way that he
could probably get it into action quicker than a man could bring
a pistol out of a holster.

"Good thing for me you went out huntin' a renegade this
mornin'," I remarked. "I might've gotten him myself, but it
would've been a close thing."

"Point is, Matt, I need to get back to the herd. Ya think ya
can ride that black horse of yours?" Mike asked.

"I feel better now. I must have been a little tired, and that's
the reason I took that unexpected nap," I said, grinnin' at him.

"Don't worry. I won't tell no one that you fainted out like
some prissy, back-East woman, and all over a little groove in the
top of your shoulder. Hell, I been hurt worse than that tryin' to
get a three-day beard off," he said, grinnin' back at me.

I rose to my feet and got so dizzy that I near fell on my face.
I stood a minute until the world quit spinnin'. I was goin' to have
to take it slow. I walked easy over to Sin and got a clean shirt
out of my saddlebag. Mike had cut my other one off, and it was
soaked with blood anyhow. If things kept on like they had been,
I was goin' to have to buy some new shirts, and I surely hated
breakin' in a store-bought shirt.

Before we left out, I went over and looked at the man Mike
had killed with the Greener. The man that had near done for me
in the oak brush was the same man that hunted wounded Indians
for a bounty. It was the skunk that I had braced on the creek over
the wounded Ute. The Beck boys must have offered a pretty fair
price for my hair, or at least someone had. He'd told me there'd
come a time, and I guessed that time had come for him.

We rode in the dark following an old Indian trail back toward
where Mike had left the herd. I could hear and smell them before
we got there. We rode right up to the fire, and Mike stepped
down. My arm had stiffened up, and I was slow gettin' off my
horse. The men that had been under their blankets had gotten up,
stomped into their boots, and were walkin' our direction.

"How's come ya brung the thievin' rascal back to camp,
O'Malley? We figured you would take care of him somewhere
out in the brush," one of the men said.

"No, ya got it wrong, Jess. This ain't the renegade. It's my brother, Matthew O'Malley. I pulled him out of a tight spot back up the trail. I never did come up with the renegade," Mike replied.

Mike explained to the cowboys what had happened during the day. "The kid told me 'bout a new shippin' point for cattle that's bein' built right now," Mike said as he was finishin' his story. "He says we don't have to go over to Missouri, or even come close to Baxter Springs in east Kansas. He says he'll show us a town to ship from that's west of the quarantine. I'm for lettin' him show us. We calculated that we'd have to pay ten cents a head to get our critters past the Jayhawkers, and even then they might try to take the whole herd. I say we take the chance on this new place."

"I am in complete agreement," one of the Eastern boys said. "I'll be the first to admit that myself and my associates are not drovers. The sooner we get the cattle to market the better off we will be."

The rest of the men also spoke out in agreement, and I quickly found myself to be a guide for the first herd goin' to Abilene. I laid my blankets out after we'd had the discussion and I'd been introduced around. My shoulder and arm were stiff, sore, and I was tired. The blankets felt good, and before I knew it, Mike was shakin' me out.

"Roll it out, Matt. Cookie's got breakfast on, and we got to get movin'. We want to get to your Abilene town before the snow flies," he said, and then walked toward the cook fire.

I got out of my blankets and rolled them into a tight roll that would tie behind my saddle. I walked over to the fire and joined the other men.

"How far do ya reckon we are from Abilene, Matt?" Mike asked me.

"What river was it we crossed last night comin' in?" I asked him.

"That was the Cimarron, and the Turkey is about ten miles farther up," he replied.

"Okay, I 'spect that makes it about forty miles to the Kansas border. We got to hold east of the Salt Fork, or we'll end up on the Salt Plains. From the Kansas border up to Abilene is about another hundred and twenty miles as the crow flies, but more like a hundred and forty for us. That's a hundred and eighty miles total," I said.

Mike turned to the other men. "That's eighteen more days if we hold to our average. Can everybody handle another eighteen days?"

"I 'spose we've come this far, we can make it the rest of the way," one of Mike's partners replied.

"We will certainly try to be of more help than we have been so far," one of the Eastern owners remarked. "We have learned a considerable amount about cattle in the last ten days, and I anticipate the learning process to continue."

"All right. We're headin' for Abilene. Matt will work the scout for us, which will give us another hand for the cattle," Mike said.

We finished our breakfast in silence, and the men drifted away from the fire one by one to go catch their morning mounts. The work was hard enough that they used at least two horses a day and sometimes three. I watched Mike and came to realize that he was as good with a rope as a two-armed man. His cast was accurate, and he was strong in the one arm he had. No one moved to help him, and it wasn't 'cause they were mean or callous. A man was expected to do his own bait of work, plus a bit more. Even a one-armed man. If he couldn't keep up, then he'd best find somethin' else to do. I caught Sin, which wasn't even a challenge anymore, and threw my saddle on him.

"Mike," I hollered across to him "if the trail gets thin or there's a branch, I'll mark it off with a pile of rocks to show you direction. You're the first up this year, and it might be growed over in spots." He waved to show he'd heard. He seemed to be as much of a boss as these men had, and he yelled back, "Matt, we'll need water 'bout ten or twelve miles out. That's where we'll bed tonight," he replied.

I waved my arm to show I understood and headed north. My shoulder was stiff with a scab, and it was darn sore. Cookie had put a fresh dressin' on it and remarked about how he'd cut himself once peelin' taters. I got the general drift that he'd been hurt worse peelin' those taters than I'd been by the rifle bullet.

I'd ridden 'bout a half hour when I came to a branch trail that headed north by a little east. I made a stone pillar on the left side of the trail and continued to follow it. It seemed fairly straight, and the brush wasn't very thick. I knew the drovers behind me would have a hard time keepin' the herd together if the brush got thick. I rode easy, makin' a stone marker about every forty-five minutes or so. I come up with the Turkey River along 'bout

midday and figured that was where we'd hold the herd come
night. I had a couple of biscuits and some jerky that Cookie had
given me after breakfast. I let Sin take on water while I tried to
choke down my dry meal. I took a small drink from the river,
and my lips pulled back over my teeth from the taste of gypsum
in the water. It wasn't bad enough to hurt the stock, but it tasted
foul. I expected it to have a taste since it ran through the salt
plains to the west. I fooled around for a while more, then mounted
my horse and headed back. I came on the herd 'bout middle of
the afternoon. It was hotter than blue blazes, and the cowboys
were havin' trouble holdin' the cattle in a bunch 'cause of the
heat and humidity. Mike rode up to me with a kerchief tied over
his mouth to filter out the dust.

"How much farther, Matt?" he asked.

"Can't be much more than three miles. You've made good
time. The water is gypie, but there's plenty of it," I replied.

"Okay, sounds good to me," he said. "We have made good
time today. The cattle are restless, and they're movin' better than
they have since we started this adventure." He looked toward the
left side of the herd and then back to me. "I reckon the boys
over on the left flank could use some help bustin' a few of the
strays out of the brush." He rode away with a wave of his hand,
and I turned Sin with a flick of the reins. Mike had put all three
of the Eastern owners on that side, and they were havin' a little
trouble. I rode up to one of the fellas. He was covered with dirt,
and the sweat that was drippin' out from under his hat cut little
trails down his face.

"Mike says you can use some help over here," I shouted over
the sounds of the cattle.

"We can use all the help we can get. My name is McCord.
Smith is the one just gettin' down from his horse," he said, pointing out the man. "My other partner is Chanlers. I think he is
riding behind the herd. His position is the most ungodly place on
earth. I am sure he would appreciate being spelled down there."

I nodded agreement and rode toward the rear of the herd. I
saw instantly what McCord had been talkin' about. The dust was
risin' in a cloud behind the cattle and the heat seemed to hold it
there. I got a kerchief from my saddlebag, dampened it with water
from my canteen, and tied it over my nose and mouth. I rode
into the cloud and managed to find Chanlers. He was coughin',
spittin', and near gaggin'. Sweat was runnin off him in rivers.
It was hotter here than it had been anywhere else around the

cattle. A thousand head of beeves put a lot of heat into the air. That, combined with a summer temperature over a hundred, made the butt end of the herd the hottest place this side of hell. I motioned him to move up on the left flank with the rest of his partners, which he did with a wave of gratitude. I started pushin' the cattle and watchin' for strays. The dust was so thick I could barely see, but I noticed movement to my right and behind me. I stopped Sin, who was sweatin' as freely as I was, and let the cattle move ahead of me. A single cow had stopped, turned around, and seemed to be headin' back for Texas. I kicked Sin, and we moved in on her. Her horns were an easy four-foot stretch from side to side, and she had a little crook in the left one. I was careful not to get dead in front of her where she could get her sights on me. Mike had warned me of the danger of these half wild cattle and their long horns. More than one horse had been killed during the roundup of the herd in Texas, and they were lucky that a man hadn't been killed or maimed.

I tried to turn the cow, and she just wouldn't have any of it. I hated to admit it, but I wasn't much better at workin' cows than were the men from back East. I'd had little experience with stock, and none at all with cattle like these. I didn't want to have to go to the fire tonight and admit that I'd been outsmarted by a cow. I crowded in close on her flank and tried to turn her with Sin and brute force. She toppled over like she'd been shot. The dust had cleared, and I could see plain that this cow was hurtin'. Now, I've hunted a lot, and I've killed animals, but I made sure my kills were clean. Pa always told us that animals had feelin's and there was no sense in makin' 'em suffer. I purely hated to see an animal in pain. I stepped down from Sin and walked up close behind the old gal. She was goin' to calve. Her timin' wasn't right, but most times nature cared little for such things. Spring was mostly when cows had calves, but this old gal had decided to hold off 'til it got hot. We'd had a milk cow at home, and I watched her have calves a number of times. I looked toward the cloud of dust that marked the rest of the herd and made up my mind to ride up and get Mike. I was over my head and I knew it. I jumped astraddle Sin.

"I'll be back shortly, old girl," I said to the cow. She didn't seem to care much right at the time. I turned Sin up the trail and kicked him into a gallop. I found Mike at the right flank of the herd and near the front.

"Mike, I got an old cow down at the rear of the herd. She looks to be havin' a calf," I told him.

"We got no time fer her, Matt." His horse spun, and he turned it back. "We've had this happen several times on the drive north. We got no place for small calves. They get underfoot, and the cows are just plain mean when they have a calf on 'em. We'll have to leave her." His horse spun again and took off for a cow headed for the brush.

I turned my black around and headed back for the drag, as the butt end of the drive was called. I raised a hand to one of the Texas men who had dropped back to bunch them up, and pushed my side up even with his. A small breeze had come up. It wasn't much, but it cooled the sweat and made the dust drift off a little faster. We rode for another hour and suddenly the herd stopped all at once. There was a concentrated surge from the rear, and soon the cattle were lined up shoulder to shoulder drinkin' the nasty water of Turkey River.

Mike rode over to me, stopped, took off his kerchief, and wiped his face with it.

"Was the cow that went down a brindle color with a little crook on the left side?" he asked me.

"Yep, that's her," I replied.

"Damn it all," he swore. "She's one of our lead cows. I missed her this mornin', but didn't really look for her." He took his hat off and wiped his hair down, holdin' the reins in his mouth. It was plain to see that Mike had made the adjustments necessary for livin' with one arm. He put his hat back on and spat the reins into his hand. "We found out early in the drive that we had two lead animals. One was the old cow that's back on the trail, and the other is a red steer that must weigh near a half ton. They's the first ones up in the mornin' and the rest of the herd follows right behind 'em. It makes it a bunch easier to drive the rest of the herd with them two old moss horns leadin' out. I hate to lose her," he said.

"I'll go back and see if I can fetch her in. She ought to be done and on her feet by now," I volunteered.

"I hate to ask ya, Matt, but this cow probably is worth the effort. If the calf can't keep up, put him sideways across your saddle. The cow will follow ya if you have the calf in the lead. And 'member what I tole ya about them cows. They will surely put a horn to ya if they get the chance."

He turned his horse away and moved up the river. I scratched

Sin between the ears and turned back on the trail. It wasn't a
hard trail to follow since a thousand head of cattle have a way
of churnin' up the ground. We made a quick trip of it, and a half
hour later I was at the spot I'd left the old cow. She wasn't there.
I figured that she'd taken to the brush once she'd had the calf,
so I started castin' around for tracks on each side of the beaten
trail. I finally came up with a set of tracks, only there wasn't just
cow tracks. There were tracks of a cow, calf, and a shod horse.
Somebody was drivin' our lead cow off through the brush. I
remembered what Mike had told me about a renegade that had
been workin' the herd since they had gotten into the Nation. It
had to be him, and pretty quick our old cow and her calf was
going to be traded for whiskey. I rode easy knowin' that if I
caught the renegade it could easy be a shootin' matter. Stock
thieves were generally hung or shot, and often without much
explanation bein' offered.

The trail turned toward the north and headed for the Turkey
River. The sun was gettin' down low, and I hoped I'd come up
on the thief before it got dark. The brush started to get thicker
as we approached the Turkey, about three miles downstream from
where the herd was bedded. The river came in view, and I took
the keeper from my Colt. It stood to reason that the renegade
would camp on the river for the same reasons that we had. It was
mighty unpleasant to make a dry camp after a hot day. Sin's
hoofs made no sound in the soft sand as I followed the tracks
around a gentle bend. I come right up to him; he hadn't heard
me comin'. His horse was tied off to a willow close by the water,
and he'd already taken his saddle off. The brindle cow with the
crooked horn was suckin' water from the river.

The renegade was greasy, with long black hair that hung down
his back in two dirt-covered braids. He didn't look to be a full-
blood Indian, which might account for his bein' a loner. Half-
breeds weren't much liked either by the tribes or the whites. He
was sneakin' up behind the cow, and had a knife in his hand that
was long enough to cut wood with. The cow's head jerked up,
and she turned a little to one side. She had a beautiful, brindle-
colored bull calf beside of her, and it was plain to see that the
renegade was plannin' on havin' calf steaks for supper. The cow
figured out the same thing and let out a beller that sounded like
a low-toned whistle on a locomotive. She dropped her head and
started churnin' the sand tryin' to get a horn into the renegade.
He took off runnin', yellin', sweatin', swearin', and generally

appeared to be havin' a hard time keepin' out of reach of old crook horn. He made it to a cottonwood tree and skinned up it faster than I would've thought possible. The old cow bellered some more, looked at her calf to make sure he was fine, and began to smack the tree with her horns.

The renegade had made the mistake of takin' off his short gun and leavin' it with his rifle at the spot where he'd dropped his saddle. The only weapon he had was his knife, and while I calculated that he was a mean man, he just wasn't up to takin' on an upset, longhorn cow with a sheath knife. I rode slow up to where his horse was tied. It had the O'Malley brand on it. Mike had come up with the brand down in Texas and put it on near everything. A brand was as good as a signature in cow country. Mike O'Malley's brand was an O over an M with a bar in between them. It was a simple brand, and Mike called it the O Bar M. It was registered somewhere down in Texas as the O'Malley brand.

The renegade wasn't only a cow thief, but also a horse thief. I had a clear memory of what happened to horse thieves from Junction City, so I had little sympathy for the man in the tree. The reason western folks were so hard on horse thieves was if you left a man afoot in much of the country, particular the wide open plains, he'd most likely die. It was a long walkin' distance between rivers, and sometimes in the summer, water was just plain hard to find. There was also the problem of Indians comin' up on a man on foot. He was usually fair game. I had little sympathy for the man up the tree. He hadn't seen me yet, and I moved slow so as not to attract his attention until I was ready. I untied the O'Malley horse from the willow and walked both horses over to the calf. I grabbed him under the middle and hoisted him up on my saddle. He let out a puny bawl, but it was enough to attract mom's attention. She come toward me snortin' and caterwaulin'. I jumped in the saddle and took out like my shirttail was on fire. I'd tied the extra horse behind my saddle, and he wasn't havin' any trouble keepin' up. The mad mama behind him kept him movin' right along. I could hear the renegade yellin', but I couldn't make out what he was sayin'. I reckoned it wasn't polite language anyhow.

Chapter Twelve

Abilene had changed so much in the month I'd been gone I hardly recognized it. There was a lot of excitement in town when we drove the herd onto the main street by the railroad. Several men swung open the gates to the stockyards, and I noticed there was a big sign over the main gate proclaimin' that this was the home of the Great Western Cattle Company.

"Matt!" I heard a voice holler from down the street. I looked and saw Joe McCoy walkin' toward me with a big smile on his face.

"Matt," he said as he got up close, "I'm glad you're back. I see you accomplished your mission." He stood beside my horse and watched as the thousand head of long horns filed into the fenced yards. "It's begun, Matt. Just as I envisioned. Abilene will soon be the biggest little town this side of the Mississippi." He laughed out loud like a delighted child.

"I got the cows here, Joe. How about the buyers? These boys have been on the trail for three months, and they're anxious to sell out," I said.

"Well, I've had a little problem there, Matthew. I sent telegram after telegram to buyers I knew in Kansas City, Springfield, Chicago, and the like. I got very little response. They don't believe I can deliver the cattle. Now that you're here I want to send a carload of cattle back to Chicago to prove that I can deliver." He looked out across the two thousand horns that filled the stock pens and then continued. "I had some of the men round up some buffalo along the Smoky Hill, and I plan on shipping a carload of them back with the cattle just to create interest."

"Well, I know the cattlemen are going to be disappointed, but if you think the buyers will come out, then I 'spose they'll just have to wait," I said. I knew Mike and the boys wanted to unload the herd as quick as they could. There were still too many things that could happen to them even behind the relative safety of the strong fences. Spanish Fever wasn't the least of the possibilities, and a good loud thunderstorm might drive them through even the railroad-tie posts.

"I'll go find the owners and let them know," I told Joe. He nodded, and I turned Sin toward the main gate of the pens. Mike was sittin' slouched in his saddle, relief showing on his face.

"Well, we made it, Matt. There were times when I wouldn't have given a wooden nickel for our chances," he said as I rode up.

"The buyers aren't here yet, Mike. Joe's havin' trouble gettin' them to believe he can deliver stock. He's goin' to send a carload of your cattle back to Chicago along with a car of buffalo to show he can do it. If the buyers decide to come, they ought to be here in 'bout four or five days," I said.

Mike looked a little sick, then his face lit up. "I'll send our cowboys back along with the cattle. They can tell the story of the drive, and I bet they create enough interest that they make the Chicago newspapers. In fact, I'll tell 'em to play it up big. That ought to help spread the word."

"That's a fine idea," Joe said. He had walked up to us while we sat on our horses and talked. "What we need to create is a carnival atmosphere. We need to make it fun to come to Abilene, both for the drovers and the buyers."

"Mike O'Malley, this here is Joe McCoy," I said introducing the two men.

"I've heard a lot 'bout ya, McCoy. If you're half the man that Matt says ya are, then ya stand good with me," Mike said as he leaned down and shook the little man's hand.

"Another O'Malley is it? You boys just keep popping up. There must be a bunch of you around," Joe said and grinned. The fact that Mike was short an arm wasn't lost on the cattle buyer. I saw him take it in, but he had too much tact to mention it.

"There's a passel of us around, or least there was before the war," Mike responded. "We got relation spread from here to yon, accordin' to what our Pa told us."

"Well, there's another O'Malley down the street at the new saloon," Joe remarked. He pointed down the street to a spot where a new clapboard buildin' had gone up since I'd been gone. "Owen and the Major have set up shop. They called the place the Alamo, thinking that the Texans would feel more at home.

By the way, the name of the street is now Texas Street in honor of the drovers.''

Mike looked over at me. ''What say we go down and cut the dust out of our throats at the Alamo?'' he asked. ''The rest of the men can finish here. The worst work's most done anyhow.''

''I'm right behind you, Mike. I'll let you go through the door first, and we'll see if Owen recognizes you,'' I replied.

He put the spurs to his horse, and we trotted down Texas Street to the new saloon. We tied off the horses and stomped up to the swingin' doors. Mike threw them open and stepped inside. Owen stood behind the bar, fit as a fiddle, as usual. He looked up and took in our dusty forms standing silhouetted against the sunlit door.

''Come on in, boys, and pull up a chair,'' he said. ''The first one is on the house if you're the ones that just brought in that herd.'' He reached under the bar and pulled a bottle from a shelf.

''I'd rather have a beer if you don't mind, bartender,'' I said. ''I can't stand the green whiskey you sell in these clip joints.''

''Matthew,'' he yelled and jumped over the bar. He grabbed me by the shoulders, ''It's good to see you, Matt.'' Then he hugged me. I didn't remember Owen ever huggin' me before. Maybe the married life was makin' him soft. He let go of me and turned toward Mike, expectin' an introduction. His eyes got as big as dinner plates, ''Mike,'' he whispered. ''God be praised, it's really you.'' He wasn't swearin'. He really meant it. He grabbed Mike around the neck and started dancin' him around. I knew it for sure now. Married life had certain sure made a soft spot in his head. Them two had been close together in age, with two years between 'em, and they'd been closest friends as well. They hadn't seen each other for near six years, and there'd been a lot of fast water runnin' under the bridge since then. The Major and Joe McCoy had come in behind us and were watchin' the carryin' on.

We finally got Owen settled down and we all sat at one of the tables. Mike and Owen had a lot of catchin' up to do, and after I'd had a beer, Joe and I went outside to leave them alone for a spell.

''It's a strange old world isn't it, Matt?'' Joe asked me. ''Who would have imagined that you would come across your brother the way you did?''

''It's pretty strange. Kind of like we was destined to come together or somethin','' I agreed. We stood quiet for a time watchin' the horses flick flies off each other's backs with accurate swipes of their tails.

"There was a little red-haired gal asking about you a few days ago," Joe said, lookin' a little smug.

"What'd she have to say?" I asked, knowin' immediately who he was talkin' about and tryin' not to sound anxious.

"Seems her brother and her had quite a long conversation, or so Brian told me a few days ago, about a certain false-gaited man that she'd been stepping out with," Joe said. "Brian says that she is starting to see the light. It also helped that this particular gent, and I use the term loosely, tried to take some liberties with her which she objected to. I heard that she told Beck off good and proper. Something like Matthew O'Malley would never think of trying to take advantage of her, and she could not imagine where Beck had conceived the idea that she was a girl he could trifle with." We stepped down from the front porch of the Alamo and stood beside the horses. Joe continued, "Brian said that Beck left the farm in quite a huff and made several threats toward both Ara and the family. That might have something to do with the fact that Turbech ordered Beck off the place and enforced it with a shotgun. I think Beck caught him a panther by the tail and got scratched up some before he could let go," Joe chuckled.

I was scared for Ara and the Turbechs. I really was. I knew what Beck was capable of, and I knew he had at least twenty men that would ride with him. He surely wasn't stupid enough to bother a girl, particular since he'd been warned off. Folks in the West just wouldn't abide a man playin' light with a decent girl. I had to admit that I wasn't particular unhappy about the fact that she'd brushed him off like the horses were brushin' flies, but I was worried.

"Folks don't want to underestimate what Beck will or can do," I commented. "He's meaner than two snakes tied together, and I don't think there's a moral bone in his whole body."

"That reminds me," Joe said. "Falcon and his brother Macon were in town right after you left out south. They made a lot of noise about killing a certain O'Malley. When they found out that you had left town, they started condemning you for a coward. They got drunk down at Colten's, broke up his place, and then shot him when he protested. Falcon told around that Colten had gone for a gun, but Tim Hersey says that Colten never wore a short gun. Beck's crowd all left town shortly after that, and then a few days later Falcon had his problems with the Turbechs. I just heard today that they all went down to Fort Hays, and they are raising hell with Hays City.''

I hadn't known Colten for very long, but he'd held no malice for any man and was always willin' to lend a hand. I'd counted him a good man.

"Did anyone do anything about the killin' of Colten?" I asked Joe.

"We sent a telegram to Topeka asking for a federal marshal, but you know how that goes. It was a local killing, and usually the Federals won't get involved in local investigations," Joe replied. "The point of my conversation is that the Beck brothers seem to be hunting you, and they have branded you a coward," he said.

"Well, I'm back now, and I 'spose me and the Becks will meet up by and by. I'm not lookin' for trouble, but if they bring it to me, I'll stand." I hoped I sounded brave. Fact was that there were too many of them. I might be able to take Falcon alone, or Macon, but not both together. And what about the rest of their men? I didn't 'spose they'd be just standin' around with their hands in their pockets while the fightin' went on. There was also the problem of a price on my head, put there by the Beck boys. I hadn't heard anything official, but the fact that a bounty hunter had tried for me down in the Nation made it appear I was worth somethin' dead. That meant that some freelancer might decide to ambush me when I least expected it.

"You have help, you know, Matt," Joe said as if he divined my thoughts. "You have two brothers here with you, and a pack of good friends that also happen to be good fighters. They will certainly fight beside you."

"Yeah, I 'spect they will, and it's a pleasant thought, knowin' I got friends that will stick by me, but it's my fight, Joe. I'd hate gettin' one of my brothers or friends killed stickin' up for me," I said.

"Well, I know some of your friends and at least one brother that would be very unhappy if they didn't get in on the fight, if it ever happens," he replied. "I don't know Mike yet, but I bet he is no different than the rest of the O'Malley clan. He looks to be a good man despite his handicap," Joe commented.

"He is that, and once you get to know him you forget that he's one-armed," I said. We stood quiet a moment listening to the sounds of hammers and saws. We were surrounded by the commotion of building. The clamor sounded disorganized, but I knew that every board, every peg, and every driven nail was designed to build somethin'. We were buildin' the future, and I was a part of it.

"I'm goin' down to our cabin on the creek. I'm tired and I want to see Kiowa. Is he still down there?" I asked.

"He has been spending a lot of time down there. I see him from time to time. He's been eating at the Alamo, and then takes a meal down to the Ute he doctored. Owen told me the other day that they have gotten to be good friends, and the Ute is about healed up," Joe replied. "I saw the Ute the other evening when he came outside for a breath of air. He's not very tall, but he's built like a bull buffalo. He might be a load for someone who's planning on fighting him," he said, grinnin' at me.

"That's real encouragin', Joe. I wouldn't doubt if somebody around has already started offerin' odds on the fight," I replied.

"As a matter of fact, Wedge has mentioned it," Joe said as he laughed.

"Well, you buzzards can forget it. The only reason I said what I did to the Ute was 'cause I wanted to help him get better," I said.

"Tell that to the Ute, or Kiowa for that matter," Joe remarked. "I think Kiowa is lookin' forward to it as much as the Ute is."

"Damned savages are always lookin' for a fight," I replied. "I think Kiowa must have a mean streak in him down under all that polish."

Joe laughed again, and I turned toward the tie rail and untied my horse. I swung aboard and looked down Texas Street. Things was changin' fast. The Drover's Cottage was goin' up and was a work of art considerin' that a month before there was only one shingled roof in Abilene. Joe had talked the railroad into givin' us a siding that held a hundred cars, and the K and P crew was workin' on it. Joe had told me that they were usin' cull ties 'cause they still had no faith in the dream. They expected to tear the siding out in the spring.

Joe had sent one of his brothers and another man south with printed circulars that promoted Abilene as the only shippin' point to consider for Texas cattle. He also made Abilene sound like a paradise, which it might prove to be for men that had been on the trail for three months. Right now it looked like a dusty little town in the heart of a summer-baked prairie. The only thing that spoiled the picture was the smell and sounds of the penned cattle.

I reckon they smelled like money, but it was still right putrid if you stood downwind.

I turned Sin around and headed toward the creek and the cabin. We were both ready for a rest.

Kiowa was sittin' out front on a bench, and Wedge was sittin' next to him. The Ute was sittin' on the ground crosslegged on the other side of the door.

"Matthew, we heard you'd made it back. We also heard that you found another O'Malley along the trail," Kiowa said to me.

"You heard right on both counts, only it's more like my brother found me instead of the other way around," I replied. I stepped down from the black and walked over to Wedge. I'd forgotten he was so dang big and ugly. It'd been a spell since I'd seen him.

"Wedge, it's good to see you even if you are offerin' odds on a fight that ain't gonna happen," I said, takin' him by the hand.

"You forget, sonny boy, I'm the man what trained ya. I'm offerin' odds only 'cause ya had such a good teacher." He laughed and nearly broke my hand. "I'm glad to see ya, boy. I come over from Junction City the day after you taken out. I have missed ya, boy," he said seriously.

"I missed you, too, Wedge. I even missed this no good savage," I said turning my attention to Kiowa.

"Be careful who you call a savage, Matthew. I might take your hair," he said laughing.

I sat down and told them most of what had happened durin' the month I'd been gone. They caught me up on the partnership. Owen and the Major had sold out Rainbow City for nine thousand dollars and signed the river farm over to the Chapman boys, who had decided to stay on the Republican raising spuds and wheat. They'd make a good life of it, and they'd always be our friends. Wedge had bought into the partnership for a thousand dollars, and I couldn't think of anyone I'd rather have than the big man. Joe and Kiowa had sold fourteen buildin' sites along Texas Street for one hundred and fifty dollars each. Seems that there were folks that did believe in what we were doin'. Course it was mostly speculation on their part, but it was money in our pocket. Owen had told Kiowa that we had near fifteen thousand dollars in cash money in the partnership fund. It was a lot of money, and only five thousand from what we figured we'd need to start out on our own little dream. We finally wound down the conversation and sat quiet with evenin' comin' on.

"Have you talked with the Major and Owen about the ranch?" I asked Kiowa.

"I did. In fact the discussion turned to goals and direction one night. I mentioned the conversation you and I had before you left and told them that we felt twenty thousand dollars would be necessary to start the ranch. They generally agreed. They also agreed that we were close to achieving the monetary goal, but there is one big hitch in our plans," the big Indian said.

"We don't have any idea where we're goin'," I interrupted. "We don't have the foggiest idea where we're goin' to set up our ranch."

"Exactly. You understand the problem completely," Kiowa said. "We nearly have the money accumulated, but it's too late in the season for us to do much this year anyway. We need to scout a location and be prepared to move by spring." The locusts had started to sing in the cottonwoods along Mud Creek, and the bullfrogs added an off-key harmony.

"I'd like a long, wide, green valley where the grass is butt-deep to a tall horse and a river runnin' cold and fast," I said to no one in particular. "I'd want tall trees with eagles sittin' in the top, and deer as thick as hair on a dog's back," I said lookin' toward the western sky. "I'd want a big wide view with a ring of mountains all around the valley holdin' up the sky. I dreamt about such a place one late night back home on the farm. It was so real that it stuck right there in my head."

"Maybe you'll find it in your dreams, Matt." Wedge smiled at me. "It'll have to be in dreams 'cause there can't be that kind of place on this earth. It's too perfect."

"There is a valley just as you have seen it in your dream." I had forgotten about the Ute. He was standin' up lookin' off to the west and pointin'. "It is there, beyond the mountains, and it is just as you have seen it. It belongs to my people. It has been our hunting place for many generations, and will be ours until the end of time."

I looked at the Ute kind of dumbfounded. So the valley of my imagination did exist. There was only one little problem. The Utes were some of the most cantankerous folks in the West, and they were known to kill other folks that edged into their country. The man I was lookin' at didn't strike me as the kind that would be likely to share.

The valley was so real to me that I could almost hear the wind in the trees and smell the pureness of the air. If it was there, then

I planned on livin' right in the middle of it. How could we get around the problem of us trespassin' on Ute tribal ground? Suddenly an idea struck me.

"You say that the valley is there beyond the mountains?" I said to the Ute.

"It is there," he assured me.

"You also say that the land belongs to the Mountain Utes and will be theirs until the end of time?" I asked.

"That is true," he replied.

"How could a man go to that valley and make a home?" I inquired.

"There is no way, unless you are of my tribe," he replied.

I switched tracks and continued. "We must fight, you and I," I said to him.

"We have agreed, and it is a thing which must be done to preserve my honor. I have been taken by you, my enemy, and we will fight. I know that I must sing my death song after I have beaten you, for your friends will surely kill me. It would not be so in the Valley of the Utes that we speak of. If I had taken you prisoner, we would fight, and if you won, we would be friends. But that is not the way of the white man," he said, looking intently at me. The Utes were great bargainers, and this man was bargainin' for his life. I had counted on it.

"We will fight as you said. I given my word to you before I left, and my word is good," I remarked. I hadn't been plannin' to carry on with the fight, but all of a sudden it had become important that I not only fight, but that I win. "We will fight, but we will not fight to kill. We fight for honor only. We fight until one of us drops in our tracks. The man left standin' is the winner. If you defeat me, then you can return to your mountains with your life. If I win, you take me to the mountains with you and speak to your chief 'bout lettin' me and my friends live in your valley. We want to raise cattle and live in peace with our neighbors."

The Ute looked toward the west again, perhaps seein' the Valley of the Utes in his mind, and then turned toward me. "It is done, O'Malley. We need not worry about speaking to the chief of my people. It is me. I am Chief of the Weminuche band. My name is Ignacio."

You could've knocked me over with a feather. I'd actually saved the life of a chief. He stuck out his hand, and I took it. He grabbed my forearm in a brotherhood shake and 'bout crushed it. I didn't let on, but it hurt. He let me go and turned toward the cabin. He stopped and turned back.

"It will be a good fight, and I will win. When I return to my valley, I will speak of the O'Malley man that I defeated on the plains, and it will become a great legend among my people," he said with a big smile on his face.

Well, I'd got lucky. There was a man once that said he'd rather be lucky than good. I just stepped into a pot of luck. The only thing that remained was to beat a man in unarmed combat to the point where he couldn't get up. A man who had been trained from his youth in all the ways and means of fightin' both with weapons and without. A man who belonged to a tribe of people who were known for their courage in war, and their absolute refusal to quit a fight 'til they was dead or the other guy was. Man, was I lucky.

Chapter Thirteen

The fight between me and Ignacio became common knowledge around town in just a few days. Abilene was a town starved for entertainment, so the fight was takin' on the lustre of a back East event. Joe had told me that he wanted to create a circus-like feelin' about the first shipment of cattle goin' east, so we calendared the fight for September fifth. The buyers had gotten in, and they had bought out Mike's herd for thirty dollars a head. The only thing he'd kept was the old lead cow with the crooked left horn and her calf. Mike and Owen figured to use them to lead our own herd someday. We kept 'em in the corral by the cabin, and they'd gotten near tame. The railroad was sittin' cars on the new sidin', and we were scheduled to ship cows on the fifth. It was goin' to be a big affair, and Joe planned on makin' it a day no one would forget soon. He wanted the word to get spread around that Abilene was the only town worth a darn in all of Kansas. He wanted everything just right for the celebration on shippin' day. He had a bunch of strange food comin' in from the East and was plannin' a big-time feast. He'd invited everybody he could think of, and even sent flyers East on the trains callin' it "the event of the year." It looked like he was goin' to have his circus.

A man named Colonel Wheeler, and his two partners, had brung in another herd of cattle. They hadn't been pointin' for Abilene to begin with. In fact, they'd started out for California with their twenty-five-hundred head of Texas longhorns, but they'd hit several spots of trouble along the trail north. The longhorns were near the same as wild animals down in the brush country of Texas. It took patience and determination to drive them any distance at all. They'd shy off at the slightest noise or movement, and Wheeler's herd had experienced three major stampedes. They'd had a brush with some Indians in the Nation,

130

and there was some problems among the partners. All in all, Wheeler had decided he wanted out. He'd come into Abilene by himself and looked over the situation. He'd liked what he'd seen and soon struck a deal for the whole herd at twenty-eight dollars a head. He'd brought them up near town, twenty-four-hundred head of cattle, havin' lost only about a hundred head in the drive. They'd camped on the Smoky Hill River where the grass was good, waitin' for the pens to empty out.

Wheeler had done it up right at the start. He'd hired near sixty Texas boys to act as drovers. He'd issued each man two horses, a new Henry repeater, a new Colt six-gun, a new rope, and two new shirts each. He'd put on two cooks in two wagons and made sure that they knew how to cook. Bein' a former army man, he knew how important a full stomach is to a workin' man. It was a hell of an outfit, and they knew how to raise hell. Wheeler let them come into town half the crew at a time, but it seemed like there was a hundred of them instead of twenty-five or thirty. Joe had put up a little tent city along the railroad to house the cowboys in, and even went so far as to put wooden floors in the tents. They slept on cots instead of the blankets on the ground they were used to. It was real luxury for them.

Wheeler had been paid half the money for his herd on delivery to Abilene. He had turned around and paid his cowboys half of their pay: They'd been on the trail for near three months, and they were ready for a blowout. Blow out they did. The Alamo was open 'round the clock. It was different than what the Rainbow City had been back in Junction City. There was no such thing as "refined trade" in Abilene. Every man there was belted and booted and stepped aside for no one. Owen hired four bartenders and two bouncers from among the K and P crew. There wasn't an hour went by that they didn't throw a liquored-up cowboy out the doors. Gamblers started comin' in, and while Owen didn't gamble, he soon saw that he'd need to run his own games, or else the cowboys would be cheated blind. He hired six of the transient gamblers to run house games, and told them to run them honest. He figured he'd make enough on the percentage. He'd fired two of them for cheatin' and they'd been run out of town by the cowboys. The Texans didn't mind losin' their money, but they wanted to lose it honest. Owen was buildin' the reputation of bein' an honest man, who gave an honest drink, and his games were straight.

The Major was cookin' meals, only it wasn't the fancy stuff

that he'd been doin' in Junction City. It was all the same meal
breakfast, dinner, and supper. A cut of buffalo or longhorn steak,
dependin' on what he had that day, two slices of bread, and taters
from the river farm, and all covered by rich brown gravy. Once
in a while he'd bake pies, but they went so fast that he felt like
it was useless to make 'em. He was always out of pie before nine
in the mornin'. He kept three big kettles of coffee boilin', and
by noon the brew was strong enough to float a railroad spike. He
was sellin' the meals for seventy-five cents each, and even with
three cooks he had trouble keepin' up. There was no division
between the saloon and the eatin' house like there had been in
Junction City. The town folk, particular the women, didn't come
up on Texas Street, so there was no need for the separation.

In the matter of one week's time three more herds arrived in
Abilene, and things got real lively. All of a sudden Abilene was
the place to be, and we jumped from a population of less than
three hundred to more than two thousand, and not all of them
was good, God-fearin' folk. We got most of the "dregs of so-
ciety" as Joe called them, that had been workin' the end of the
track towns as the railroad was bein' built. Abilene was really
jumpin'.

Cowboys from the three herds that come in after Wheeler's
complained about not havin' a guide to help them through the
brush and sand hills after they hit Caldwell in southern Kansas.
They'd lost some cattle in the brush, and they told McCoy that
it could harm his chances for drawin' in the herds. McCoy got
worried, and the more he considered, the more he worried. He
finally got hold of Tim Hersey, who was a civil engineer of sorts,
and commissioned him to plow a guide furrow all the way from
Caldwell to Abilene. Hersey turned around and hired a dozen
teams with plows and over fifty men to plow the furrow. Hersey
surveyed it, and the men he hired plowed it. Folks around figured
it was the longest furrow ever plowed in Kansas, and it might
even have been a world record. Joe was good at things like that.
Kiowa said that Joe was the best promoter he'd ever met, and he
had a way of gettin' things done. Trouble was, he had no head
for money. That was the topic of conversation out in front of the
cabin late in the afternoon, the first day in September.

"I am becoming concerned about our continued involvement
with the McCoy brothers," Kiowa said to the gathered partnership. "The promotions that Joseph is involved in are certainly
getting Abilene noticed, but they are also very costly."

"Kiowa is right," the Major agreed. "We have not realized a single dollar's profit from our partnership with the McCoys. However, his advertisings have brought in a large number of people. In fact, would Abilene even exist without what Joe has done?" he asked, not really expecting an answer. "Of course not. This is Joe McCoy's town. As a direct result of his imaginative efforts, we are making excellent money from the Alamo."

"The issue is," Owen said, "our continued participation in the partnership with the McCoy brothers. The reason I brought it up in the first place, is that Joe told me today his brothers are unhappy with the agreement. They want us out, and they're tellin' him that if they can't buy us out they're goin' back to Illinois. He feels bad about it, but there's not much he can do. They're offerin' five thousand dollars for our share, which doubles our original investment, and I say we ought to take it. I think Joe is headed for more problems than just his brothers. He spends money like it was free. I really like Joe, but I say we get out."

"It's really not a matter of whether we like Joe or not, and I don't feel like we are leaving him stranded," the Major said. "He has asked us to sell out, and I think we should."

A vote was taken, and it was agreed all around to sell out our partnership with the McCoys. Mike and the Ute were the only ones that didn't vote. Mike had just bought into the partnership, after he sold his herd, and didn't feel like he ought to have a say in a decision that had started before he came. The Ute didn't care. All he was stickin' around for was to kick my tail.

I felt kind of bad about Joe 'cause what they said was true. Joe was headin' for some real money problems if he kept spendin' like he did. We heard the crash of gunshots and some yells up on Texas Street. It was gettin' to be a pretty common occurrence with all the trash that had come in. You throw the bad folks in with the Texas boys, shake up 'em up real good, and they 'most always came out fightin'. We were havin' three or four fights every night, and some of them had ended up in shootin' matches; two cowboys had already been killed. There was some talk around town of gettin' a town meetin' together and electin' some officials, includin' a marshal. I didn't figure it would happen this year and maybe not the next, since most folks in Abilene hadn't been together long enough to get to know each other. Politics is one of them things where you got elected if you was popular. Nobody stuck out as bein' popular yet. They was all too busy tryin' to make a buck.

"Let's go down by the creek, Matt," Wedge said. He'd been workin' out with me since I'd been back. I was his pupil, and he sure didn't want me to lose the fight to Ignacio. He also had some money bet on me. The fight was only four days away, and I was gettin' nervous. The Ute stayed close by the cabin 'cause he knew that the Abilene folks didn't hold much with Indians who had a price on their head. I'd been watchin' him, and there were times, usually in the afternoon, when he'd go down on the creek and be gone for a couple hours at a time. He was lookin' fit, and except for the bad scars he had, a fella wouldn't know he'd been shot up. I calculated that he was goin' down on the creek doin' some kind of workin' out to build his strength back. Kiowa and him had got real thick, and I wasn't so sure that Kiowa wasn't coachin' him a little. It was kinda strange that they'd got so friendly considerin' that their people were traditional blood enemies, and had been for generations. Kiowa was big on fair play, although not all that particular about a fair fight, and there was a difference.

Wedge and I started wrestlin' around and then got down to some serious head thumpin'. We both pulled our punches so as not to hurt each other, and after an hour I'd worked up a good drippin' sweat. Wedge tried to come in under my fists. I back-stepped, then let go with my left fist. It took him right in the side of the head.

"Damn it, boy. This ain't the real thing. You got to remember it's just a little exercise. That last smack you gave me hurt," Wedge said, sounding a little miffed.

I grinned at the big man and stepped back. "I'm sorry, Wedge. I'm gettin' a little anxious, and I hit you harder than I meant to."

"Yeah, well, let's call it off. I'm tired, and ya raised a lump on me," he replied.

I got my shirt from where it was hangin' on a limb and wiped myself down with it. As we started walkin' toward the cabin, I saw that we had company drivin' up in a wagon. It was the Turbechs, and I could see the womenfolk under the wagon tarp.

"I'll be up in a minute, Wedge. I'm goin' back down to the creek and wash up," I said. He followed my gaze and looked back at me, smilin'.

"You want I should bring ya back down some of that good smellin' rum that Mike puts on after he shaves? I'd hate havin' ya smell like a polecat in front of decent women." He laughed.

"I think I'll get by without it tonight, but bring me down a clean shirt would ya?" I asked the big man.

He chuckled and walked up the hill. I went down to the creek and washed up. Wedge was right; I didn't want to smell like a polecat. I'd seen Ara a time or two since I'd been back, and I even spoke to her at Seely's new store. She'd been polite and friendly, and I was some encouraged. It was the first she'd spoken to me since Owen's weddin'.

"Matt, are you down there?" It was Brian Turbech. He'd been out on the farm for a spell helping his pa and uncle with the work.

"Yeah, Brian. I'm down at the creek," I hollered back.

I heard him comin' through the trees, and when he got up close, I could see that Wedge had sent my clean shirt down with him.

"How's things goin', Brian?" I asked him.

"Pretty good, I guess. We got most of the summer work done, and it'll be a while 'fore the fall crops come in, so Pa says I can stay in town and work 'til harvest," he replied.

"Did everyone come in with you?" I asked.

"If you mean did Ara come in, the answer is yes. So did everyone else. They're up to the cabin talkin' with the other men. We come in for the shippin' celebration. Pa said we needed to get off the farm for a few days and see some different people," Brian said.

I finished cleanin' up, dried with my dirty shirt, then slipped into my clean one. We walked up to the cabin talkin' about things that mattered, like horses and guns. Brian had bought him a new Colt pistol with some of the money he'd earned, and he was right proud of it. We walked up to the cabin, and everyone was sittin' around outside 'cause of the heat. The sun had gone down, but the heat seemed to hang on. There was just enough light left in the sky to see Ara. She had on a delicate blue bonnet that matched her dress. I reckoned right then that she was the most beautiful girl in all of Abilene, maybe all the world.

"Hello, Matthew. Please sit down with me." She patted the bench beside her where a spot had been left vacant. Everyone else seemed to kind of fade out like it was just me and her there all alone. I sat down beside her, and our arms touched lightly. I got all hot in the face and had trouble catchin' my full wind.

"How have you been, Matt?" she asked.

"I estimate that I'm doin' pretty fair," I said in kind of a hushed tone.

"Have you killed anyone lately?" her voice mocked me.

I looked at her, kind of shocked and then stood up. I just plain didn't know what to say. I could feel the hurt startin' way down deep, and I realized that maybe she wasn't as pretty as I'd thought.

"I got to go tend my horse," I said with a stammer and turned away from her. All the other folks had gone quiet like they knew somethin' had happened. I walked away with my shoulders squared to them, but on the front side my lip was quiverin' and my eyes felt like bawlin'. I wouldn't let her see it, but she'd sure stuck me good. I got my black out of the corral, slung my saddle on him, and headed off down the road. I remembered Ara at the sunflower patch when I'd first fell in love with her, and I wondered how a man could misread another person so bad. Part of the problem was that she was a woman, and I knew horses a lot better than I'd ever know women.

I rode out past where I could see the lights of town and lay down in the deep prairie grass holdin' the reins of my horse. He was content to chomp grass, and I lay watchin' the stars pop out and feelin' miserable.

I wasn't far off the road, and after 'bout an hour I could hear some horses slow walkin' toward town. I was down behind a little dip at the crest of a small hill, and I stuck my head over to take a look. It was the Butterfield stage, and somethin' was wrong. I pulled Sin over to me, jumped into the saddle, and galloped down to the stage. The shotgun rider was up on top, and he'd bled down the side of the coach. He was dead. Nobody bleeds that much and lives through it. The reins were still up over the driver's seat, but they was tied off to the brake. It was plain to see that they'd been attacked. There were bullet holes all over the coach. I grabbed the lead horse to stop 'em, and then dismounted and climbed up on the driver's seat. The driver had crawled down under the platform, and he'd been shot twice through the body. He was still alive, but just barely. I climbed down and tied my black to the back of the stage. I'd have to drive them in, and hurry, from the looks of the wounded man. I opened up the passenger compartment and saw a big, fat man lying on the floor. He'd been shot through the head. He must have been the only passenger. I started to step down, but then I heard a voice.

"Mister, if you ain't a bandit, I'd be obliged to ya if you'd get this carcass off from me." It was a girl's voice.

I grabbed the fat man and moved him onto one of the seats. She crawled out, all covered with his blood.

"He saved my life, but I was about to suffocate. When they started runnin' us, I got down on the floor, and when he got shot, he fell on me. They just checked his front pockets and must've found his wallet in his jacket. They didn't move him, so they didn't find me. It's just as well they didn't. I got me a little Smith and Wesson, and I would have sure blown a hole in at least one of 'em." She stopped talkin' for a minute to catch her breath and take a look back inside.

"I didn't like him much," she said, lookin' in at the dead man. "For a spell there, just outside of Hays City, I thought he was gonna try and put his hands on me. I don't look like much, but Pa brought me up to be a good girl, and I'd have had to cut him up a little to teach him some respect. I didn't wish him dead, though," she said and started cryin'.

Holy hoot owls, what was I supposed to do anyhow? I went back to my horse, got my canteen, and took a clean shirt out of my saddle bag. I tore it for a rag, wet it down, and wiped the blood off her face.

"You hurt anywhere?" I finally asked.

"No, except for maybe a bump or two from the rough ride on the floor." She'd quit bawlin' and managed a smile. "I'm beholdin' to you for rescuin' me, and tearin' up your shirt."

"That's fine, only that was next to my last shirt, which means I'll have to go buy some at Seely's store tomorrow. I surely hate breakin' in new store-bought shirts." She laughed with me; then I remembered the driver. "We got to get to town as quick as we can. The driver's up top and he's hurt bad," I said.

She didn't waste around. She jumped right up on top and settled into the seat. I untied the lines and grabbed the whip. We fair stirred the dust gettin' into town, and by the time I'd drove the stage full tilt all the way up Texas Street to the stage station, we'd drawn quite a crowd.

"I got a bad shot man up here," I yelled, and I laid on the brake. Several men climbed up, lifted the driver down, and took him into the station. We didn't have a doctor in Abilene yet, so Kiowa was the next best thing, maybe better. I saw Brian standin' at the edge of crowd and beside him was Ara.

"Brian, go down and fetch Kiowa up here. We need him to

tend a wounded man,'' I yelled. Brian took off like he'd been shot out of a cannon. I glanced at Ara. She was white as a sheet with her hand held over her mouth. I stepped down, and then helped the girl down. She hung a heel on the last step and fell into my arms. I looked over her shoulder and saw Ara watchin'. She looked mad. We went into the station.

Kiowa came on the run and pushed men back from the table where the wounded man had been stretched out.

"Please, I need more room, and better light," the big Indian said. Some of the men went out the door, and one man brought back two lanterns. Kiowa worked on the man for over an hour and then stepped back. "He is going to die. There is nothing I can do." He had a defeated look about him, and I knew he hated givin' up.

There was kind of a collective sigh from the men that had gathered in the room, and they began to file out.

"What happened?" someone asked outside the station.

"We was robbed by a gang of men 'bout three miles east of Salina," the girl piped up.

Questions started comin' at her from every direction, and she held up her hand until it was quiet.

"I can't tell you much except they started runnin' us and shootin' up the stage. They finally got the coach stopped and shot the driver, and him not even offerin' no argument. I was layin' under that fat drummer man on the floor and couldn't see much, but I could hear. A man that talked like the leader told another man named Macon to climb up and throw down the express box. That's all I know."

She took a couple of steps back toward the station, and I got a clear look at her. She had an unruly mane of chestnut-colored hair and a pert upturned nose with a sprinklin' of freckles over it. I figured her to be a year or two younger than me, and she was small. I guess she was what folks called cute. She was wearin' pants, which was real different. I don't reckon I'd seen a girl in pants more than two or three times. They fit her bottom end pretty snug, although I never noticed that sort of thing usually. I'd noticed when I caught her that she probably didn't weigh more than a full bag of wheat. She looked at me and smiled. The lantern hit her just right, and I saw she had the biggest, greenest eyes I'd ever saw. She walked back over as the crowd cleared out and looked up into my face.

"My name is Lewara Conall, but most folks just call me Lee," she said as she stuck out her hand.

I took her hand in mine and shook it friendly-like. Her grip was firm, nearly manlike, and surprising since she was so little. "My name is Matthew O'Malley, and most folks call me Matt," I responded.

"Okay, Matt. I already told you I was 'bliged for your help, and I still am. Can you tell me a place I can stay for the night that don't cost much, but where I won't be bothered?" I hesitated for a moment.

"She can stay with Owen and I, Matthew." It was Patty. She and Owen had walked up close to us. I hadn't noticed them in the crowd. Owen stood close behind her 'cause decent women didn't come out on Texas Street without an escort, particular at night.

I introduced Lee to Patty and Owen, and Patty put her arm around Lee's shoulders. "I'm beholdin' to you, ma'am," Lee said to Patty. "I've had an uncommon hard day." I saw the tears well up in her eyes though she fought them back. The two women walked off towards Owen's house with Owen trailin' close behind. He'd gotten lucky and bought the one original Abilene house that had roof shingles when he'd first moved to town. Patty had made it nice.

We counted the bullet holes in the stage and came up with a total of thirty-one. There had surely been more than just two men involved in the holdup. It was more likely a gang of men, and there was only one man that I knew of that carried the name of Macon. It looked to me like the Becks had finally gone full out-law. I happened to look over where I'd last seen Ara, and she was still standing there with Brian close by. She had watched us count the bullet holes, and I thought she looked a little green around the gills. I could still feel the hurt she'd put on me, but along with it I felt the deep start of anger. Didn't she see that good men didn't kill just for the sport? It was forced on folks just like it had been on me. If I hadn't got into action fast, Owen would be dead, and maybe Patty. I turned away, untied my horse from the stage, and started walkin' him toward the cabin on the creek. I was bone-tired, and the hurt was still there like a lump of lead just above my stomach. I got to the cabin, unsaddled Sin, and turned him into the corral. Then I walked up to the door and jumped as someone moved close to me. It was the Ute. He had taken to sleepin' outside when he'd healed up some. He looked at me close in the starlight, and then grinned.

"I think you are a good man, O'Malley, and I will hate to make you bleed. But I will be standing over you when the fight is finished. Otherwise it will not make a good story to tell my people when I return home." He went back around the cabin, and I went inside. I'd better forget Ara and concentrate on a certain Ute.

Chapter Fourteen

He was big through the shoulders and arms, even if he was short. I reckoned that Ignacio was an uncommonly strong man and a born fighter. It wasn't goin' to be an easy thing to whip him, but all of my plans centered on the fact that I must fight and win.

September fifth had arrived, and the celebration was beginning. The K and P had moved the rail cars onto the new siding, and just after the fight, McCoy and his brothers would commence loadin' longhorns for back East. There was a big crowd of people in Abilene. Folks had come from all the surroundin' towns, and there had even been a special trainload of people come in from Chicago. Shippin' day was goin' to be a day to remember. The fight between me and the Ute wasn't the only thing that Joe had put together. He had arranged at least five horse races, a buggy race, a horse pullin' contest for the farmers, a pie sale, and there was goin' to be a big dance in the evenin'. It was gonna be quite a day.

I was standin' across from Ignacio, sizin' him up. It was obvious that the large crowd bothered him, but once the fight started he'd forget the crowd. Joe had put up a rope on the street to keep the crowd back, and to keep us in one spot.

The Ute smiled and walked toward me. Kiowa was actin' as his second, and Wedge stood behind me as my second. It was a duel of sorts. The Ute walked up to me and held out his hand in a show of friendship. I took it, which proved to be a mistake, since he hit me with his other hand and knocked me down. It didn't hurt much but my pride, and it brought a laugh from the crowd. I figured the fight must have started.

I moved toward him, he backed away, and then came running at me and clinched. He was powerful, and his grip around my waist hurt like blazes. I couldn't get my breath. I dropped on my

141

back and kicked my feet up, throwing him over my head. It broke his grip, but he jumped quickly to his feet and kicked me in the side before I could get my feet under me. It rolled me, and I kept rollin' 'til I was away from him. The kick had hurt and put a stitch in my side. It felt like I'd run ten miles without stoppin'. I jumped to my feet and saw the Ute running at me with his head down and his arms spread. This was one of the things that Wedge had schooled me on. Indians weren't much for hitting with their fists. They would rather clinch and throw a man to the ground, then kick him senseless.

I timed his running stride, and just as he got to me I stepped aside and hit him a solid blow in the temple with my right fist. It knocked him down, and as he tried to get to his feet, I knocked him down again. He blinked his eyes and made a grab for my legs. I stumbled back away from him, and he came after me. I was worried. I'd hit him hard, and all he'd done was shake his head.

I staggered, and he was on me. He knocked me down with his body, and then dropped on my chest with his knees. I felt the air rush out of me, and stars started spinnin'. I couldn't catch my air. He'd taken hold of my hair and was poundin' my head on the rock-hard street. I forced my arms up into his face between his arms and grabbed his ears. I started pullin'. He grimaced, but wouldn't let go of my hair. I pulled harder. I'd made up my mind that I'd pull 'em off if he didn't let go real soon. His knees were shuttin' off my wind. Just when I thought his ears were gonna start rippin', he let go. I flipped him over my head again. I jumped to my feet, not wanting to get kicked again. I caught him comin' at me, and I nailed him with a left cross on the point of the chin with him comin' in. It hurt him, and I followed with a right that was nearly as hard. He backed away.

My breath was comin' in long, ragged gulps, and I was bleedin' from a cut over my eye that I had no memory of gettin'. Ignacio wasn't even breathin' hard. He was smilin' at me. Wedge told me that the one thing I didn't want to do was get mad. He said if I got mad I'd quit thinkin', then I'd get whipped. It made me mad as hell when Ignacio grinned at me. I headed for him with my hands clenchin'. I was seein' red, and I meant to rip his head off. We went at it then. There wasn't nothin' purty about it. It was just two men standin' in the dust swingin', bitin,' scratchin', kickin', tryin to put each other down.

I got too close, and he grabbed me by the hair and the crotch.

He lifted me over his head and slammed me down. He dropped on my chest with his knees again, and I felt something pop. He sat straddle of me and started workin' on my face with his fists. He didn't seem to be hittin' hard, but he was poundin' 'em in fast. He'd either took a lesson from me smackin' him, or Kiowa had been givin' him lessons. He picked me up again and threw me into the street away from him.

I was nearly done for. I couldn't breathe, and it felt like I had a broke rib. He came at me with his feet as I lay there. He got me once, but I managed to roll and get to my feet. I stood there swaying, just barely able to stand, with blood drippin' into my eyes. Ignacio came runnin' at me again. I wasn't mad anymore. I was scared. I sidestepped him, and as he went rushin' by, I hooked his ankle with my toe. It was near accidental, but it worked. He skidded on his face for a ways, and I followed at a run. As he stood, I swung a roundhouse left that took him right in the nose. This was a man that had to be proud of his nose. It was straight and narrow, and was one of his best features, or least it was 'fore I smeared it all over his face. His hands went up to his broken nose, and I hit him in the gut. It was like hittin' a nail keg, but it made him grunt and drop his hands. I hit him in his damaged nose with my left again, and I hit him hard. Suddenly I was feelin' good. I couldn't hear the crowd. I didn't feel the pain in my ribs. I didn't notice the blood. I swung with both hands, first one and then the other. I hit him in the face, then countered with a blow to his body. I moved him back a step at a time. I brought an uppercut in with my right hand that started down around my shoe tops. It rocked his head back like it was on springs. I brought my left in straight from the shoulder and pegged him between the eyes. I brought the right up from the ground again. It sounded like an ax splittin' a green log. The blood splattered from his face, his eyes crossed, and his head flew back. He landed on his back in a little cloud of dust. I stood over him a moment, then turned toward Wedge. I took a step and fell flat on my face. I could hear the crowd screamin' as I kind of drifted out.

"I never seen anybody get hit that hard." It was Wedge. "I seen people get hit a hundred times, maybe more. Hell, I probably hit people a hundred times if ya get down to it. I never, in my life, seen anybody get hit as hard as Ignacio was with that last thumper of Matt's."

"We know, Wedge. That is the tenth time, at least, that you've told us." Kiowa sounded a little unhappy.

"I want my money as soon as we get to the cabin, Kiowa," Wedge said. "It ain't that I don't trust ya, but I do savor the sight of ya countin' out them pretty gold pieces into my hand."

"And they call us savages," Kiowa commented.

I could tell that I was in the back of a small spring wagon, and we were movin' slow. I'd have taken a look, but my eyes were near swollen shut, and it was easier to leave them closed. I hurt everywhere, even on the bottoms of my feet. We pulled to a stop, and I felt the wagon bounce as Wedge jumped down.

"How long you think they'll be out?" Wedge asked.

"I expect that Matt is awake now, but Ignacio may be out a while longer. I don't think I have ever seen anyone get hit harder," Kiowa said.

Wedge burst into great whoops of laughter. "See I told you I'd never seen anybody hit harder, and now ya finally admit it."

"I only said that because you had made the statement so many times it became ingrained in my mind," Kiowa defended himself.

"I don't care what kind of grain it is. You admitted that Matt hit the Ute harder than anybody's been hit before. It's the only time we been together that you ever agreed with me on anything. I want my money," the big man said.

Kiowa laughed, "Okay. Let's get them into the cabin, and I'll pay up."

They lifted me gently from the wagon, took me into the cabin, and laid me on my bed. I could hear them shuffle around, and I 'sposed they were doin' the same with the Ute. They probably put him on Kiowa's bed. I didn't bother to look.

Kiowa came over and put his hand on my head.

"Did I win?" I managed to croak through broken lips.

"I guess you did if you want to call it that. You look more like you lost, but I have to admit that Ignacio looks worse," he said.

"How is he?" It was Owen. He'd come down to check on me.

"He will be all right," Kiowa replied. "He has a broken rib or two, and that cut over his eye is going to take some stitches, but he'll live."

"How's the Ute?" Owen asked.

"He hasn't come around yet, and his nose is never going to be the same. I don't know why his jaw isn't broken, but it seems

intact. I think he will be okay, but neither one of them is going
anywhere for a few days,'' Kiowa said.

"Do you need some help puttin' them back together?'' Owen
asked. "Lee said she'd come down and help if you needed.''

"It might not hurt to have some extra hands. I am going to try
and straighten Ignacio's nose while he's still out, and Matt is
going to need a wrap on those ribs. Send her down and tell her
she's welcome,'' Kiowa replied.

"Wedge, let's you and I go up and watch the horse races.
There's not much we can do here,'' Owen said to the big man.

"That suits me, Owen, but Kiowa owes me some money on
the fight. If'n I leave, he'll forget to pay me. He might even try
and forget permanent,'' Wedge said.

"I'll pay you tonight. I certainly wouldn't try and cheat you
out of it,'' Kiowa said a little testily.

Wedge could tell he'd gotten under the big Indian's skin. "I
know you wouldn't cheat me, Kiowa. I was just rubbin' it in a
little,'' Wedge said apologetically.

"You guys go on,'' Kiowa said. "I'll stay here and play nurse.
Don't forget to have Lee come down, Owen.''

"Right,'' Owen replied as the two men walked out the door.
It got quiet. I drifted into sleep.

"He looks terrible, Kiowa. You sure he ain't hurt permanent?''
It was Lee, and she was standin' over me.

"No, he will be fine. There will be a few scars, but he wasn't
that pretty before the fight,'' Kiowa said.

"I don't know. I thought he was kind of purty. Leastways
better than some I've seen,'' she replied.

"That's the difference between you looking, and I,'' Kiowa
laughed.

I felt her cool hand on my forehead, followed by a damp cloth.
She was washin' the blood from my face, and it felt right nice,
except when she hit a raw spot.

"What happens next, Kiowa?'' Lee asked the big Indian.

"Well, first, these two have to heal, and then I think we are
heading west. Ignacio is a man of his word, and he made Matt a
promise. We are going to the Valley of the Utes somewhere in
the Shining Mountains and look for a place to start our own
ranch,'' Kiowa said. "What about you, Lee? Do you have any
plans?''

"I haven't had many plans since Pa died. I heard there was

work here in Abilene, and that's the reason I ended up on that stage. I only got 'bout forty dollars left between me and starvin'.'' She dipped the rag into a basin, rinsed it out, and continued workin' on my face.

"Pa never 'mounted to much, particular after Ma died in St. Lou. It wasn't 'cause he didn't try. It was just the way things went. He wasn't much at farmin' or anything else he turned his hand to. He weren't much, but I sure miss him. He was all I had.'' There was a catch in her voice, and she rubbed a little harder than she needed to on my face. I flinched, and she let up.

"Are you awake, Matt?'' she asked.

I tried to say yes, but all that came out was a little grunt. "You just lay quiet, and I'll get you cleaned up,'' she said.

I sure as heck wasn't goin' to get up and run a race.

"Anyhow, I think I got a job today,'' she said, returnin' to her conversation with Kiowa. "The Major said he would put me to cookin'. One of his cooks quit, and he was lookin' for somebody anyhow. That's one thing I can do. I can cook. Owen said I could use the extra room over at his and Patty's house. I'm beholdin' to him. He wasn't goin' to charge me rent, but I won't stay free. I'll pay my own way.'' There was a touch of pride in her voice. Lee was a gal that planned on makin' her own trail.

"Owen and Patty are like that,'' Kiowa said. "They are probably the nicest folks I know.''

I tried to open my eyes just a bit to get a look at the girl that was workin' on me. I got 'em opened a slit and watched her as she talked. I tried to compare her to Ara, but it was hard to do. Ara was a beautiful, full-figured woman with refinement. Lee was small-figured with big eyes, a nice face, but no ravin' beauty. She was a sharecropper's daughter without much education, and she carried a gun and a knife. I couldn't imagine Ara packin' a knife, let alone a gun. Yet, there was somethin' about Lee that stuck with a man.

She finished with my face and walked over to where Kiowa was takin' some stitches in Ignacio's head. I watched her go, and I had to admit that her britches fit her bottom end real nice. I went to sleep with Lee on my mind.

The next three days were hell. I was so sore the first day that I laid flat on my back most of the time. The trips to the little house out back were torture. I couldn't eat, and my stomach thought sure a rope was tied around my neck shuttin' off my gullet. The second day was some better, and I was able to eat a little, although it had to be soft stuff. The third day I was up and around, but it was real slow. I thought out each step before I took it, and I didn't do no laughin'. My ribs hurt real bad when I laughed, so I made Wedge stay away from me.

The Ute was worse than me. He stayed down two days, but was gettin' around better than me by the fourth day. On the evenin' of the fourth day followin' the fight, we were all sittin' around in the cabin talkin' over what we were goin' to do.

"I would suggest that we get started west if we are going this fall," Kiowa said. "It won't be long before it starts getting cold."

"It is as the Kiowa says," Ignacio agreed. "We must be in the valley before the snows come."

"Who all's goin'?" Wedge asked.

"Well, Owen shouldn't go. He has responsibilities here in Abilene that should be his first concern," the Major said.

"The same is true of you, Major. We will need to accumulate as much money as possible before spring. The more we save, the better our life will be while we are building a herd. You need to manage the restaurant," Kiowa remarked. "We know Matt is going. It was to him that the promise was made, and he was the one that earned it."

"I think I ought to go," Wedge said. "Ignacio and Matt are goin' to need someone to keep 'em out of trouble." That brought a general round of laughter since the big man had whipped nearly every cowboy that had come to Abilene.

"No, you are needed here, Wedge. I am afraid that Joe McCoy's promise of finishing the Drover's Cottage in twenty days would be extended to several years without you. It will still be spring even if you fulfill your contract with him," Kiowa said. "It is my opinion that Matt, myself, Mike, and Ignacio should be the ones to go. We have no obligations here in Abilene, and I would like to see the country."

There was some discussion, but finally everyone agreed that Kiowa was right. It was also agreed that we would begin the trip in two days. That would give me and Ignacio a little more time to heal, and it would take us that long to get ready. I went to bed that night with excitement buildin' in my gut. I reckoned not too far down the line I was goin' to be seein' the Valley of the Utes.

"Matt, make sure that pannier is tied tight to the pack saddle. We don't want it floppin' around," Mike hollered. I went to do as he told me and looked over the outfit. We made a pretty good crew with the four men, our ridin' horses, and a pack horse each.

"Where did Kiowa go?" Mike asked as he rode over to me.

"I don't know. He was here just a minute ago," I replied.

It was early mornin' of our leavin' day near the middle of September, and Mike was plum ready to go.

"I am here," Kiowa said from the door of the cabin.

I turned to look, and took in a breath. Kiowa was there all right. He'd changed out of his white man clothes and was dressed in fringed deer hides. They'd been worked so nicely that they were a beautiful tan color, and the beadwork was outstanding. He was an Indian from headband down to moccasins. He was quite a figure of a man regardless of the clothes he wore.

"What are you staring at, Matthew? Haven't you ever seen an Indian before?" He was grinnin' at me.

"Dressed up like that you could near pass for a Kiowa," I said grinnin' back at him. "Where'd you get those?"

"My sister made these with her own hands just before I went to England. They made quite an impression on the English ladies," he said.

"I didn't know you had a sister, Kiowa."

"She died of smallpox, along with the rest of my family while I was gone," he said as he turned toward his horse.

He mounted and looked toward the west. No question about it, he was every inch a warrior.

Mike had ridden over to Ignacio and was talkin'.

"Let's go," I hollered over at them.

We grabbed the leads on our packhorses and headed west out of town. I looked back once. I saw Lee standin' on the railroad platform wavin'. I waved back and turned my face toward the Valley of the Utes.

We rode two by two. Mike and Ignacio led the way. Kiowa and me followed behind, a little off to one side to stay out of the dust. We'd planned on stoppin' at most of the army forts on the journey out. That way we could gather the news of what was ahead of us, and we could replenish our supplies as we went. We'd heard several reports of the Plains tribes raidin' west of us. A troop of cavalry from Fort Leavenworth had been hit by Arapaho a few weeks earlier up on the Solomon. The army had been out all summer tryin' to get a handle on the tribes, but they'd had little success. The way General Hancock had been treated by the Cheyenne and Sioux at Fort Larned in the spring showed the way most of the tribes viewed the army. With pure contempt. The Indians had been invited to a confab, and the army had gathered up every trooper they could find to impress them. The Indians weren't impressed. The two tribes left out in the night, and the army never even knew they was gone. Over two thousand Indians packed up, rode out, and never even woke the army sentries.

There was still some mighty nasty feelin's between the whites and the tribes over the Sand Creek fight, and the Indian raids were happenin' more often. We figured we could talk to the Kiowas. That was part of the reason that our Kiowa had dressed up as a warrior. The Kiowa tribe packed a real hate for the whites. They had even gotten to the point where they wouldn't let any traders set up shop in their territory. We hoped we could talk to 'em, but Indians were real notional. You couldn't be sure of anything.

Black Kettle's Cheyenne would as soon kill us as look at us, since they were the ones that suffered most at Sand Creek, but we counted on them bein' north. They ought to be settin' winter camp, and hopefully not out raidin'.

The Comanche worried us most. They weren't notional at all, they flat hated everybody. They claimed all of western Kansas as their huntin' grounds, and while they were allied with the Kiowa, that didn't make them bosom buddies. The Kiowa name for the Comanche was *Gyai'-ko,* which meant "enemies," and we didn't reckon we'd be able to talk with them. It didn't help much that we had a Ute with us. The Utes were traditional enemies to all the Plains tribes. They'd been killin' each other for generations, and rarely trespassed onto each other's territory.

We were heading for Fort Harker first, and then on over to Fort Hays. Both of these army posts had been built with the sole purpose of dealin' with the Indian problem.

We rode all day at a steady gait, stoppin' only for a bite to eat around noontime. We'd bypassed Salina, stayin' on the north, and makin' good time. We crossed the Saline River, left the trail, and pointed a little south. We figured we could make better time cuttin' straight across the prairie.

I hadn't been doin' all that much ridin' since I'd come in with Mike, and my butt was sore by evenin'. My ribs were wrapped up pretty tight, but after ridin' all day I could hardly get a good breath. We stopped at a little spring that had two cottonwoods standin' guard over it. We judged we were 'bout fifteen miles east of Fort Harker, so we'd make it in easy the next day. The country around was easy, rollin' hills with grass that was belly deep to our horses, so there wasn't much need to put 'em too far out for feed. We'd seen a wealth of wildlife durin' the day, but we hadn't done any huntin'. We had side meat and beans, and we hated to cut loose a shot unless we had to. No use attractin' anybody's attention.

"Kiowa, if you want to build a small fire, Matt and I will water the horses. Ignacio's gonna take a look around," Mike said as we stepped out of the saddles. We'd kind of elected Mike as the boss, and he took to it natural.

Kiowa nodded, and I took hold of a handful of reins and lead ropes. We watered two animals at a time since the spring was small, and as we finished the waterin' we put them on pickets close in by the fire. Kiowa had made a fire from dry wood, so there was almost no smoke. Ignacio had gone over the crest of a nearby hill, and I could see him comin' back through the grass.

Kiowa had the dutch oven settin' over his fire. He was burnin' side meat and throwin' in beans for flavor. The beans had been soaked, then dried enough to pack, but they was still like eatin' bullets.

"Good grief, Kiowa. You tryin' to kill us with these beans?" I smiled across the fire at him.

"You heard him, Mike, Ignacio?" he asked, lookin' at the other two men. They both nodded their heads.

"There is an old campfire tradition that goes back for centuries, Matthew. The first man to complain about the meal gets to cook for the next week, and that includes washing dishes." He laughed. The other two men laughed with him. It wasn't the all-out gut-bustin' laugh that they'd have gotten in town. They laughed soft, makin' some concession for where we were, not wantin' to have a belly laugh echo through the hills.

"It is true, O'Malley man," Ignacio chimed in. "It has been so with the Utes for a long time."

I knew he was lyin', but he was havin' so much fun at my expense I hated to spoil it by whippin' him again.

"I hate to tell ya this, Matt, but Kiowa is right. I seen it happen a dozen times durin' the war, and more than a few times since." Mike laughed. My own dern brother was sidin' with a couple of savages against me. I'd always thought the O'Malleys hung to-gether and told him so.

"That only happens with fightin'. It don't apply to cookin' and washin' dishes," he explained.

I grumbled and gathered up the dishes after we'd eaten. I washed 'em in the lower end of the spring, not wantin' to get goobers in the good drinkin' water.

"I 'spect we'd be smart if we'd kill the fire, then go back into the fold between the hills to sleep. We ain't far from the river, but ya never know when some thirsty Kiowa might decide to stop here and get a drink," Mike said. He looked over at Kiowa and smiled. "He might even kill ya before ya had a chance to tell him ya was cousins, it bein' dark and all."

We gathered up our gear and moved back to where two hills came close together. It gave us considerable shelter from both the weather and unexpected visitors.

"Matt, you take first watch. Ignacio will take second. Kiowa third, and I'll take the last," Mike said. "Watch the horses, Matt. They know when somethin's around. If their ears all come up same time, and they all look the same direction, wake us up."

They all rolled up in their blankets and soon were sleepin' sound. It was so quiet I could hear my heart beatin'. Once in a while a horse would drop his head and take a small bite of grass at his feet. I'd never realized that it was so light at night out on the grass. We didn't have a fire, and there was just a sliver of moon, but I could see the horses silhouetted perfectly against the stars. I watched them for several minutes before I realized that their ears were up, and they were all lookin' the same direction. I stood up and looked where they were lookin'. The grass was silver in the starlight, and I could see somethin' dark movin' down the opposite hill. I gently kicked Mike's foot. He came awake with his pistol in his hand.

"Over there," I whispered and pointed.

He looked toward the dark shadow movin' through the grass. Both the Kiowa and the Ute had gotten to their feet. They watched the movement for a few minutes.

"Wolf," Ignacio said out loud, breakin' the deep silence.

"Yep, and it's a big one," Mike agreed.

"It's a buffalo wolf," Kiowa said. "He is alone, which is unusual. They customarily run in packs."

Just as he said that another shadow appeared at the crest of the hill and then several more.

"Must be a herd of buffalo close about," Mike said. "They generally don't get far from a herd." He turned toward me.

"Good eyes, Matt. That could have been a 'Rapaho brave lookin' for a horse."

They laid back down and were soon asleep again. I woke Ignacio when his turn came, and went straight to sleep as soon as I was flat on the ground. Mike shook me out just as the sky was turnin' pink. It was chilly enough that it made a man wonder what he'd done with his summer wages. We packed our gear and then chewed some jerky for breakfast, washin' it down with water from the spring. The horses watered, and we were on our way west as the sun peeked over the hills.

We made the fort by mid-afternoon. I had to admit it weren't much. They were short of supplies, and there wasn't much game left in the creeks around. Mike and I went out to see what we could round up. We rode into the cover on a little creek, and a turkey jumped out. I palmed my Colt and dropped him 'fore he'd taken two good wingbeats. I thought it was mighty good shootin'.

Mike got down and picked the turkey up. "Good grief, Matt. Look what ya done. Ya near blew both legs off, and them bein' the best eatin'. Next time try for a head shot."

"If you think you're so blamed good, Mike O'Malley, you take the next one, and use your pistol," I said a little aggravated. He'd taken to wearin' a short gun along with his shotgun, but I'd never seen him use it. On the way back to the fort a prairie chicken jumped up between us. Where the turkey had been slower than molasses in January with those first wingbeats, the chicken was like greased lightin'. Mike drew and fired, knockin' the chicken out of the sky. I stepped down and picked up the bird. It didn't have any head. I reckoned I wasn't the only O'Malley that could shoot.

"You let him get out too far," was all I said to Mike.

When we got back to the fort, Kiowa had most of the army boys laughin' at some story, and Ignacio had told them all how he'd whipped some guy named O'Malley in Abilene, but not all the army posts were that friendly to Indians.

I did the cookin', and we shared some with the army. Nobody complained, although the turkey was tougher than a piece of cured rawhide. One sergeant commented on the turkey havin' flavor and character. I waited to pounce, but nobody said one bad word about my cookin'. Seems that the whole world had heard about the complainin' rule 'cept me. If one of the army boys would've complained I'd have sure made him go with us to cook. A rule is a rule.

We left out in the mornin' and landed in Fort Hays two days later. It wasn't in much better shape than Harker had been for supplies, and they had four wounded men. They'd crossed trails with Indians they hadn't identified and had a runnin' fight. We didn't stick around since the post commander had laid the blame on the Kiowas, and we were ridin' with one. We headed straight south for Fort Dodge. We calculated it would take us three or four days to get there, and there was nothin' between us and the fort 'cept maybe Indians. We stopped the first night on the Walnut river 'bout ten miles east of the forks, or so we figured. We spent the next night on the Buckner havin' crossed the Pawnee earlier in the day. The next mornin' we was up and out of camp by first light wantin' to make the fort before it got dark.

The country had changed some. The grass was short, and there weren't near the trees even along the rivers. We rode most of the mornin' headin' south. We went through a gully, and as we came out the other side I saw Mike's arm go up, signaling us to stop. We pulled in, and I looked toward the crest of the hill we were climbin'. There were Indians headin' right at us. They was wearin' paint, and there was a lot of 'em. They spotted us about the time we saw them. They was close enough that I could clearly see the look of surprise on their faces.

"Comanches," Kiowa said in a low voice. "It's a raidin' party, Mike. They got fresh hair, and extra horses with 'em."

The Indian in the lead raised his rifle and let out a screech.

Mike jerked his horse's head around and faced toward the gully we'd just cleared.

"Run!" he yelled at the top of his lungs.

Chapter Fifteen

"Try to make the wash," Mike yelled.

There was a blast of gunfire from the Comanches, and my packhorse went down. I dropped the lead rope and spurred Sin. I drew my Henry from the boot as we raced toward the gully. I could hear the Indians shriekin' behind us. We went into the gully in a cloud of dust. It was fairly deep, but the sides were cut with buffalo trails that led into it. I was a little ahead of the others, not havin' a packhorse to slow me down. I plunged off Sin, scrambled to the lip of the gully, and started firin' the Henry as fast as I could work the lever. Two of their horses went down, and I shot a big brave right through the brisket who was gettin' ready to club Ignacio.

Suddenly, there was a blast of gunfire as the other men got their feet under them. Both Kiowa and Ignacio had Henry repeaters, and I could hear the hollow boom of Mike's Greener. It could do terrible damage the way the Comanches were packed together. I fired until my rifle was empty, dropped it, and palmed my Colt. The air was gettin' thick blue with powder smoke, and my ears were hammered by the sounds of shouts, screeches, and gunshots. I shot a man between the shoulder blades that was ridin' away from me. There was a blur of motion and color, and abruptly it was quiet, except for the sound of retreating hoofbeats. The last Comanche was ridin' over the crest of the hill where we'd first seen 'em.

"Get loaded. They'll be comin' again," Mike yelled.

I picked up my Henry, ran over to Sin, and got a fresh box of shells from my saddlebag. I started shovin' them into my rifle as fast as I could make my hands move. I grabbed the extra cylinders for my Colt and put one in place. I was shakin' like an old hound trying to puke a peach pit, and I was scared.

"Matt, grab the horses and put 'em under that lip of the gully," Mike said, pointin'. "They'll have some protection there."

I started grabbin' horses, glad of havin' somethin' to do. I got them all tied off to a handy root and went back to where the other men were lookin' up the hill. I could see three dead Comanche in the grass in front of us, and there was the first one I'd shot layin' right at the edge of the gully. The only thing we'd lost so far was my packhorse. We'd been lucky.

"I think they'll try to ride right over us this time," Mike said. "If we can hold 'em off, we might have a chance."

"Yes, they have already lost more men than they would like. They didn't count on us being so well armed," Kiowa said. "If they lose two or three more men, they may begin to feel their medicine has gone bad."

"That may be, Kiowa warrior, but if they were Ute, they would not quit until we were dead. We have spilled Comanche blood on the short grass of their hunting grounds. They will want blood in return. We must make the price of revenge too costly if we will live, but I don't believe they will quit," the Ute said.

We heard them comin' before we could see them.

"Hold 'em steady and squeeze your shots. We got to make every one count. Don't panic," Mike said in a quiet voice. He had his Greener in his hand. He put extra shells in his mouth as I watched him. He couldn't work the lever on a rifle one-handed, so he'd stuck with the Greener. He'd have to wait 'til they was up close.

They come over the hill in a rush of horses and screams. They was dodgin' and jerkin' around so, that it was hard to pick a target. As they come roarin' down the hill, I had to admire the way they sat their horses. They had to be the finest riders I'd ever seen.

I picked a painted warrior who had a nice scalp lock and tracked him with my sight. Soon as he got to the point on the hill where my packhorse lay, I dumped him from the saddle. There was firin' all around me. I worked the lever on the Henry, tryin' to pick targets. I shot a horse as the rider swerved, and he went over the horse's head as it fell. Kiowa knocked him back to the grass with a nice shot. They weren't slowin' down any. It was plain that they planned to ride right into the gully. My Henry ran dry, and I shucked the Colt again. I shot a man on a paint horse as he made the cut that led into the gully. I heard something behind me.

"Matt, look out," I heard Mike yell, and then I was knocked down as an Indian jumped from the lip of the gully onto my back. I heard the blast of Mike's Greener and felt a burnin' sting as a piece of stray buckshot hit me. The Indian on my back was smashed against the side of the gully. I jumped up and swung toward Mike just as he cut loose the second barrel over my head. A dead Comanche fell from the lip of the arroyo and landed with a dull thud at my feet. I swung around, climbed up, and looked back over the edge. They were ridin' away again. I counted seven dead out in front, and there were three in the wash. I turned to look at the other men with a smile that froze on my face. Kiowa was down in the sand of the gulch, and there was blood on his beaded, deer-hide shirt. Mike was kneelin' beside him. I went runnin' over to where he lay and dropped to my knees.

"Kiowa," I managed to gasp. He was bad shot.

The big Indian took hold of my hand and looked into my face. Mike got to his feet, looked down at me, and shook his head. He walked over to where Ignacio was watchin' the crest of the hill.

"Kiowa," I said again, not knowing what else to say. I could feel the tears start in my eyes.

"Remember your promise to me, Matthew," he said in a weak voice. He winched as the pain hit him, and he squeezed my hand. His eyes closed.

"I love you, Kiowa," I whispered.

A small smile came on his lips as his hand relaxed in mine.

The world around me turned red, and then black. I felt something terrible inside me.

I jumped to my feet, grabbed my Henry, and ran to my horse. I tore the reins from the root, and leaped into the saddle. I turned the black's head toward the cut out of the wash and hammered his sides with my spurs. He took off like he'd been shot from a cannon. We pounded up the hill toward the Comanche position, me shovin' shells into the Henry as we went. There was a deep, black rage on me like I'd never known. I was blinded by fury and grief. I heard Mike shoutin' at me, but it was far removed and meant nothin'. I blasted over the crest of the hill and came face-to-face with a single Comanche wearin' three feathers in his hair. I screamed at the top of my lungs and ran Sin into the side of his horse, knockin' him down. As the Comanche jumped to his feet, I turned my horse and shot into him as fast as I could work the lever. I kept shootin' until my rifle was empty. I screamed again as the sounds of my last shots echoed across the

hills. I turned toward the rest of the Comanches. They were ridin'
away toward the south. They were ridin' fast, and I knew I'd
never catch them.

"Come back and fight!" I screamed across the hills at them.

"They are gone, O'Malley man," Ignacio's voice said behind
me. "You killed their war chief, and they have decided that the
fight is bad. He was coming to see what manner of men we were
from the top of the hill, and you attacked him. He is finished,
and they are finished."

Mike and Ignacio had followed me up the hill when I'd gone
berserk. I walked down the hill toward where the Comanches had
disappeared, leadin' Sin with one hand and carrying the Henry
in my other. I knelt down in the short grass and felt a sob rip at
my throat.

Kiowa had been more than just my friend. He'd been family,
and he'd been my teacher. He'd taught me to laugh at myself
when I'd gotten too serious. He'd taught me to love life. He'd
taught me to love learnin' new things.

I knelt there in the grass a long time. Mike and Ignacio had
gone back down to the gully. I stood up and stepped into my
saddle. I rubbed Sin between the ears and headed back for the
gully. They'd gathered up the dead Comanches and laid them in
the wash under an overhangin' bank. They were cavin' the dirt
in over them when I rode up.

Nobody said much as we finished the job. A lot of men had
died in less than half an hour. Truth was, I doubted if the actual
fightin' took in more than ten minutes all told. We'd killed more
Comanches in our fight at the ravine than the army had killed all
summer.

"We will not put dirt in the face of our Kiowa warrior," Ignacio said. "We will send him to the world of spirits the mountain way."

The Ute pointed down the wash where there was a group of
cottonwood and elm trees. We went over, picked up Kiowa, and
carried him down to the cluster of trees. They looked out of place
on the short grass prairie, but there was a little seepin' spring that
kept the ground moist, and the trees had taken root. We laid
Kiowa down and watched as Ignacio put together a platform between four of the close standin' trees. He cut several branches
from surrounding brush and tied them all together with a rawhide
rope that he cut in pieces. It took an hour or so to build it, and

Mike and I helped where we could. Mainly Ignacio acted like he wanted to do it himself. Kiowa had been his friend, too.

After the platform was built, we laid Kiowa's blankets on it. We lifted him up and laid him gently onto the platform. Ignacio crossed Kiowa's arms over his breast, and then placed a blanket over him up to his neck. We put his saddle up beside him, as well as the rest of his stuff. He'd brought a volume of English history along, which I put under the cover next to his hands. Ignacio made sure his weapons were close by his side.

"Now, he will go in peace to the land of the spirits," Ignacio said. "No Indians will bother a mountain burial. It is a sacred thing." We stood back and the Ute sang and chanted a death song. It seemed a fittin' prayer for a departed warrior. When he was finished, I looked up at Kiowa one last time. A small breeze moved his black hair gently. I remembered the way he'd been, and the memories were good.

I turned away and walked to my black horse. My shoulder blade hurt like blazes where I'd been hit with the buckshot, but I knew it wasn't real bad. I still had the use of my arm. I rode out to where my packhorse lay and worked the pack saddle and panniers from under him. We had several extra horses left behind by the dead Comanches, and I could see the marks of pack saddles on at least two of them. They'd probably been stolen from some settler that had been raided. I didn't recognize any of the brands as I caught a nicely built, brown horse with gentle eyes. I loaded my gear on him. He made no complaint.

We rode toward Fort Dodge. Three men riding now where there had been four.

"They was Comanches, Colonel. They was identified by both the Kiowa that was ridin' with us and killed, and the Ute that is with us out front," Mike was reporting the action to the commander of Fort Dodge.

"I believe you, O'Malley. It's just that we'd had no recent report of depredations by the Comanche this far north," the colonel said.

"I'd bet before the week is out you'll get some reports. They had fresh hair on their lances, and quite a few stolen horses," Mike told him.

"Yes, well, you are probably right. Would you show me exactly where the action took place?" he said, unrolling a map on his desk. "I'll send out a patrol tomorrow to confirm what you've told me. It's just for the report, I'm sure you understand. The army runs on paper.''

Mike plotted on the map exactly where the action had taken place, and the commander made note of casualties for the report. After we'd finished he called in an orderly.

''Show these men to barracks B, corporal. They can rest the night there.'' He turned to us. ''Barracks B is empty at the present time. We have detached a troop of cavalry south, and B is their billeting area. You will be comfortable there. I'll also send over the surgeon, and he can check your wound,'' he said, lookin' at me. I near forgotten that Mike had hit me with a piece of buck-shot.

''Thanks, Colonel. We appreciate the hospitality,'' Mike replied.

We turned and followed the orderly out the door. Several of the army men had gathered around outside and were watchin' curiously.

''You pilgrims actually kill near a dozen redskins?'' one of the blue-shirted men asked Mike in a nasty tone of voice.

''I'd be real careful how you talk to us, army boy,'' Mike said quiet-like. He was touchin' the Greener when he said it. ''We've had a powerful hard day.'' The blue-shirt took the hint and left.

''I hear they got 'em an even dozen if ya count the one that got kilt that was ridin' with 'em.'' The man that spoke was a very large, redheaded, blue-shirt, with sergeant stripes on his sleeves. He had a bushy, red beard, and his open shirt revealed tufts of red hair on his chest. ''I reckon if we do fer the redskin out front of the gate, we can have us a baker's dozen today.'' He stopped and looked around at the crowd of men that was gatherin'. He wanted to make a show at our expense. ''I can't imagine you pilgrims killin' them Comanches with ya lovin' Injuns the way ya must to ride with 'em.''

I started to move toward him, and Mike grabbed my arm. ''He's army, Matt, and we're inside a fort. There'll be no help for us if we tangle with 'em. Let's ride out right now.'' I didn't say anything, but I could feel that black rage startin' to work down in my gut again.

I followed Mike out the front gate of the fort to where we'd tied the horses. Ignacio was off his horse and surrounded by army men. The sergeant had followed us out.

''Look what we got here, boys,'' he yelled makin' his show. ''We got us an Injun and two Injun lovers. I say we hang the

redskin and dip the Injun lovers in tar.'' There was a shout of
agreement from the bystanders. They started to move toward us
and stopped when Mike eared back both hammers on his Greener.
These were men that knew guns, and they knew what a short
shotgun would do up close.

The situation was about to get ugly, and I could feel my control
slippin' away. I made the big step that it took to get next to the
sergeant, and I hit him as hard as I could right in his vile mouth.
It felt good. He landed on his back and lay there a minute.

"Come on big mouth," I said to him. "Just you and me, I'm
goin' to kill you with my hands." I meant it. I wanted desperately
to kill him.

He stood up with a grin on his wide face, but I could see a
little fear behind his eyes. Maybe he could see the devil ridin'
my shoulders. He took a step toward me, and I hit him three
times as fast and as hard as I could, knockin' him down again.
It was quiet. Usually with a fight, the men standin' around would
be yellin' themselves hoarse, but this wasn't a fight. I meant to
kill him. The spectators knew it. He came at me again, and I
waded in jabbin' and throwin' punches with both hands. Suddenly all the rage, fear, and grief that was in me came into my
hands. He put his arms up in defense, and I beat them down. I
felt no sympathy for him, and I showed no mercy. I hit him until
his face was a bloody mask. I followed him as he tried to back
away from me. The men split apart as we moved, and I continued
to beat him. His hands were down at his sides, and he was
swayin' on his feet. Every blow I struck rocked him to his heels.
Finally, he fell over on his back, and I jumped straddle of him,
grabbing him around his bull-neck. I started squeezin' my hands
together, and his legs started jerkin'. I was past all reason.

"That's enough, Matt." Mike's soft voice cut through my
mind like a sharp knife. "Ya done whipped him. Ya don't need
to kill him."

I stood up and backed away from him, flexing my hands. I
looked wildly around, and the army men moved quickly away
from me. Ignacio had mounted his horse and untied the rest of
them. He rode up beside us with his Henry over the saddle.

"Let us go, O'Malleys. We are not welcome here," he said. I
reckoned that might be an understatement.

We swung into the saddle and kicked our horses into a gallop,
leaving before the army could react.

We rode south for a few miles and then turned west. We rode

for a couple of hours, not sayin' anything. We stopped by a little dry creek that had a few scattered trees along the banks. Ignacio found a small pool of stagnant water upstream from our camp, watered the horses, then put them on the picket. Mike stirred up supper, not sayin' anything about me cookin'. I sat on the ground and watched the small flame burn yellow and orange.

After a while Mike spoke. "I never seen anythin' like that, Matt. You flat took that man apart. Why, he never even got a chance to hit ya." He stirred the bacon in the pan. "Ya got the devil's own temper, Matt. It could get ya killed, someday."

I didn't reply. I didn't need to. Mike was right and I knew it. I just couldn't help it.

Ignacio walked up behind me. "Take off your shirt, O'Malley man. I will dig out that piece of lead." I did as he told me. I was too exhausted to resist. He pushed around for a minute and then squeezed on my back, right in the middle of my shoulder blade. It hurt somethin' fierce.

"Here you are," he said, and handed me a piece of buckshot. "It was stopped by the bone. Remind me that the next time we get in a fight with Comanches, not to let your brother save my life. He nearly killed you."

He walked over to the fire and fished a piece of hot bacon from the pan.

We ate, and I rolled up in my blankets. Mike said he'd take the first watch. Ignacio laid down beside me. I looked up at the crystal clear sky. There were at least a million stars winkin' and blinkin'. The night before, Kiowa had been with us.

"He is there, Matthew," the Ute said as if he could read my thoughts. "He is right there on the warrior's trail." I could vaguely see the Ute pointin' up to the sky. "You white men call it the Milky Way, but it is the warrior's trail. When a man dies in battle, he sets his feet on the warrior's trail and makes his way to the land of the spirits. Right now, I would say that the Kiowa warrior is unhappy with you."

"How's that?" I asked.

"The Kiowa warrior is walking. If I would not have had white men with me, I would have killed his horse under his burial. He would have ridden his horse on the warrior's trail instead of walking. I knew you would not let me kill his horse. You would have felt sorry for the horse. I feel sorry for the Kiowa warrior. No Indian likes to walk when he could have ridden. He is up there now, walking on the warrior's trail."

Ignacio fell quiet, and I could hear a family of coyotes mournin' to the stars.

Chapter Sixteen

"I think we'll ride wide of any towns and forts. We got enough supplies to last a while," Mike said as we rode west. "Ignacio says there's a fort not too far into the valley, and they know him pretty well. We can get supplies there without any trouble."

"I'm needin' cartridges for my Henry. I got some, but if we get in another scuffle, I'd probably run short," I replied.

Ignacio was out in front of us scoutin' a trail. He never got completely out of sight, but there was times when he was a mighty long ways off.

We were riding close to the Arkansas River again, but it a much different river than it had been in southern Kansas. It was clear as crystal and runnin' fast. I could see the rocks down in the bottom any time we stopped to get a drink, and once in a while I'd see a fish. The trees were pretty thick in some places, and we always had a nice campin' spot for the night. The country away from the river had changed a lot. It was plain to see that we had gotten into a dry country. The grass was pretty short, except where the river watered it, and there were clumps of cactus every now and again. Once in a while we'd see a real strange cactus that grew tall and had arms on it. The first one I come across I nearly shot. It was almost dark, and I rode up on it sudden-like. Mike and Ignacio got a real laugh out of it. Mike said he'd heard 'em called Joshua trees. We'd figured to ride the Arkansas until we hit the fork of the Purgatoire, then we'd turn south.

The days stacked up one behind the other with none of 'em being different. We were makin' good time, but winter was comin' on, and it was plum chilly at night. The ducks and geese had made up their minds to take out, and there were places where the sky was near full of 'em. We were workin' the horses hard enough that I started ridin' the packhorse every other day to save

162

Sin a little. He didn't think much of carryin' a pack saddle, him
bein' a war horse and all.

"Two more days and we will be home," Ignacio said one night
after supper. I finally gotten out of cookin' every meal, and we
were takin' turns. Ignacio had taken an antelope late in the afternoon, and we were fryin' some of it in bacon grease. It tasted
like a goat that'd been eatin' sage.

"We will go through Cordova Pass. There is an easier way,
but you will like Cordova. From there you can see almost all of
our valley," Ignacio said.

"Where do you think the best place will be for us to situate
the ranch?" I asked the Ute. The question had been on my mind
since we'd made the fork of the Purgatoire the day before.

"I think you will like the western side, O'Malley man. It is a
long distance from the fort, and there are no other white men
there yet."

"You mean there's white folks already in the valley?" Mike
asked.

"Yes, there have been white people coming to our valley for
over three centuries. The Spanish were the first white men to
come. They gave many places names. They found much gold and
took away some of my people as slaves. We did not like them
and hid from them, or so the legends say. Then in my grandfath-
er's and father's time there were men who came to trade with us
and trap fur. We got along with them well, and some even lived
with us in the winters. Now, in my time, men have come search-
ing for gold again. There are even a few who try to grow crops,"
Ignacio replied.

"I thought you told me that the only way we could come into
the valley was if we were Utes, or at least we had to have your
blessing," I said.

"Well, I lied. You were my enemy then, and there is nothing
wrong with lying to your enemy." He laughed. "Besides, it will
be better this way. We will give you the land. You can have the
paper signed by me that gives you the land forever. My people
will not steal your horses or cows, at least not many, because
you were invited. Your government forced us to give these other
white men land. It was in a treaty we signed in 1863. We did
not want to, but we have been friends to the whites. We do not
want to be enemies, but I fear that they will want more and more
land until there is no more to give. Your land is a gift of friend-

ship. Besides, you won the fight.'' He laughed again as he got a piece of antelope out of the pan.

Mike stood up and walked out to check on the horses.

"I have the place all picked out for you, O'Malley man. You will like it. It will be a place where your sons and my sons can grow up together and become great and mighty men, as we are," Ignacio said. Nobody ever said that one of his faults was bein' humble.

Mike came back to the fire and sat down. "There's goin' to be a good moon tonight, and I think it's gonna get cold," he said.

"If they got a sutler's store at the fort, I'm goin' to need to buy a coat," I said. There'd been a few mornin's when I'd wished I'd had one.

We doused the fire and rolled out the blankets. I lay on the ground lookin' up through the leaves at the big moon. A flight of geese went by, a dark wedge against the silver brightness of the moon, honkin' and chatterin' as they flew. Kiowa would've loved it.

It was cold come mornin', and there was frost on my saddle for the first time. I reckoned that the ducks and geese knew what they was about. I went down to the river to fill my canteen and looked straight across the clear blue water. There was a giant bull elk lookin' back at me with water runnin' off his bottom lip. He had seven full points on each side of his head, and they were heavy. He was one of the most magnificent animals I'd ever seen.

"Go in peace, big fella. You're carryin' too much meat for just the three of us," I said out loud to him. When we did hunt, we tried to take a small animal, so we didn't waste much. His head came up as I spoke. He turned and walked majestically away like the monarch he was. It was a grand and beautiful country we'd come to, and if it weren't for my dream valley, I'd be content to settle right along the Arkansas River.

We rode out a little later than usual, takin' time to repair a rein that had worn thin on Mike's rig. We left the riverbed, as we usually did, and rode the hills. The river had too many bends in it. If a man followed it along too close, he'd end up traveling twice the distance. We stayed within easy ridin' distance of the water, so we could camp comfortable. 'Bout mid-mornin' we rode over a little swell, and off in the distance was a range of shinin' blue mountains that reached up and touched the sky.

"I never seen anything like that before," I gasped.

"We will sleep in their shadows tonight, and tomorrow you will see the valley of your dream," Ignacio said. He kicked his horse and trotted off toward the mountains. I'd seen what folks called mountains back home, but they was little hills compared to these monsters.

We got up to the base of the mountains by late afternoon, and we started climbin' up their flanks. The air was noticeably colder, and it was scented with the strong smell of pine. We camped in a little meadow where the grass was deep. There were wild flowers scattered along in the grass, and there was one tall pine right in the middle.

"We are home," Ignacio said. "We will not need to set watch tonight. No other Indians dare to travel this way. This is the land of the Utes."

"How can you be so all-fired sure about that, Ignacio?" Mike asked.

The Ute didn't say anything. He raised his arm and brought it quickly down to his side. I saw movement from the corner of my eye and turned to look. Five warriors materialized from the edge of the forest and stood looking at us. My hand dropped to my Colt.

"Hold steady, O'Malley man," Ignacio said. "These are Weminuche men."

"How long've they been close to us?" I asked.

"They started following us as soon as we began climbing up the mountain," he replied. "That is why no other Indians come this way. They know the Weminuche watch."

It was eerie knowin' we'd been followed for several miles, and I hadn't even noticed it. The Weminuche braves rode toward us. Ignacio went to meet them. They met near the single pine tree. It was obvious that they were glad to see each other. Ignacio talked to them a while, and then rode back to us as the other Indians disappeared into the trees.

"They will watch tonight, then ride with us into the fort tomorrow," he said.

"Where are they goin' now?" Mike asked.

"They have a camp made back down the mountain close to the trail. They will stay there. They say the white men smell strange and make funny noises in their sleep." He laughed.

I cooked supper, since it had come around my turn again. I thought I was gettin' pretty good at this cookin' thing. I sure didn't hear any complaints from the other guys, although I

listened close. It got cold early, and Mike built up the fire for
warmth. The burnin' pine smelled nearly as good as the trees
themselves. I wrapped my blanket over my shoulders and looked
into the fire. Tomorrow we would see the valley. Ignacio had
said that it was another day's ride to where he'd picked out the
spot for the ranch. I figured we'd ride down there, pick out the
site, and then come back to the fort. We could telegraph the rest
of the partnership and tell 'em we'd found a spot. I reckoned
we'd have to tell them about Kiowa, too. There were times when
I'd turn around to tell him something and realize he wasn't there.

It had gotten dang cold, so I got my blankets together and laid
down. My eyes got used to the dark, and I could plainly see the
Warrior's Trail. Someday I'd travel that trail, just as Kiowa had.

"Man-oh-man, it's one cold puppy," Mike said the next morning, as he hopped around on one foot tryin' to get his other boot
on. He'd been right about it gettin' cold. I was real reluctant to
get out from under the blankets even if my feet was cold. Ignacio
laughed as Mike fell on his rump.

"It ain't nice to laugh at a one-armed man who can't get a
boot on, ya heathen," Mike said to the Ute. That made Ignacio
laugh harder. He really enjoyed bein' a heathen.

It didn't take us long to get our stuff together and get packed
up. The horse's breath was showin', and there was deep frost on
the saddles. Sin gave me some trouble about puttin' on the saddle
for the first time in a long while. I 'sposed that havin' a cold
saddle slapped on your back wasn't real comfortable.

We'd just got a seat in our saddles when the other five Indians
rode into our camp. They'd brought some roasted deer, and we
chewed on it as we climbed the side of the mountain. The trail
we followed was steep, and as we neared the top there were
places where the horses really had to scramble. We made the top
in just over an hour. As we made the last scramble, Ignacio motioned for me to take the lead.

As we hit the summit of the pass, I looked out ahead of me
and sucked in my wind. I'd never seen anything so beautiful in
my whole life. In fact, I doubted if there was anything as beautiful
as the Valley of the Utes on the whole face of the world. It
stretched out in front of us as far as I could see toward the west.
To the north and south, the mountains swung in wide circles,
corralling the valley with a fence of peaks. I could tell we was
high up 'cause I could make out a settlement below me. The
buildin's looked as small as toys, and there was a hairline of

smoke comin' from one of the bigger ones. Suddenly, I knew that I'd seen this scene before. Somehow, I'd seen this very view of the valley. I belonged here. It felt right to me. It was more than just the dreams I'd had. It was more like the hand of destiny had directed me to this very spot.

"You can't see the land I have picked out for you, O'Malley man. It is over to the west, and a full day's ride from the fort," Ignacio said. He had pulled up beside me, and I hadn't even heard his approach I'd been so taken by the scenery.

"It's beautiful ain't it, Matthew?" Mike said in a hushed voice from behind me.

"It is that, Mike. But it's more than beautiful. It's gonna be home to the O'Malley clan," I replied

"Is that the fort down there, Ignacio?" I asked, pointing at the little buildings.

"That is Fort Garland," Ignacio replied. "They promised to move it away, but it is still there."

"Well, we'd best ride down there before they do," I grinned at him.

"Yes, I would like to stop at the fort, and then move on to the river. My brothers told me that my people are camped on the river not far from your land. I will be glad to see them," Ignacio said.

He kicked his horse and began the descent, as did the other braves. Mike and I were a little slower. The trail was steep, and there were times when Sin sat right down on his rear to keep from slidin' to the bottom. Ignacio beat us to the fort by half an hour.

"Where have you been, O'Malley man?" he asked. "We thought maybe a bear had eaten you and your brother." The other Indians thought that was really funny and laughed out loud.

"We value our hides more than you do," I replied.

"No, you just do not know how to ride down a mountain like a Ute," he said. I reckoned he was right about that.

Mike and I walked in through the gate of the fort. It looked like it hadn't been much even in its best day, and its best day was long past. A blue-shirted captain came walkin' up to us and held out his hand to Mike.

"I'm Captain Moorhead," he said. "I'm acting commander of Fort Garland."

"Looks kind of dead around here," Mike said.

"The army has decided to close this post down, so most of

the detachment is being moved to Fort Lewis, west of the San Juan Mountains. The colonel and half of the troops have already gone over. I'm waiting for orders to join them,'' the captain explained.

"My name's Mike O'Malley, and this is my brother, Matt. We plan on takin' up ranchin' herebouts. We come in with Ignacio and his boys.''

The captain looked surprised. "I wondered why the Utes came in today. Most of the band are camped up on the Rio Grande toward the west end of the valley. I expect they will winter there this year. How is it you became acquainted with Ignacio? We'd heard he'd been killed.''

"He nearly was,'' Mike replied. He went ahead and told the captain the whole story.

When he'd finished, the captain took off his hat and scratched his head. "I would guess that if Ignacio is willing to give you title to some ground, your claim will be good. But if I was you, I'd also file some homestead claims with the government. That way you won't have anybody crowding you later on. I expect this country to open up once the army gets the Plains tribes under control.''

"That's right good advice, captain. We'll do just that when we get to someplace with a land office,'' Mike replied.

They talked for a few minutes more, and the captain turned and strode off. He stopped abruptly and turned back to us.

"You wouldn't be kin to a Dan O'Malley would you?'' he asked.

"Yeah, he's our brother. We ain't heard nothin' 'bout him fer quite a spell,'' Mike replied.

"Well, you might be hearing from him soon. Not sixty days ago he was at this very fort. He rode in at the head of his troop on a long patrol. He was in charge of Troop D at Fort Lewis, and had some action with the Navajos over toward the Blues. He has the reputation of being a good commander, and he is a hell of a shot with either hand. He's a good man to have with you in a fight,'' the captain said.

"That sure sounds like him,'' Mike said. "I used to outshoot him left-handed, but I 'spect he could beat me now.''

The captain laughed. "Last I heard, Dan grabbed the stage for Fort Leavenworth. He was supposed to muster out almost a month ago. Hope you are able to find him. All the times I rode

with him I don't remember him ever mentioning family,'' the
captain said as he turned and walked away.

"Well, Mike, things are comin' together," I said. "If we could
get Dan back with us, I could finish with the promise I made Pa
before he left."

"Yep, it'd be right nice to see Dan again, although he could
be the meanest ol' son ya ever seen if ya made him mad. Ya
didn't know him too well, Matt, but Dan was powerful strong
and real quick on the fight." We turned to walk back out the
gate. "It's kind a funny ya think about it. Our trail must have
near crossed Dan's somewheres along the way. There's been a
time or two recent when I'd like to see big ol' Danny boy standin'
with us. He always stood good to trouble," Mike said.

We walked out of the gate of the fort and continued toward
the sutler's store. It served not only as a store, but, with a plank
over a couple barrels, it was also a bar. We walked out of the
bright sunlight into the relative darkness of the store. There was
a quiet hum of voices, punctuated with a loud laugh comin' from
behind the curtain that separated the store from the drinkin' area.
A bearded man came from behind the curtain when he heard the
bell over the door tinkle.

"Can I help ya, gents?" he asked.

"I reckon ya can, if you run this place," Mike said.

"That's me. Sutler to the fort and storekeeper to the San Luis
Valley, not to mention part-time barkeeper."

"I need three boxes of forty-four metallics for my Henry, a
can of powder, three boxes of ball for my Colt and a coat if you
have one," I said.

He looked up at me. "You plannin' on startin' a war?" he
asked.

"Don't plan on it, but I want to be prepared if one comes
lookin' for me," I replied.

"I need some cartridges for my Greener and a coat. We could
also do with some grub. Maybe some pig bacon, beans, flour,
soda, salt, and some canned peaches. I got a hankerin' for somethin' sweet," Mike said.

The storekeeper started hustlin' around gatherin' up our order
and puttin' it up on the counter. Mike grabbed a can of the
peaches and cut them open with his knife. He started slurpin' 'em
down, soundin' like a big hog in a little trough.

"Barkeep, get your ass in here. We need another drink," a
loud voice came from behind the curtain.

"Hold on, I'm fillin' a store order for some people. I'll be over there in a minute," the storekeeper said. We heard a glass crash against a wall behind the screen.

"Ya drunks. I ought to quit servin' whiskey, but I need the money, particularly with the army movin' out," the sutler said.

A greasy faced man threw aside the curtain. "You pork-faced jerk, I told ya to get in here and get us a drink. I mean right now," he yelled.

Mike moved toward the man. "You're gonna have to wait your turn, mister. The man is gatherin' up our supplies."

"Get out of my way, ya one-armed monkey," the man said, and pushed Mike hard. Mike lost his balance and landed on his butt.

I walked over to Mike and helped him to his feet.

"Easy, Matt," he said to me. I could barely hear him. There was a roarin' in my ears, and I was seein' through a red haze.

I walked over to the greasy man.

"What do you want, kid? You needin' a spankin'?" he said to me.

I hit him in the throat with my elbow. Wedge had taught me that an elbow thrown as a sideways punch has about twice the power of a fist. The man's eyes got as big as silver dollars, then he fell flat over on his back gaggin' and chokin'. Three men in the drinkin' room jumped to their feet, their hands goin' for their guns. I felt the devil jump on my shoulders.

"Wait," one of the men yelled and dropped his gun on the floor. My gun was comin' level, and I was ready to kill. "Wait, please," he yelled again, this time pleadin' for his life. The other men hadn't drawn their guns yet, and they were lookin at him curiously.

"I know ya, O'Malley. You're Matt O'Malley from Kansas. I seen ya there." The man was near sobbin'. "I don't want to die here, O'Malley." The other men's hands had moved off their gun butts like they was on fire.

"They say you've killed more than twenty men, O'Malley," one of the other men said in awe. I felt the anger go out of me like water down a sink drain.

"That's strechin' it a mite, and I got no need for the story to build. I never killed a man that didn't come askin' after it. You boys come mighty near buyin' more than a drink," I said to them. "Pick up your loud-mouthed buddy and get out of here." They scrambled to do what I'd told them.

I put a hand over my eyes and shook off the feelin' I had in my gut. I'd never tried to build a reputation, and I didn't want to be known as a killer.

"Ya okay Matt?" Mike asked.

"Yeah. Let's get our stuff and get out of here," I said.

I helped Mike gather up the packages, and he paid the sutler. I walked out the door and went over to where the horses were tied. Ignacio and his braves had done their buyin' while we'd been talkin' to the captain. They was waitin' on us, sittin' their horses easy. I packed the supplies in the panniers on my pack horse and then mounted Sin.

"Let's go, Ignacio. There's daylight wastin'," I said.

Ignacio and the Utes led the way west. I brought up the rear, thinkin' about what had happened. It was there inside me, and Kiowa had seen it long before I had. I was a killer, or at least I certain sure had the skills to be. I could have easy killed the four men in the store, and I'd nearly killed the one man with a single blow. I was walkin' the edge, and one step in either direction and I'd be what I'd promised Kiowa I'd never become. I realized that I was lettin' grief and anger lead me by the nose. I wasn't thinkin' anymore. I was just jumpin' in and doin'. I had to go back to thinkin'. I had to remember what Kiowa had said to me before he'd died. I had a sacred promise to keep.

Chapter Seventeen

Ignacio had been right. The valley was everything I'd seen in my dream, and more. I was sittin' easy on Sin with grass clear up to his tail. The river runnin' beside me was fast and clear. There was a ring of mountains all around holdin' up the sky, and we'd seen more deer than I'd ever seen in my whole life.

"He done real good by us, didn't he, Matt?" Mike asked.

"Ignacio gave us the best spot in all the valley. There's no question of it. It's the best watered, has the biggest trees, deepest grass; it's the prettiest spot we've seen," I agreed.

It was perfect for our purposes, but to the Utes it was nothing special. The Utes weren't given to stayin' in one spot, and they had no interest in ranchin' or farmin', so one piece of ground was 'bout the same as another to them. As I looked around, I could nearly hear the cattle bawlin' and the cowboys yellin'. I already knew the spot where I wanted to build the house, and Mike had agreed with me. There was a gray lava outcrop that formed a straight narrow ridge running east and west. It lay a short way to the south of the river, was probably sixty or seventy feet tall, and near a quarter mile long. With a house and barn backed right up against it, the winter wind could howl in, and what wasn't broke by the trees along the river, would be turned by the ridge. It was a wonderful place to winter even if the winters were harsh, as I suspected they would be.

"Was Ignacio goin' back over to Garland with us?" Mike asked.

"He said he would. He wanted to make sure the army was really leavin'," I replied.

"You ever seen such carryin' on as when them Indians seen Ignacio?"

I laughed, remembering what had happened when we'd ridden into the Ute camp. Anyone who said that Indians didn't have or show emotions should've been there. The whole durned tribe had set to celebratin'. They'd heard that Ignacio had been killed just like the captain at the fort had.

We'd been at the spot that Ignacio had picked for us for two days. We'd ridden with him and his braves around the perimeter of our new holdin' the first day. He showed us landmarks that marked the edges of what would be our ranch. Mike and I reckoned that the total gift was somethin' just over twenty thousand acres, all of it well watered. I had written the description of the land as we rode, and then over the campfire that night we had a ceremony with the Weminuche tribe. The two-hour ritual made the gift official, so far as the Indians were concerned, and it would live in their memories longer than any book would last. Still, I had Ignacio sign a paper that described the acreage. We'd use it to file our claim with the land office. Most times the government would recognize title given to a white man by the Indians if it was surveyed and witnessed. Them was all things we'd have to deal with later.

"Let's go over to the camp and get Ignacio," Mike said. "I'm right anxious to tell the rest of the boys what we got here."

"I don't 'spose they'll come out this winter, but they'll want to get a good start in the spring. It'll take a while to get a herd from there to here," I remarked.

"Just 'cause there's a house to build don't mean they'll let us out of helpin' drive the herd. You and me is the only ones that have been on a drive. I'm bettin' they'll want us back in Kansas just as soon as the snow's off," Mike said.

"Well, it's certain one of us has to go. They'll need a guide." I didn't relish the though of ridin' back to Kansas. It was a far piece of travelin', particular if a man went alone.

Ignacio came ridin' up with ten men as Mike and I were sittin' there talkin'.

"Let us go to the fort, O'Malleys. I am sick of listening to the chatter of women."

We headed for the fort at a good clip. We had no extra supplies, but we were each leadin' an extra horse, so we could take it easy on our mounts. We wanted to get there, send the telegram, and get back as quick as we could. There was a lot of work to do, so we could survive the comin' winter.

We got to Fort Garland just as the sun was goin' down. The air was cold, and the troopers had fires goin' to keep warm. Me and Mike rode in the gate of the fort, but the Utes waited out front. The army was right touchy 'bout them coming inside in a bunch.

I was just swingin' down from the saddle when the captain came from one of the buildings.

"O'Malley," he said to Mike, "I was just getting ready to send a patrol out to find you. We got a telegram in from Fort Riley today. It's addressed to you and your brother."

He handed him a folded paper, which Mike took, unfolded and read aloud:

TO: KIOWA MIKE AND MATT O'MALLEY FORT GARLAND COLORADO TERRITORY
FROM: OWEN O'MALLEY ABILENE KANSAS
BECK GANG HIT TURBECH HOMESTEAD STOP DILLEN KILLED STOP ANGUS AND BRIAN HURT STOP ARA LEWARA UNA ALL TAKEN STOP BECKS HEADING WEST STOP MAYBE HEADING FOR CHERRY CREEK STATION STOP SMALL POSSE FOLLOWING BECKS FROM HERE STOP YOU START NORTH AND MEET US STOP SEE YOU THERE STOP OWEN.

I was shook all the way to my roots. I couldn't imagine Ara, Lee, and Una bein' taken by the Beck gang.

"They sent this to Fort Dodge first, but when they found that you had already been there, they decided that you were either here by now, or else getting close," the captain said. "It's a day old now."

"We best get goin', Matt. Owen will be havin' a need of us, not to mention the girls," Mike said. I was still stunned. I knew the Becks were bad, but to kidnap women put them way beyond the bounds of even outlaws. There wasn't many men would take the chance on messin' with womenfolk in the west.

"I can't send any men with you, but I do have some extra horses. You will need them as well as some supplies," the captain said. "Sergeant, get the troop out. We have to lend a hand here," he yelled. Men started runnin around, gatherin' up horses and supplies.

"I'm goin' out and tell Ignacio what's happenin'," I said to Mike. He nodded as I turned Sin through the gate. I rode up to Ignacio and filled him in on the predicament we had.

"I will go with you, O'Malley man," the Ute said.

"You don't have to do that, Ignacio. You got to help your people get ready for winter," I argued.

"I will go, and five of my warriors will go, also. You and I have fought, and I have that story. We have fought the Comanche together and lived to tell the story of that fight. We will fight this Beck tribe and tell the story of their defeat around the fires. Let the women prepare for winter. The men will make war," he said.

He turned to his men and began to speak in Ute. I went back into the fort and told the captain we'd need a few more horses. It flat swelled my heart to know we'd made a friend like Ignacio. We surely needed the help. Last I'd known the Becks had a small army with them, and they was all fightin' men.

We rode hard, changin' horses often, and stoppin' only to feed and water the stock. We'd grab a couple hours of sleep, let the horses have a breather, and then we were off to the north again.

We made it to Cherry Creek in four days of hard ridin'. We were ready for anything, but the Becks weren't there. We checked every saloon and store. We knew if they'd made it this far, they'd have come in town. We were ahead of them. We started ridin' east.

I was scared. I feared for the girls. These were mean and lawless men. I swore if they did anything to harm the girls I was gonna see every one of them hang, particular Falcon. I had no good feelin' for the man, and Macon wasn't far behind. I calculated that Falcon was runnin' wild. He would be the brains of the gang. Macon would just follow along. Falcon must've decided that there was no law that could touch him, and no one dared to come against him. Well, he was wrong about that. He hadn't reckoned on the O'Malleys.

We rode east easy. We didn't want to miss them, and it'd be a simple thing to do. There was a wide stretch of ground east of the front range of the Rockies. It was all cut with dry creeks, gulches, and broken hills. An army could hide for months and never be seen. We spread out with the six Utes ridin' scout.

The afternoon of the second day one of the Utes come bustin' up on a winded horse.

"Ignacio says to come. He has found their trail," the man said. We'd agreed that if someone spotted the trail we'd raise a smoke. I looked north and seen a small finger of blue smoke liftin' to the sky. I might've missed seein' it, so Ignacio had made sure of findin' me by sendin' one of his men. I dropped out of the saddle and pulled together some sticks. I started a fire and then threw some green grass on it. A pillar of dark gray smoke lifted to the sky. Mike ought to see it and come a foggin'. I wasn't waitin'. I climbed back up on Sin and headed for Ignacio's smoke with the scout trailin' me.

"It must have been the Beck tribe, O'Malley man. There were many of them, and they are well mounted," Ignacio said.

I looked across the little plain readin' what must have happened. Beck's men must have come upon the Indians unexpectedly. There were ten dead Cheyenne braves lying in a group. They weren't wearin' paint, and there was a lot of pots and other camp gear spread around. It looked to me like it had been a small band headin' for the main winter camp.

"These warriors dropped back to try and fight. They sent the women and children on ahead." Ignacio was down from his horse readin' sign. "They went north," he said.

I heard a runnin' horse and turned toward the sound. Mike came poundin' up.

"Beck's gang?" he asked pointin' at the dead braves.

"Looks like. I hate to think what we're goin' to find along the track," I replied.

We started followin' their trail and almost immediately we found some of what I had feared. There was a small Indian boy lying on his face with his skull crushed. We rode a few hundred yards and found an older woman, dead, with a bullet through her back.

"They have not caught up to all of the women and children yet. These two could not keep up," Ignacio said, readin' the sign like it was an open book. "There is another thing. There are tracks of three Cheyenne braves following behind. They are not behind the women, they are behind the horsemen. They are on foot. Their tracks are over the top of the horse tracks. The braves will try to get the women and children away if they are captured."

We rode on, continuing to follow the trail. We came up with a dead antelope that was dressed out.

"It is plain, now," Ignacio explained. The three braves that are following were out hunting. They came back after the attack. They are trying to catch up."

We continued to ride, and not far from the dead antelope we found a dead white man without his hair. Ignacio stepped from his horse to see what had happened.

"The men on horses overtook another woman. This man got down to have his way with her. The other horsemen went ahead without this man. The three braves that are following have had a small bit of revenge," he said. "The woman is now with them. We are not far behind."

Another half an hour we came to where Beck's gang caught the fleeing Indians. The Cheyenne had tried to shelter in a small natural bowl between two hills. There were four dead braves and six dead women. There were fourteen dead children. I was sickened when I saw the faces of the children. They'd had no chance. No chance at all.

I had recommitted myself to the promise I'd made Kiowa when I'd first left Junction City. I had made up my mind to think each situation through and avoid killin' if I could. I'd already thought this situation through. Every man that was ridin' with the Becks needed killin'. I looked over at Mike. He was still lookin' at the youngsters.

I caught a movement from the corner of my eye and jerked my pistol. Three Cheyenne warriors came over a small hill. They were on foot and followed by a woman. The man in the lead had his hand up givin' the sign for friend. Ignacio was closest to them, and he returned the sign. Their hands fluttered and floated for a spell, and then Ignacio came down to where we sat our horses.

"When the Cheyenne first saw us they thought we were part of the gang, but after they watched us they knew we were not. They are seeking permission to come down and care for their dead. All three of the braves have wives and children lying here," he said. I could tell that the tough Ute was visibly shaken, as we all were.

"Of course, they can come down. We'll help if they want," Mike said.

"They will not want our help. The Weminuche have fought the Cheyenne many times. We will fight them again. They are enemy to the white man as they are the Ute. They know that we mean them no harm now, but that does not make us friends."

Ignacio waved the Cheyenne down into the bowl and mounted his horse.

"We must leave now. These are proud men. They would not have us see their grief. I have told them that we go to make war with the Beck tribe who did this. They have wished us well. They say that the Beck tribe are camped on Deer Trail Creek about five miles from here. They have seen them. They still have four Cheyenne women, but they won't live much longer.''

''Let's leave them off four of the horses that don't belong to the army,'' Mike said. ''I got a feelin' that by this time tomorrow we're not goin' to need 'em one way or the other.''

We rode out of the bowl leaving behind four horses. Ignacio sent his best scout ahead of us with instructions to find the Becks and report back. My nerves were on edge, and I had a rotten feelin' in my gut. Mike was right. By this time tomorrow, we might not need any horses at all.

''What do you think?'' I asked Mike. The scout had found the Beck camp, and we'd waited 'til dark to get a look at it.

''They feelin' pretty safe if ya ask me,'' Mike responded. ''They got several bottles out, and the sentries are smokin'. They also got big fires. They pretty much act like they got the world by the hind pockets.''

''I think we ought to shake 'em a little, but I don't know exactly how to go about it,'' I said.

''Well, we got surprise on our side. That will give us an edge. We need to find the girls, if they still be alive, and then make a plan.''

Ignacio crawled up to us. He'd gotten down close to the camp, and we'd told him what to look for. ''There are three white girls at that fire over there,'' he said, pointing to a fire that was off to one side. There are four men with them,'' he said.

''Okay. I'm goin' on in and look the situation over, Mike. If I start shootin', you and the Utes mix it up with 'em. Keep your heads down,'' I said to them.

''All right, Matt. Don't try to take 'em yourself. Just get the lay of the land, and see if ya think we can get the girls out,'' he replied.

I went back to where we'd tied the horses and traded my boots for a pair of Ute moccasins. I started workin' my way to the fire that Ignacio had pointed out. There was sage, short grass, and occasional clumps of prickly pear. That wasn't a lot of cover, but it was enough.

After 'bout an hour, I was right up close. I could hear their voices plain.

''You saw what happened to those Indian women today, Ara. I can only hold my men back for so long. If we were married, I know that they would not bother you as my wife. If you don't

marry me soon, I may lose control of my men." It was Falcon
Beck talkin'.

"I will not consent to marry you, Mr. Beck, until you have
agreed to release my sister and Lee," Ara replied to him. She
sounded like she still had some spunk left.

"We have had this discussion before, Ara. I cannot let them
go. My men have been promised Lee because she killed one of
my men when we took you, and Macon wants your sister." He
walked over and threw a log on the fire, sending sparks cascading
upwards and lighting up the area. I hunkered down. "You don't
have much time to answer, Ara. To maintain control of my men,
I must deal with you. You have one hour, and then I will have
you one way or the other. I have tried to be a gentleman, but my
patience has run out." He walked away from the fire back toward
where the rest of his men were gathered, leaving the girls with
their three guards.

There was no countin' on some folks' thinkin'-machines. Here
Falcon Beck was, probably the worst outlaw this side of hell, and
he was still tryin' to impress Ara how much of a gentleman he
was. Well, so be it. It probably had saved the girls from bein'
raped and killed. At least to this point. It sounded like their time
was runnin' out. I could see them plain in the light of the fire,
and I noticed that Lee had moved maybe three foot since I'd
taken my position. Whatever we were gonna do, we'd best hurry
up about it.

I could tell that Lee was movin'. She had somethin' in her
head, and it was likely to get her killed if she acted on it. Suddenly, she bolted straight at me. It was purely luck, but she rated
a break. She'd had her share of bad luck. She come runnin' like
the devil hisself was comin' after her, and she wasn't far wrong.
A man was sprintin' after her and gainin' by the step. She got to
me, and I knocked her feet out from under her. I grabbed her
around the mouth to keep her from screamin'.

"Keep it shut, Lee," I said in her ear. "It's Matt." She quit
fightin' as soon as she realized it was me. The man chasin' her
had been about forty feet back, and he lost sight of her when I
knocked her down. I slipped my Spanish steel from its sheath
and waited for him. He walked right up on us. His night vision
wasn't good 'cause he'd been lookin' into the fire just before Lee
took out. I swung my arm in a wide arch and took his legs out
from under him. He hit on his shoulders knockin' out his wind.
My Spanish blade took care of the rest of the problem. I looked

toward the fire where the other two girls were. Falcon Beck come runnin' into the light with Macon close behind.

"What the hell's goin' on here?" he asked one of the remainin' guards.

"The one what killed Duffer took off runnin'. Jenkins took out after her."

Falcon looked out in our direction and started to move.

"Start screamin', Lee. Make it sound like you got caught and the man is gonna have his way with you. Hurry," I said to her.

Well, she let out a caterwauler they could probably hear back in Abilene. Then she started makin' noises like she was fightin', and I started makin' noises like I was wrestlin' with her.

Beck stopped walkin' and turned back to the fire. He walked right up to Ara.

"You hear that, Ara?" he said. "It has begun. In less than an hour you will know what she is experiencing. The only thing that will stay my hand now is your consent to marriage." He walked around to where Una sat and looked back across at Ara. "I am going to be king of these western lands, and I need to own a woman who looks good and makes me look good. She has to know all the ways of a lady. You are that woman, Ara. I would think you would be grateful. I will break you just as I would break a horse. I will either break you gentle, or I will break you like rough stock, but I will break you." He reached up and put his hand under Una's chin, liftin' her head to look at him. "I am going to let my brother have Una." He dropped his hand and walked back toward the other fires. Ara looked mighty green around the gills, and Una was cryin'.

"Give me a gun, Matt," Lee whispered.

"What for?" I whispered back.

"I'm goin' to kill me a man. It was him I was aimin' for with my Smith when they took us, but he moved and I got the man behind him," she said.

"You just hold your fire, Lee. We got to figure a way to get the girls out first. Then we'll worry about Mr. Falcon Beck," I replied. "Let's move back away from the fire."

Lee scooted back with nary a noise. I followed close after her. We got back to the rest of our crew, and I told 'em what was goin' on.

"Where are the horses, Lee?" Mike asked.

"They're all tied to a line over by the creek," she replied.

"Well, we're bad outnumbered, so we need a diversion. If we

was to run the horses through their camp, we might be able to get the girls away,'' he said.

"Let's do it then. Time's wastin','' I said.

"Ignacio, take your boys and go after the horses. Cut the lines, run 'em through the camp, then get the hell out. We'll meet you over at the hollow where the Cheyennes are,'' Mike said.

"Is this gonna work?'' I asked my big brother.

"We'll know shortly,'' he said.

"Lee, ya can't go with us.'' Mike said to her. "We're facin' up to shootin' trouble, and it'd be easier knowin' you're safe. Look against the sky over there,'' he said pointing toward the west. "Ya see that clump of trees?'' She nodded. "I want ya to go there and stay. We'll be along shortly, I hope. If we ain't, just follow the creek south, and you'll hit the main trail.''

"I want a gun, Mike,'' she said.

"Okay, there's a .36 Navy in my saddlebag, and a extra cylinder. The horses are behind us 'bout a quarter mile. You get the gun and then get to them trees,'' he said.

She moved to leave, then turned toward me.

"I'm most 'bilged for ya savin' me again, Matthew.'' She stretched up and kissed me full on the mouth, then turned and ran for the horses. I was fair surprised. It was the first time a female had ever kissed me on the mouth. It weren't all that bad.

"Let's go, Matt,'' Mike said. We started ghostin' for the Beck fire where the girls were. We got up close and lay quiet. Everything depended on timin' now. That and the Utes gettin' to the horses before they were spotted. They'd been stealin' horses for a long time, so they'd had a lot of practice. The three men that were guardin' the girls were playin' cards and suckin' on a bottle. They was all sittin' on the opposite side of the fire from us, and I knew that their night vision would be no good. Ara and Una were off to one side, and Ara was watchin' out toward where we were. I knew she was thinkin' about Lee. Falcon Beck came walkin' back into the firelight.

"The time has come for an answer, Ara,'' he said.

Suddenly, out of the quiet of the night, came the war scream of a Ute warrior and the poundin' of hooves. Things were about to get downright interestin'.

Chapter Eighteen

When the war cry echoed across the hills, Beck turned and ran toward the other camp. Me and Mike got our feet under us and took off runnin' for the fire. The guards had turned to look at the commotion that was happenin'. We come bustin' up, and they turned toward us. I wasn't figurin' on bein' polite, so I shot one right through his left shirt pocket. Mike cut loose with the Greener and blew another man backwards ten feet. I shot the last man right in the face.

"Ara, Una, quick," Mike yelled.

They didn't waste around. They come on the run, and we taken out across the short grass and the sage.

"Mike, get 'em out of here," I said quiet. "I'll cover our tail and be up with you shortly."

He didn't ask no questions, but took off runnin' south with the girls. A man came runnin' out of the shadows, and I dropped him with a quick shot. The sounds of runnin' horses was gettin' louder, and I heard a man scream with pain. Suddenly, there was a tremendous crash of gunfire from the direction of Beck's main camp. There had been a few scattered shots before, but this was concentrated. I reckoned we was gettin' some help, only I didn't know who. I'd have to be careful who I shot at. It might be somebody friendly. There was a rush of horses came past me. I could see the Utes were ridin' some of em', and screamin' at the top of their lungs. A man came ridin' behind them, shootin' their direction. He wasn't actin' friendly, so I blew him out of the saddle. The heat of battle was on me, and I started runnin' toward the shootin'. I knew there was a man over that direction what needed killin'.

A bunch of men came runnin' out of the dark. I tipped the Henry up, but waited.

"Get them dirty son of a bitches," a man shouted. It was

182

Macon Beck. I cut my wolf lose. I fired the Henry as fast as I could work the action. It snapped on an empty chamber. I dropped it, drawin' the Colt. I felt a wicked blow to my left leg, and I knew I'd been hit. I shot into the group makin' five shots sound near like one. They started to scatter. The sound of gunfire was almost to make me deaf. I dropped the cylinder from the Colt and slipped in another. I shot a man comin' at me and hammered the rest of the shots at indistinct runnin' targets. My guns were empty, and there was no one left around me.

There was shootin' over to the south, but nothin' close about. I fished around for my Henry and found it layin' under a dead man near my feet. He'd gotten in close, and I didn't remember killin' him. I was feelin' weak as a starved-out pup, and I had a leg that wasn't workin' good. I sat down abruptly and checked over my wound. I'd been holed right through the thigh, but the ball seemed to have missed the bone. I dropped my britches and wrapped the wound with my kerchief. It was startin' to hurt some, and I knew it'd hurt worse later on. Main thing was to stop the leak. I got my pants back up and started hobbling off toward where I figured the horses were.

I got lost. It weren't a hard thing to do. It was darker than the inside of a black cow, and I wasn't trackin' straight anyhow. I walked awhile and come up to a little seepin' spring with a ring of cottonwoods. I was powerful thirsty, and my leg hurt like blazes. I decided to get a drink and wait for light.

I got a nice cold drink from the spring, then moved back a little distance. What had happened? Were Mike and the girls safe? Did the Utes get clear? Was Falcon Beck dead? Things kinda went black as I passed out with my mind full of questions.

"Look what we got here," a voice said. I opened my eyes and looked. It was daylight, and Falcon Beck was standin' near the seep with his gun pointin' at my gut. He had a bullet burn across his face, and a wild look to his eyes. "I just stopped to get a little drink, and I ended up with an O'Malley as well." I didn't say nothin'. What was there to say? I was layin' on my back with my Henry flat beside me. The keeper was off my pistol. My right hand was close, but still too far away. Too far to take on a fast man that had the drop on me. "I should have killed you a long time ago, O'Malley. I should have killed you back in east Kansas. You still got that watch? I guess I will own it after all." He was really enjoyin' himself. "They killed or captured most of my men, but I got away. I can raise another army, and I will still become king of this western land." I realized I was dealin' with a crazy man.

"It's been tried, Beck," I said.

"What?" he exploded. He was on a short fuse.

"I said it's been tried. Back in 1806 a man named Burr tried to set up his own western kingdom. It didn't work. In fact, they tried him for high treason." Here I was talkin' history with a crazy man holdin' a gun on me. What I needed was an edge, and talkin' history was the only thing I had goin' for me. A branch snapped loudly behind Beck; his eyes wavered from me, and his gun swung toward the sound. I went for my Colt.

Beck saw the movement and fired. He missed, shootin' before his pistol came back on line. He started walkin' toward me. I fired and saw him bend over as if he'd been hit in the gut by a fist. He fired again, and I felt the blow of the bullet. I blasted shots into his body, but he kept on walkin'. I fired again, and he fell down. He got to one elbow and shot into me again. My pistol was empty, and I was shot to rags. I had only one arm workin': my gun arm. I pulled my blade. He got his feet under him and come walkin' at me again. Things were gettin' dim, and I couldn't see him good. He stumbled and fell toward me. I felt a great weight on my chest. I heard another shot from a distance, and then I kind of floated away.

I felt a cool hand on my forehead, and then a wet cloth. Seems like I'd had that kind of attention before.

"I love you, Matthew O'Malley, and if you die, I'm goin' to be powerful mad." It was Lee, and I surely didn't want to make her mad. She was hell on wheels when she got mad.

When I woke again, it was day, and the light hurt my eyes. Lee was asleep in a rockin' chair across a well-furnished room. I was layin' in a feather bed. The first one I could remember sleepin' in for a spell of time.

"Hello, Matt. Welcome back." It was Owen, and he was standin' on the other side of the bed away from Lee.

I looked at him, then back toward Lee. "She's spent the last week right here beside you day and night. I think the girl's got a case on you."

"Water," I managed to croak. Owen got me a drink, and it was wonderful good.

"Lee's the one that found you. We'd all gathered in the Cheyenne hollow after the action. It was comin' light, and you hadn't shown up. She took Sin and left out. She told us later that she rode into a little bunch of trees around a spring. Then there was enough shooting for a whole war. When she got to you, Falcon Beck was fallin' on you. She shot him with Mike's Navy, and then rolled him off you. Your knife was stuck in his chest, and he had five bullet holes in him, countin' the one she put in his back. You were nearly as bad. You have three in your upper body and one in the leg. You nearly checked out on us, boy,'' he said, looking gravely at me. "Lee got you up on Sin somehow and brought you in.''

So Lee and Sin were the ones that broke the stick behind Beck and gave me the chance.

"The Utes took the horses through the Beck camp just as our posse was gettin' ready to hit them,'' Owen continued. "We almost wiped them out. They had thirteen dead and ten wounded, with five of the wounded bein' bad. A few of them got away. The ten wounded ones are looking at hanging right here in Cherry Creek. The story has gotten around about what happened, and there's a lot of bad feeling for them here.'' He walked over to the window and threw it open. A cold breeze come in, and he shut it again, leavin' the smell of pine in the room. "Only one thing,'' he said, lookin' at me. "Macon Beck got away. We think he lit out west, but we're not sure.''

"Mike?'' I whispered.

"He's fine, and went back over to the ranch site as soon as the doctor said you'd live. Ignacio is doing well. He and his braves did a courageous thing with that horse herd. He lost a brave in the fight, but he has a new story. He went back with Mike.'' Owen turned to leave. "You get some sleep now. We can hash this out later.''

I looked over at Lee. She was darn good-lookin' with the sun shinin' off her hair, and I must've dreamed about her while I was out. I dreamed she said she loved me.

I looked out the window that faced out toward the mountains. I'd come near to walkin' the Warrior's Trail. Maybe I'd stuck around 'cause I still had a couple of promises to keep. For one thing, I still had to find Danny, and Pa might still be kickin' around lookin for us if he'd made it through the war. I also still had to prove to Kiowa that I was more than just a gunslick killer. I went back to sleep.

A few days later, when my talker was workin' better, I got to conversin' with Lee. She was workin' on some little piece of needlework, and she was wearin' a dress.

"How'd you come about bein' out at Turbech's when the Becks hit there?" I asked.

"Well, Ara had come into town a couple of times, and we'd gotten to be friends. She was the only girl around near my age, ya know. Anyhow, she said she'd made up her mind to go back East to school, and her folks had okayed it. She asked me if I'd come out and help sew up some new clothes. The Major said I deserved a leave from work, so I went out. I don't know how to sew much, but both Patty and Mrs. Turbech been teachin' me. I even got a dress of my own now, and Owen said he'd buy me another 'fore we leave out.''

So Ara was goin' East. Well, it was a good thing. Ara wasn't cut out for the frontier life. She needed to be back where there was regular police and laws that protected folks. I didn't judge that she'd ever be able to understand a man fightin' for what was right. She'd marry some high-toned lawyer and they'd have a house full of little lawyers. I wished her well.

I looked Lee over close as she rocked in the chair. She looked right fetchin' in girl clothes. Maybe down the road there'd be some little O'Malleys runnin' around the O'Malley spread in the Valley of the Utes.